The
Curiosities

The
Curiosities

SUSAN GLOSS

wm

WILLIAM MORROW
An Imprint of HarperCollins*Publishers*

THE CURIOSITIES. Copyright © 2019 by Susan Gloss. All rights reserved. Printed in the United States of America. No part of this book may be used or reproduced in any manner whatsoever without written permission except in the case of brief quotations embodied in critical articles and reviews. For information, address HarperCollins Publishers, 195 Broadway, New York, NY 10007.

HarperCollins books may be purchased for educational, business, or sales promotional use. For information, please email the Special Markets Department at SPsales@harpercollins.com.

FIRST EDITION

Designed by Diahann Sturge

Library of Congress Cataloging-in-Publication Data has been applied for.

ISBN 978-0-06-227036-8 (trade paperback edition)
ISBN 978-0-06-293376-8 (hardcover library edition)

19 20 21 22 23 LSC 10 9 8 7 6 5 4 3 2 1

For Bill and my boys, with love

The
Curiosities

Prologue

Nell stood atop a stone retaining wall, next to a frozen lake, clutching a shoebox full of the remnants of a dead woman's dreams. Her coat pockets bulged with the credit card bills she'd nabbed from the mailbox that morning before her husband could see them. She knew they were marked Past Due without even opening the envelopes.

A gust of wind whipped up from the rippled banks, causing her to turn her head away from the shore and toward the mansion behind her, dark except for the lamp she'd left on in the office. *What on earth am I doing here?* she wondered.

The wind died down and Nell looked at the box in her hands. Nestled inside were notes written in the sort of perfect, slanted cursive no longer taught in public schools. Jumbled along with them were pages torn from catalogs of galleries long since shuttered and snapshots of people Nell had never met.

She felt as drained of color and life as the frozen landscape laid out at her feet. A year earlier, she never could have imagined keeping secrets from her husband. She would have pictured herself rocking a baby to sleep at the end of each evening instead of slipping into bed alone. She would have predicted that by now she'd have found a tenure-track teaching position.

Instead, her next career move hinged on a box full of paper scraps, a cast of unpredictable artists, and a turn-of-the-century mansion in need of modernization. Nell had no idea how she was supposed to make sense of it all. All she knew was that she had to figure it out, somehow. She had no choice.

Chapter One

Nell

PIECE: *Edwin Blashfield*, Pioneers, *circa 1917. Oil painting. Currently on long-term loan from the Elizabeth Barrett Trust for the Fine Arts to the University of Wisconsin.*

Outside the windows of the dean's residence, white lights left over from the holidays twinkled on bare tree branches, lending a festive glow to the otherwise quiet neighborhood. But inside the walls of the stately brick home, Nell Parker wasn't feeling particularly festive, despite the cocktails being passed and the red dress she'd bought for the occasion.

She hadn't wanted to come. Not today, when she was expecting news. But Josh had insisted. Rumors had already begun to circulate among the law faculty that in the wake of his recent award, the young professor might leave Madison for one of the East Coast schools that kept courting him. He and

Nell both needed to be at the reception, Josh had said, to show people that they planned to put down roots here.

"To be honest, I don't really want to go, either," he'd said earlier that evening. "I'd much rather just put a movie on and stay in tonight. But showing up at stuff like this is important for tenure. And maybe the party will help get our minds off waiting."

Nell had zipped up her dress and said, "I don't think there's much chance of that. But I'll go." She'd walked over to where he stood in front of the mirror and kissed him just below his earlobe, her lips brushing against his short-clipped beard.

Now, she set her still-full wineglass on the windowsill and dug in her purse for her cell phone. She stole a glimpse at the screen to check the time. 4:47. The clinic would be closing in thirteen minutes.

What could possibly be taking so long? she wondered. She curbed the impulse to call the clinic yet again. She'd already called three times since she went in for blood work that morning. Each time, the receptionist had told her, "Your lab results aren't in yet. A nurse will call you as soon as they are available." The woman's tone was calm and even, which only served to highlight how frantic Nell felt, how light-headed and desperate. The receptionist talked about how the wait time so far wasn't outside the "usual time frame" it took "the lab" to process samples. It all sounded so neutral, so medical. Nothing about any of this felt neutral to Nell.

She stared at her phone and watched the digital display turn from 4:47 to 4:48. She'd give the clinic five more minutes and, if she still hadn't heard anything, she'd call again. The last thing her nerves needed was to be in limbo all weekend, waiting for the clinic to open Monday.

Across the wood-paneled room, Josh looked to be deep in conversation with an older, taller version of himself, right down to the square glasses and sweating glass of Scotch. Nell recognized the other man as a member of the law faculty, but couldn't remember his name. She and Josh had lived in Madison for a year and a half now, but Nell still couldn't keep Josh's colleagues and all their disciplines straight, even with mnemonic devices. *Square glasses and Scotch go with Stanley Something Something*, she remembered. But did he teach Constitutional Law or Contracts?

Josh caught her eye and made a beckoning motion, as if to invite her into the conversation. She took a few steps toward them, enough to hear the older professor discussing an exhibit he'd seen at the art museum on campus, of paintings by Edwin Blashfield, the same artist who'd done the ceiling mural inside the dome of the State Capitol building.

"My wife has a PhD in art history," she heard Josh say. "I'm sure she'd love to check it out." He nodded in her direction. "Nell, you remember Stan . . ."

But her phone buzzed in her hand just then. Nell held it up to show him and said, "Excuse me, I've got to take this."

She hurried out to the foyer. More partygoers flowed into the house, checking their coats with a young hostess in a sparkly green dress, probably a student. Nell envied her. Not just for the way she wore the flimsy garment without even a suggestion of self-consciousness—no tug at the short hemline, no pulling up of the thin straps—but also for her station in life. Nell thought back to when she'd been around the same age, early twenties, maybe. She'd been living in Chicago and just starting grad school. Back then, her cares never extended beyond considering which jeans best flattered her backside when she went out with friends or which seminar to take (Poststructuralism or Postminimalism?). How things had changed.

Nell answered the phone. "Hello?" Her eyes darted around for a private place to talk. She tried the door to a powder room she'd spotted earlier, but it was locked.

"Hello," said a familiar male voice. "Is this Nell?"

"Yes," she managed to say. "Dr. Lynch?" She could feel her heart thumping inside her rib cage. She had been expecting one of the nurses to call.

"Are you able to talk?" he asked.

"Of course. Just give me a moment to get somewhere quieter." Nell eyed the white-shirted servers flitting into and out of the kitchen. She followed one of them and crouched in the corner of a walk-in pantry, where she pulled the pocket door shut behind her.

The voice on the other end cut in and out. "Can . . . oooo . . . hear—?"

Of course her reception would decide to fail at this very moment. She silently cursed both her cell phone provider for having such crappy coverage and the walls of the old house for being so thick.

"Hang on a second." Nell got up and went back through the foyer, pushing open the heavy front door.

The hostess called after her. "Wait! Do you want your coat?"

Nell ignored the hostess and shut the door as a wall of frigid air hit her face.

"Okay," she said, exhaling.

"Nell, I want you to know how sorry I am that it took us so long to get back to you today. There was a huge backup at the lab," the doctor said.

The results are bad, Nell thought. *He wouldn't apologize first if he were going to give me good news.*

"I'm not pregnant," she said. Maybe if she said it first, tested out the words herself instead of hearing them from Dr. Lynch, their meaning would hurt less.

"I'm afraid not," he said. "Your blood test was negative."

So much for her theory about the words hurting less if she braced herself for them. The January wind against her bare legs stung much less than the harsh finality of what the doctor said. Nell wavered in her high heels, feeling light-headed again. She leaned against the wrought iron railing of the front porch, pulling gasps of icy air into her lungs.

"Those were our last frozen embryos. And you put *two* of them in there." Nell clutched her midsection with one hand, reeling with anger at her body. "I can't believe neither of them took."

"I don't understand it, either," Dr. Lynch said. "I thought

we'd gotten your meds just right this time. You seemed to be responding well to the hormones. I truly hoped this would be it."

"You and me both."

The doctor went on to talk about options and next steps. Something about a new IVF protocol that had been published for women of "advanced maternal age"—the medical terminology for women who, like Nell, were over thirty-five.

She barely heard him, staring instead at the trees lining the sidewalk. The twinkle of lights strung up among them did little to hide their spindly, barren branches. Nell wondered how she'd possibly get through another winter without a baby—or at least the hope of a baby—to fill the hole left by the one she'd lost.

When she hung up, she realized she'd been holding her breath. She let it out, and a puff of water vapor rose toward the sky like so much hope, then dispersed and disappeared.

When Nell stepped back inside, shaking, she spotted Josh in the foyer, already waiting for her. He pulled on his gray wool jacket, his face creased with concern. He dangled his keys in one hand and Nell's coat in the other.

As soon as they made eye contact, Nell's throat constricted and her eyes filled with tears, but she blinked them back. Josh closed the distance between them and put a hand on her shoulder. Stunned, Nell let him help her into her black dress coat and guide her to the door.

As they walked down the porch steps, another couple was coming up. Josh gave them a polite nod, but Nell turned her face away, not wanting these strangers to see the tears that now fell freely down her cheeks.

When they got to the car, Josh started the engine, but didn't drive. Instead, he leaned his head back against the seat. "Shit," he said. He leaned over to the passenger seat and wrapped his arms around Nell. "I'm so sorry. I was really hoping it would work this time. I mean, we doubled our odds, right? By transferring two."

Nell wiped her cheeks on his coat, then pulled back. "Apparently, increasing really crappy odds still gives you crappy odds."

Josh sighed and put the car into drive. He pulled away from the curb. "I just can't believe we're in the same place we started, after all the shots and surgeries . . ."

And all the money I've spent, Nell thought. But Josh didn't know about the cost, at least not the full extent of it. She pushed that thought aside and instead said, "Don't forget no caffeine. And no vigorous exercise."

"No dairy, no gluten."

"And no alcohol," Nell said. "I think I need a drink."

"Do we even have anything at home you like to drink? It's been so long. We could stop somewhere if you want."

"Like a bar?" Nell shook her head. "I don't really feel like dealing with humanity right now."

"I was thinking more like a liquor store. I could just run in."

"Sure," Nell said. What she really wanted was to crawl into bed and sleep for days.

They drove through the campus area, past high-rise apartment buildings and dormitories. The sidewalks were crowded with kids walking and texting, smoking, or standing in line outside of bars. *Friday night*, Nell remembered.

"I thought it was winter break," Nell said. "Shouldn't all the students be gone?"

"A lot of students come back early for jobs and stuff. And some of them probably just come back early because they can't stand living with their parents for a whole month," Josh said.

As he stopped the car at a red light, a group of girls in miniskirts darted through the crosswalk. Nell put her palm on the fogged passenger window and said, "You're probably not thinking about babies right now, girls, but if you had any idea that some of you might struggle to have them later, you'd be freezing your eggs instead of freezing your asses off in those skirts."

Josh let out a half-hearted laugh and stepped on the gas when the light changed. "I'm sure you weren't thinking about your ovaries when you were twenty."

Nell shook her head. "It's a cruel joke of nature, really, that our bodies are ready for babies long before our brains."

"Biology hasn't caught up yet, I guess," Josh said.

He pulled into a curbside parking space outside a liquor store on University Avenue. Nell opened her door.

"I thought you said you don't want to deal with humanity right now," Josh said.

"I can make an exception. Liquor store people are my kind of people at the moment." Nell knew her attempts at humor did little to diffuse the disappointment practically suffocating her, but it was the only way she could keep the tears at bay. She got out of the car and stepped over a snowbank onto the sidewalk. Inside the shop, she walked straight over to the shelves stacked with spirits. She grabbed a bottle of midrange bourbon and brought it to the register. The cashier, a girl with a pierced nose and lip, looked up from the hardcover novel she was reading and eyed Nell's selection.

"Good choice," she said, shutting her book. Nell recognized the title from the list of National Book Award finalists she'd seen online somewhere. A few years ago, Nell probably would have read most of the books on that list. Even when she was in grad school, she'd always managed to carve out time to read for pleasure. But in the last year, her reading had focused mostly on PubMed articles about IVF, with the occasional infertility blog post thrown in.

The clerk swiped her credit card and picked up a brown paper bag. Nell held up her hand. "I don't need a bag. I'm bringing this right home."

The girl gave her a knowing nod and opened her book again.

In the car, Josh sat hunched over his phone, typing something onto the tiny screen.

"Work stuff?" Nell asked.

He nodded. "One of my students wanting to know if grades have been posted yet."

"Is this the same kid that emailed you on Christmas Eve?"

"Yep. And New Year's Eve, too."

"That was just a couple of days ago. Don't you have, like, a portal where you upload grades when they're ready? Why is he emailing you?"

"My thoughts exactly, and that's what I told him for the third time." He looked over at the bottle of amber-colored liquid in Nell's lap. "Bourbon, huh?"

"I need some Southern hospitality," she said.

On the way home, they passed by the park at B. B. Clarke Beach, which in the summer would be crowded and noisy, with teenagers sunning themselves on the sand and children jumping off the swim raft. Now the park looked desolate, its outbuilding shuttered for the season.

Josh parked the car in the driveway next to their gray stucco bungalow, small but sturdy. Built in 1928, it would need some work eventually. An update of the tiny kitchen and a new roof, for starters. But the house was within walking distance of one of the best public elementary schools in the city, which was one of the reasons they'd chosen it.

Inside, Josh stacked logs in the potbellied stove while Nell went upstairs to put on her sweats. She made the mistake of standing in front of the mirror as she stepped out of her party dress. Bruises and needle marks formed a purple map across her belly and backside from the hormone shots she'd given herself in the weeks leading up to the embryo transfer ten days earlier. She ripped a Band-Aid off her arm that had been covered by her three-quarter-length sleeves. Beneath the bandage was a small red dot left from that morning's blood draw. When she'd sat in the chair at the clinic for her serum pregnancy test, she'd still felt optimistic, if cautiously so, chattering with the nurse about whether the forecast for six inches of snow that weekend was accurate or whether it was just the local meteorologists getting overexcited.

Nell wished now that she could preserve those moments, those snapshots of hope before the wide window of possibility came slamming down on her fingers.

She slipped on a sweatshirt and a pair of yoga pants and went back downstairs, where a fire now flickered in the woodburning stove. Josh came out from the kitchen and handed her a tumbler containing a single ice cube and a generous pour of whiskey.

He held up his own glass in his other hand and tapped it against Nell's. "Here's hoping the rest of the year turns out better than it started."

"I'll drink to that."

They each took a long sip before settling on the couch next to the fire. Nell pulled a crocheted blanket onto her lap—one her mother-in-law, Judy, had made her as a going-away gift when she and Josh had left Chicago.

"I've heard it's even colder in Wisconsin than it is here," Judy had said. "You'll need this."

Little could she have predicted that Nell would need not just the warmth, but the comfort as well. Or maybe she *had* known. The liquor thawed Nell's throat as she swallowed. Josh kicked off his dress shoes and stuck his legs under the blanket so they were intertwined with hers.

"Dr. Lynch said there's a new protocol I could try if we do another egg retrieval," Nell said. "Something about immune suppression." She watched her husband's face for a reaction.

Josh set his drink down on the coffee table with a thud. "No," he said. He shook his head. "No more. I can't do it again. *You* can't go through it again."

"I could," Nell insisted. And she meant it. She'd endure all of it—the injections, the procedures, even the heartache—as many times as she had to. "If I knew we'd have a baby on the other side of it, I'd start another treatment cycle tomorrow."

"But that's the thing—you *don't* know. There aren't any guarantees."

"But if we don't try again, we'll never know if maybe the next cycle would have been the one that worked."

"And we could keep saying that, month after month, cycle after cycle. But at some point, I think we need to say enough."

"It sounds like you're saying it now," Nell said. She'd suspected Josh felt that way, but it hurt to hear him say it.

"I *am* saying it now." Josh ran his hands through his short brown hair. Back when they were both in grad school, he used to keep it longer, collar-length. She remembered how she loved to tangle her fingers in it. But ever since he started teaching, he got it cut every three weeks.

Nell bent her legs and hugged them to her chest, so that she and Josh were no longer touching.

"Listen," he said. "It's hard for me, too. Especially to see how unhappy this whole process has made you. But we used to think our life was pretty great, even without kids. Remember that? I want to get back there."

Nell knew Josh had a point. But a familiar ache welled up inside her, drowning out everything but the palpable, biological desire to be pregnant again. Because she had been, once. And she would give anything—go into any amount of debt, endure any type of medical intervention—to experience that again and to take home a baby, this time, at the end of it.

Early on, before any of the treatments, she and Josh had discussed adoption. But Josh said that with his legal background, he knew of too many stories where birth parents exercised their parental rights at the last minute, leaving the adoptive parents heartbroken. And then there was the cost.

"I just don't see how we can afford it, with the house and car payments, and you not working," Josh had said. He'd gone along with the plan for fertility treatments because he believed they were covered by their health insurance plan. And they were . . . at first. But Josh wasn't the one who handled all the bills and paperwork for their household. Since moving to Madison, with Josh so entrenched in his new job, Nell had taken over that task.

Josh hadn't read their insurance documents in all their excruciating detail like Nell had, so he didn't know that there was a cap on what their plan would cover, and that they had reached it before they'd even finished their first IVF cycle. But by that point, Nell was already injecting herself with hormones and felt like there was no turning back. She was invested, both physically and emotionally, in the idea of getting pregnant again. So much so that she gave the clinic the numbers of credit cards she and Josh hardly ever used and told them to charge the cost of the rest of the treatments. Nell felt guilty about keeping Josh in the dark, but she justified it by telling herself that she'd have a job soon. Once she was pregnant, and the card balances were paid off, she could fill him in on the details. She was sure he would see then that it had all been worth it.

Now, Josh shifted his legs under the blanket. "Just think about how much freer you'll feel. No more taking your basal body temperature at five a.m., no more blood tests, no more pee sticks, no more hormone shots."

Nell had to admit that it did sound freeing, after months of pumping herself full of what she referred to as "the Acronyms"—FSH, LH, hCG, GnRH—but it also terrified her. She wasn't one of those people who'd grown up always knowing she'd wanted to be a mother. As a child, she'd been more interested in drawing than in dolls. And even as she turned the corner into her thirties, she'd been focused more on finishing her PhD than starting a family. But then, shortly after she and Josh got married, she'd gotten pregnant. They'd been one of those couples she now envied—not trying, really, but not preventing, either. And poof! Two pink lines on a pregnancy test. That was the last and only time their baby-making journey had been easy.

"I'm thirty-seven," she said. "It's not like we have all the time in the world to try again."

Josh crossed his arms. "You're not hearing what I'm saying. I don't mean taking a break. I mean no more trying. Because that's where my head's at. I think we're getting a pretty strong signal from *somewhere* that this isn't supposed to happen. If we have to work this hard at it, maybe it's just not meant to be."

"Since when do you think anything worth doing is easy?" Nell asked, thinking of how doggedly he'd worked through three years of law school and two years of a federal clerkship.

"I don't see it as giving up," he said. "I see it as deciding not to let this whole thing run our lives anymore."

But giving up is exactly what it felt like to Nell. And she didn't just feel like Josh was giving up on their dream of a baby. She felt like he was giving up on *her*. Her body and its ability to do what women's bodies were supposed to do.

Her younger self, the one who'd taken college classes with names like *Feminist Theory in Twentieth-Century Painting* and *Gender Identity in the Visual Arts,* would have shrunk in shame at such thoughts. Rationally, she knew that she was no less of a woman or a wife for not being able to produce offspring. She knew, too, that her struggles were the type that only fortunate people could afford to have—people who didn't lie awake at night wondering how they'd pay the grocery bill or mortgage. If Nell were the tweeting type, she'd have to lump her failed IVF treatments in with other complaints under the hashtag #FirstWorldProblems.

Still, putting her problems into perspective didn't stop Nell from feeling, in the murky recesses of her thoughts, that she was a failure. Since they moved to Madison a year and a half earlier, Josh had climbed the academic ranks at warp speed, collecting award nominations and committee chair appointments like shiny pennies. Meanwhile, Nell had yet to find a job in her field, which didn't bother her quite as much at first, back when she still had high hopes of having a family. But now she had neither. Instead, she had the added burden of a lot more debt, and the stress of keeping it hidden.

She kicked off the blanket and set down her now-empty tumbler on the coffee table. "I'm exhausted," she said. "I'm going to bed."

The next morning, Nell put on her stretch tights, running shoes, and a fleece pullover. Before starting fertility treatments, running had been her sanity. She'd given it up, though, when Dr. Lynch advised against strenuous exercise while undergoing IVF. Nell had followed his instructions without a second thought, just like she did with everything else that might help her chances, even incrementally, of getting pregnant again.

Now, her legs felt tight as she headed west toward campus, following the snowy sidewalks down her street, lined on both sides with small bungalows painted green, yellow, and pink. The tops of her running tights squeezed her stomach, still swollen from the pounds she'd put on.

She kept running, though, cutting through Orton Park, past its stone gazebo and the stately Victorian homes on its perimeter. She struggled to breathe, and her legs burned after just few blocks. But at least she was breathing. And at least while her legs and lungs hurt, she couldn't think about the deeper pain slicing through her heart.

There were only a few other souls out at his early hour, people clad in down parkas, out walking dogs and clutching coffee cups. Nell's feet made a solitary thudding sound on the snow-dusted pavement. She ran down to the bike path, past the sprawling conference center designed by Frank Lloyd Wright, following its curves along the frozen lakeshore. The wind coming off the waterfront stung Nell's cheeks, but she kept running.

She indulged in a memory of when she'd first told Josh she was pregnant, now almost two years earlier. When he came home from teaching that evening, Nell had thrust a plastic test stick in his face. Josh had squinted at it for several seconds before understanding lit up his eyes.

"Does this mean what I think it means?" he'd asked.

Nell had nodded and let him fold her in a hug, lifting her feet off the ground. They'd been so happy then, so hopeful. They both had thought, naively, that a positive pregnancy test meant holding a newborn baby nine months later. That myth, and all the others they believed about having babies, had been shattered in the long months since then.

Her foot skidded on a patch of ice on the path. The thin, top layer cracked under her feet like the crust on a crème brûlée. Her feet landed in the cold puddle underneath, saturating her socks and the bottoms of her tights.

She kept running.

Nell felt, as she so often did when she thought about the baby, phantom kicks in her lower abdomen and a letdown sensation in her breasts. It was as if her body refused to accept the fact that she was no longer pregnant. And she couldn't blame her body, really. She'd confused it with synthetic hormones and herbal supplements. Coaxed it into a constant state of waiting to harbor life again.

She kept running. She hardly noticed when a man atop a bike equipped with thick, studded snow tires whizzed toward her, coming the opposite way down the path. Just as Nell tried to dodge out of his way, he swerved in the same direction and nearly ran her over. His wheels spattered gray slush all over her clothing.

"Watch where you're going!" he yelled over his shoulder.

Nell stopped and sat down on the edge of a concrete pier, brushing grime off her sleeves. Her legs shook as they dangled over the edge toward the jagged ice below. As her heart rate slowed, the tears she had been holding back finally flowed, dripping down her chin and nose. As the tears fell faster, Nell realized she was no longer crying over her lost baby, or even the fact that her attempts at another one had failed. She was crying for the loss of the person she'd been before she ever waved that positive pregnancy test in Josh's face.

She knew he was right that she needed to focus on something else, but she'd forgotten how.

She got up and half ran, half walked back home. She grabbed the mail sticking out of the mailbox affixed to the house, beside the front door. It had become a habit of hers to always get to the mail before Josh did. She plucked an envelope from the credit card company off the top of the stack and tore it open, her eyes darting to the balance on the front page.

Had it really gone up so much, so fast? She didn't think the last payment to the fertility clinic would show up until next month's bill. She crumpled the paper in her fist, then walked around to the side of the house and tossed it in the recycling bin next to the garage.

When she went inside, Josh sat at the kitchen island reading the Saturday *Chicago Tribune*, which they still got delivered on the weekends.

He smiled when he saw her. "I was wondering where you went."

Nell grabbed a glass from the cabinet and filled it with water. "Bet you wouldn't have guessed I went running."

He shook his head. "It's been a while."

Nell gulped down half the glass before sitting down on the stool next to his. "So," she said.

Josh set down the paper and leaned toward her. "So."

"Let's just say, theoretically, that we're done with fertility treatments," Nell said. "I guess what terrifies me the most, even more than not having a baby, is the idea of how I'm going to fill that space."

And how I'm going to pay off the credit card bills, she added silently.

"You mean now that you don't have to see Dr. Lynch every other day?"

"Yeah, that," she said. "But what I really meant was the headspace. My brain is so jammed up with all this obscure information about reproductive science that I can't even remember what I *thought* about before."

"Oh, you just thought about other obscure stuff," Josh said. "French futurist painting, ancient Byzantine art . . ."

Nell smiled. "Seriously, though. I'm going to start my job search back up. For real this time."

She'd been looking for jobs at a casual pace since they'd moved to Madison the previous summer. But she'd been pregnant when they arrived, in her second trimester. She and Josh decided it didn't make sense for her to begin a teaching job in September, only to go on maternity leave shortly thereafter. Then, after they lost the baby, the hope she'd get pregnant again any month now had kept her from looking in earnest. But then she didn't get pregnant, month after month. More recently, as her credit card debt grew, she'd ramped up her search efforts, only to get discouraged, probably too easily, by the lack of positions in her field.

"I was going to suggest a job search if you didn't," Josh said. "I think it would be good for you."

"Maybe I should have taken the university up on their offer to help me find a job before we moved here," she said.

Josh shook his head. "You can't second-guess yourself. The timing wasn't right."

Nell knew, though, that her refusal to accept the university's help wasn't all about timing. It had also been about pride. After working for years on her graduate degree, she felt uncomfortable riding her husband's coattails in order to secure a spot on the faculty here in Madison. If she was going to get a teaching position, she wanted to earn it herself.

"They still might be willing to help," Josh said.

"I doubt it." Nell took another sip from her water glass. "The offer was all part of their strategy to lure you here. And now that you're here, they won't be as motivated."

"Well, I can ask, anyway. And you can reach out again to some of your contacts in Chicago. Maybe they have some connections here."

Nell nodded. "I guess this means I'll have to reopen my Facebook account."

She used to keep up with her old colleagues' personal and career developments through social media, but she shut down all her accounts after she lost the baby the year before. It was just too painful to have to explain to acquaintances why she wasn't posting newborn pictures once her due date rolled around. Not to mention the fact that other women she knew seemed only to *think* about reproducing and then, *voilà*, they were updating their profile pictures with nine-month-pregnant bellies and blissful smiles.

"People *do* still email, you know," Josh said. "Sometimes."

"Okay. I'll start putting out some feelers. Maybe after I take a shower." Nell got up and tucked a sweaty strand of hair behind her ear. She couldn't tell if the sweat was from the run or from her moment of panic at the mailbox. Maybe both.

Chapter Two

$\mathcal{N}ell$

PIECE: *Megan Gladwell,* Elizabeth Barrett at Home, *circa* 2005. *Oil painting on canvas.*

$\mathcal{N}$ell shut her laptop and put her head down on top of it. Looking for job leads turned out to be more difficult than she had anticipated. A year and a half had gone by since she defended her dissertation. She'd assumed that at the slow pace academia moved, the gap between her degree and whatever postdoctoral work she could find would be, to borrow one of Josh's law terms, de minimis. Something she could explain away with a witty interview answer.

But during the last eighteen months, while Nell had been consumed by all things baby-making and only half-heartedly looking for jobs, her colleagues had been busy. Out of the four other people who had finished their degrees at the same time as Nell, two had landed tenure-track teaching positions. Another lived in Amsterdam, doing postdoc research at the

Rijksmuseum with the help of a hefty grant. And the fourth had secured a spot on a Smithsonian advisory committee to the White House, curating new acquisitions and making recommendations regarding display and preservation. Nell wondered what she might have accomplished in that time frame, had things been different.

"Is everything okay?"

Nell popped her head up at the sound of Josh's voice.

"Just looking for jobs," she said. "Again. I didn't know you were home."

"I just got here." He set down his keys on the kitchen counter.

"Did you make any progress grading?" Nell asked.

Josh nodded. "I like the university when it's not in session. It's so quiet. If it were like this all the time, I could get so much more work done."

"You also wouldn't have a job because you'd have no students to teach."

"Oh, right." Josh went to the fridge and grabbed a bottle of beer. "Want one?"

"Sure," she said. "I need one after all the roadblocks I'm hitting."

Josh took out a second beer. He opened both and handed one to Nell. "It probably doesn't help that most universities are still on winter break," he said. "Maybe you'll have more luck in a couple of weeks when the semester starts back up and people are actually in their offices."

"I've lowered my standards at this point. Anything—even

an adjunct or a fill-in position would be fine for now. I'm just not seeing anything remotely related to my field." Nell looked down at the label of the microbrew Josh had given her. The sticker depicted a kitten riding a fire-breathing unicorn. "The breweries around here keep getting more and more creative with their labels." She squinted at a pixelated picture of a fortress. "Is that Bowser's Castle? From *Super Mario Bros.*?"

Josh looked at the picture on his own bottle and laughed. "You're right. Good call. I forget you used to be a gamer."

Nell remembered all the lonely hours she'd spent playing video games while her mom, a single parent, worked late evenings as a pharmacist. She shook her head. "If only I'd taken all that time playing Nintendo and applied it to something more useful."

"Like, say, learning to repair cracks in plaster . . ." Josh waved his arm toward the curved, ninety-year-old kitchen ceiling, which was embossed with a decorative scroll pattern.

"Never," Nell said. "You can't touch those moldings. Whoever did the plaster in this house was an artist. And, anyway, the cracks are part of the house's charm. Like how the Winged Victory sculpture at the Louvre wouldn't be the same with an intact head."

She took a sip of beer and skimmed the list of job postings she'd been perusing online. "Let's see here . . . 'Females wanted, age 18 to 30, for independent film project. No prior acting experience needed.' Too bad I'm too old. This could have been my big break."

Josh set his bottle down on the counter. "I don't even want to know what sort of film they're making."

Nell read the listings aloud. "Line cooks, office temps, baristas. Wait a second . . . 'Private nonprofit arts foundation looking for director. B.A. required, graduate degree preferred. Call for inquiries.'"

"Sounds interesting," Josh said. "At least worth a call."

"Well, considering it's the only posting I've seen with the word 'art' in it, I think I'd better check it out. Hopefully it doesn't involve any independent film projects."

When Nell called the number from the ad the next morning, a cheerful-sounding woman answered. "Peterson Law. How may I direct your call?"

Nell paused. She hadn't been expecting a law office. Perhaps she had misdialed.

"Hello?" the woman said.

"I'm calling about a job listing for an arts foundation," Nell said. "Perhaps I have the wrong number?"

"No, this is the right place. Let me transfer you to Don, he's in charge of that."

Nell waited on hold, tapping her foot to the *1812 Overture*, until a booming voice came over the line.

"Don speaking."

"Hello. My name is Nell Parker. I saw a listing in yesterday's paper seeking a director for a nonprofit arts program. I'm calling to find out more information."

There was a long silence, followed by "Of course! The Barrett Foundation. Thank you for calling."

"Can you tell me a little bit more about the position and what you're looking for?" Nell asked.

"Certainly. Are you available to come in at two o'clock today?"

"You mean for an interview?" Nell looked at the clock on the kitchen wall. Two o'clock was just a few hours from now.

"You could call it that," Don said. "Or an informational appointment. Whatever you'd prefer."

"Two will be fine," Nell said. She wrote down the name of the law firm and the address Don gave her and said, "I'll see you then."

Shit, Nell thought as soon as she hung up the phone. What had she gotten herself into? She didn't have an interview outfit that still fit her. She didn't even know if she had any printer paper for her résumé.

She went upstairs and paused with her hand on the door of what Josh called the "home office." Nell never went in there. Although she and Josh had not gotten to the point where they'd painted the walls or bought any furniture or anything, she still thought of the room as the nursery.

When they first moved in, Nell had stored the few baby items they'd already acquired in this room. The tiny, yellow crocheted hat that her mother-in-law had given them after she and Josh told their families they were pregnant. The onesie that Josh's former colleagues had given them as a going-away gift, with the words "Future U of C Law Grad" printed across the chest.

And then, for months after their loss, the room had sat

empty. Nell kept the door shut, unable to set foot inside without feeling the weight of what the room signified. When she first started fertility treatments, she'd admonished Josh not to use the room as a storage area.

"I don't want to have to move a bunch of crap out of there when we need the space for a baby," Nell had said. It hadn't occurred to her—not in any real way, anyway—that the treatments might not work. She wouldn't let herself believe it.

Slowly, though, Josh started to take over the room. First he put just a folding table and his laptop in a corner and used the space for grading papers and doing late-night reading. Then a bookshelf. One day he came home from work with an antique desk hanging out of the hatchback of their car, secured with bungee cords.

"I picked it up at a garage sale," he'd said. "Fifteen bucks. I couldn't pass it up."

Nell had stayed quiet as he and a neighbor hoisted the desk up the stairs and set it up in the room. But after that, she'd been furious for days.

Josh tried to reason with her. "This house is small to begin with and we only have two bedrooms," he'd said. "It doesn't make sense to have one of them sit unused."

Nell eventually stopped sulking about the desk, but she'd never forgotten the realization that dawned on her as she watched, from the hallway, as Josh filled the drawers with pens and legal pads and stacked the bookshelves with thick treatises. She knew for the first time, then, that Josh had moved on from their loss, leaving her behind, still in the midst of mourning.

Now, Nell squared her shoulders and pushed open the door. She walked straight to the computer and pulled up her résumé on the screen. After a quick skim for any obvious errors, she hit print. It wasn't until she'd grabbed the warm papers off the printer that she stopped for a moment to look around the room. Since the day he brought home the desk, Josh had also moved in a floor lamp and an old armchair. Every piece of furniture felt, to Nell, like further proof of his lack of faith in their ability to have a child together. And, worse, his acceptance of that fact.

She didn't have time to dwell on those feelings, though. Not today. She needed to find something to wear to her interview in just a few hours. A new suit would have been nice, but she winced when she remembered the large, looming balance on the credit card statements that kept coming in the mail—all the more reason she needed today's interview to go well. She managed to suck in her stomach enough to zip up the same pair of dress pants she'd worn to defend her dissertation. The button, though, was another story. She looped an elastic hair tie through the buttonhole and around the button, employing a trick she'd learned in early pregnancy. She let the matching black blazer hang open over an oxford shirt, which she left untucked to cover the hair tie holding up her pants. It would have to do.

At two o'clock sharp, Nell sat in the reception room of Peterson law offices on the Capitol Square. She could feel herself sweating beneath her blazer. *Damn hormones,* she thought. She tried not to be too obvious as she fanned herself with the *Wall Street Journal.*

Fifteen minutes later, Don, a stout man in a gray suit, ushered Nell into his office. "I apologize for the delay," he said. "I had a very talkative client on the phone. And my living clients have to take priority over my dead ones."

Nell's confusion must have shown in her expression because Don laughed as he settled into his leather desk chair. "Please, sit down. I can see I've got a lot of explaining to do."

She handed him a copy of her résumé and sat down across from him.

Don looked down at the paper. "I reviewed the copy you emailed over. So, tell me, Eleanor. How did you hear about this job?"

"Please, call me Nell," she said. No one called her Eleanor, not even her mother. "I read the listing in the paper and it seemed like a good fit for my background."

"You're probably wondering why you're sitting in a lawyer's office to interview for a job with an arts foundation." Don leaned back in his chair. "This firm represents the Estate of Elizabeth Barrett. Have you ever heard of her?"

"Barrett...," Nell said. "I think I've seen that name around. Isn't there a Barrett Gallery at the art museum on campus?"

Don nodded. "That's the same one. Betsy was a well-respected philanthropist in the community before she passed away recently from cancer. She was particularly known for her patronage of the arts."

"Ah," Nell said. "That's wonderful. With public resources constantly being cut, the arts are in dire need of private funding."

Don nodded. "That's what Betsy was always saying. So, when she died, she left the bulk of her estate to a private trust I helped her set up—the Barrett Foundation for the Arts. And the foundation needs a director. We had someone lined up, but we just got word that she had a job offer from the Guggenheim Foundation. Can't say I blame her for taking it, but it would have been nice if she'd given us a little more advance notice. So that's why you're here."

"Well, I'm intrigued so far," Nell said. She tried to strike a balance between enthusiastic and desperate.

"So, tell me, do you have any management experience with nonprofit organizations?" Don asked.

Of course he has to start with my area of weakness, Nell thought. She took a deep breath and said, "About that. I don't actually have any experience with nonprofit work, unless you count a few days spent swinging a hammer for Habitat for Humanity when I was in college."

Don's bushy eyebrows scrunched together.

"But, as you probably saw on my résumé, I have a PhD in art history, and I'm passionate about art—especially the visual arts," she said. "I finished my dissertation just before my husband and I moved to Madison. Since then, I've been looking for the perfect position." She hoped she sounded breezy rather than defensive.

"Well, I'm not sure how you define 'perfect,'" Don said. "But what I can tell you is that as director, you'd have a lot of independence. Within the parameters set by the trust, of course."

"Of course," Nell said. Although she didn't understand exactly what Don meant, she figured Josh could help her sort through any legal documents.

"The salary is a livable one," Don said. "Not luxurious by any means, but livable. Betsy made certain that was one of the terms of the trust—that the director be compensated fairly. She thought it was essential for attracting the right candidate." He pushed a piece of paper toward her with columns of figures on it. "The director's salary is listed on there at the top."

The first number Nell noticed was not the salary, though. Instead, she was distracted by the bolded total at the bottom of the page—the foundation's net assets—and nearly fell out of her chair. There were six zeroes behind the number. She was so stunned by the idea of someone leaving *millions* to an art foundation that she almost forgot to look at the line that showed the director's salary. When she located the figure, she saw that Don had been right—the salary was not a lavish one. The position certainly paid less than what she'd make in a tenure-track teaching position. It might be enough to chip away at her debt, though, if she could negotiate just a little bit more.

"Would that number work for you?" Don asked.

Nell paused, thinking of the credit card bills. "I could do it for another three thousand a year," she said.

Don blinked, as if he hadn't been expecting her to push back before she'd even been offered the job. But then he smiled, and Nell could tell he respected her for it. "I think Betsy would have been amenable to that, given your qualifications," he said. "As director of the foundation, you'll report to me, as trustee, for accounting and tax purposes. But I don't plan to be involved in the day-to-day happenings. I don't know the first thing about art, other than what I managed to absorb from Betsy."

A dozen questions buzzed in Nell's brain. "Would you mind explaining to me exactly what the foundation is supposed to do?"

"Certainly," he said. "Betsy's vision was that her home, which she left to the foundation, would serve as an artists' colony, taking in a handful of artists at a time for half-year residencies. The hope was that by providing a grant from the foundation for living expenses, plus a bedroom and studio space at the mansion, the artists would be freed up to focus on their work."

"That's very generous," Nell said. "I wish I could have met her."

Don nodded. "She really was an extraordinary woman. She wasn't one of those people who just wrote checks and sat on boards. Though she certainly did plenty of that. She also got to know the art community here in Madison and, to a certain extent, around the country. One of the things she often talked about was how nearly all the artists she knew spent most of their time doing something else that wasn't art—working day jobs in order to eat and support their families. Creative work was something that happened in the margins of their lives. Betsy wanted to bring it to the center, even if just for a short period of time, through the residency program."

Nell nodded. She didn't know many artists personally, which was rather strange, now that she thought about it, given the fact that she'd dedicated six years of her life to the intensive study of art—ten, when you factored in undergrad.

"How many artists will there be?" she asked.

"Three," Don said. "This year's class has already been chosen. Betsy wanted to be sure she was involved in that process. It was one of the last things she did before she died. I know I have their names written down somewhere. I remember one of them is a student from the university who came highly recommended by the art faculty. Betsy had close ties there and wanted to keep up that relationship through this program." He fumbled through some papers on his desk. "I'll have to get back to you with the artists' names. That is, if you decide to accept the position."

Nell blinked. "Are you offering it to me?"

Don crossed his arms in front of his chest, pushing his striped tie to one side. "You seem like you're well qualified. Probably overqualified, to be honest. And with our previous director gone and the candidates already planning to start soon, we're in a bit of a lurch. So, yes, I'm offering you the position."

A rush of surprise and excitement rose up in Nell's chest. She had been expecting to go through a call-back interview, at least, maybe some reference checks.

"Thank you," she said. "I'm thrilled. I'll still need to discuss the details with my husband, though, before I can give you a definite answer."

Talking it over with Josh wasn't the real reason she wanted to wait to give her answer. There was no question in Nell's mind that Josh would be happy to hear she'd be making more than minimum wage. And with a job in her field, no less—at least sort of. But running an artist-in-residence program wasn't exactly what Nell had envisioned when she went to grad school. In some ways, it sounded more interesting than teaching undergrad classes and grading countless papers. But the details of the position sounded largely unknown, and that scared her a little.

"Certainly." Don gave her a knowing smile. "My wife would kill me if I made such a big decision without consulting her."

"It shouldn't take long for me to get back to you," Nell said.

Don turned his chair slightly, glancing at his computer. "Take your time," he said. But his attention had already shifted to something on the screen. "You know where to find me."

Nell waited until she got home to call Josh. With the snow-covered streets and icy intersections, she didn't trust herself to talk and drive. Even though Chicago got its fair share of snowstorms, Nell had usually been able to avoid driving during them by taking public transport. Her winter driving skills were rusty.

She dialed Josh at work as she unlocked the side door of their house. Josh finally picked up on the fifth ring.

"Hey, what's up?" he said. "Sorry, I was just getting off the phone with the dean. Some big-shot Yale law professor is coming here the first week of the semester and we all have to volunteer to show him around for part of his stay."

"I got the job," Nell said, pushing the door open with her hip.

"Congratulations. Wow, that was quick."

"I know, I can't believe it." Nell stepped out of her heels and took off her coat.

"I can," Josh said. "You're probably overqualified."

"That's what Don said—he's the lawyer who interviewed me. The trustee of the foundation. I might need you to give me some basics on trust law. Turns out this whole thing was set up by a rich lady who died recently and left all of her money to a residency program for artists."

"So are you going to take it?" Josh asked.

"You know what?" Nell tossed her coat on the bench in the hallway. "Yes. I wasn't sure until just now. I'm a little afraid of jumping into a job I don't know very much about, but I think it will be a good challenge for me to do something different."

She didn't mention that her other fear—the fear of Josh finding out about the debt before she had a chance to pay it down—outweighed any lingering doubts she had about the directorship.

"Great," Josh said. "Listen, I've got to go, but I'll pick up a bottle of Champagne on the way home. Tonight, we're celebrating."

If Nell had known her first day of work would be the very next day, she probably would have stopped after one glass of Champagne instead of three. She slept in after Josh got up for work, waking past nine when her phone rang.

"Hello?" she said, sitting up in bed.

"Hello, Eleanor?"

"Don?" Her voice came out gravelly. She covered the phone with her comforter and cleared her throat. When she raised the phone to her ear again, she said, "What a coincidence. I was just going to call you."

"I hope it was to accept the job," he said. "Because I could use your help."

"As a matter of fact it was," she said. "I accept."

"Great," Don said. "I'll need you to fill out some paperwork, but we can do that later."

"So what can I do for you?" Nell asked.

"Remember when I told you how one of the artists selected was a university student?"

"Sure," Nell said. "For one of the three slots."

"Well, I just got a call from the chair of the art department there. She wants the young woman, a senior, to come and meet with you before the program starts and was wondering if today would be okay. Could you come by Betsy's house later? I'm sorry for the last-minute notice. Apparently the student is flying out to Rhode Island tomorrow morning to do an intensive interim class before winter break ends. When she gets back, it sounds like she'll be quite busy with both the residency and her spring semester classes starting up around the same time."

"Uh, sure, I can meet you at the house," Nell said, grabbing a paper and pen. "I just need to know where it is."

After they hung up, Nell opened her closet to search for something to wear. She couldn't wear the same suit she'd worn to the interview the day before. And, anyway, she wasn't sure she wanted to look quite so formal when meeting with a college student. She settled on a black jersey wrap dress that mercifully still stretched to fit her.

That afternoon, Nell left the house earlier than she probably needed to, taking her time on the slippery streets leading to the Mansion Hill Historic District. Some of the homes here had been lovingly restored and now housed B&Bs or law offices. Others, sadly, had been divided into crowded student apartments. These could be identified by slumped porches and crude For Rent signs tacked onto peeling siding. Only a few of the buildings in the district had remained single-family homes.

So much for historical preservation, she thought.

A light snow started to fall, and Nell slowed down, checking the addresses. The numbers matched those on a white Greek Revival mansion with black shutters, a red door, and a charming third-floor cupola that overlooked the lake. Its architectural style was simpler than that of the homes that bordered it—a multicolored Arts and Crafts beauty on one side and a blue Queen Anne Victorian on the other.

The house's clean design provided the perfect backdrop for a sculpture garden in its yard. A bronze tree stood in the middle of a berm topped by snow-covered bushes. A stone sculpture of a mother and child holding hands stood at the edge of a border made from tall grasses, now flattened by snow. The figures didn't have faces or really any detailed features—just two assemblies of rounded bodies and limbs. Still, the way the small figure's head was turned upward toward the taller figure brought a lump to Nell's throat.

A black Lexus sat idling in the mansion's brick driveway. Nell parked behind it and, before she could even get out of the car, Don already stood at her driver's-side window, tapping on the glass. Nell rolled the window down, shivering at the blast of cold air from outside.

Don thrust out a leather-gloved hand dangling a set of keys. "Here you go," he said.

She took them and got out of the car. "So this is Betsy's place?" she asked, staring up at the massive house. A wrap-around porch hinted of lazy summer days spent staring out at the lake.

"You should see it in spring," Don said, gesturing toward the front yard. "Betsy had her gardener rip out some of the grass and plant a native prairie garden. It blooms from April to October."

Nell took a few steps toward the mother and child sculpture. "I bet it's gorgeous, with all the sculptures."

"They're by Wisconsin artists," Don said. "Inside there are plenty of pieces by artists from all over the country, even the world, but Betsy said she felt strongly that if she was going to put artwork outside the house, where everyone would see it, she wanted it to be 'native,' just like the flowers she had planted." He looked at his gold watch. "I only have a few minutes before I need to head back to meet a client. But I can let you in and show you a few things."

He jiggled the key in the lock and pushed open the front door. Nell followed him into a foyer with marble-tiled floors, high ceilings, and a curved staircase lit by a crystal chandelier. She noticed a huge portrait of an elegant, gray-haired woman hanging on the wall of the landing. The woman wore a pale blue tailored jacket and diamond cluster earrings.

"That's Betsy," Don said. "It was painted several years ago, before the cancer diagnosis. She wasn't the sort of person to put a portrait of herself on the wall, but she cast the winning bid in a charity auction on a commissioned portrait by a local artist. I'm the one who hung it there, actually. Found it in a storage closet after she died. I thought that if this place was going to serve as her legacy, people might as well know what she looked like. Come on, let me show you where the trust documents are."

He led her to a room in the back of the house with large windows overlooking Lake Mendota. Out on the ice, Nell could see a few lone shanties and red tip-up flags signaling where fishing holes had been drilled. She turned around to look at the fireplace on the opposite side of the room flanked by built-in bookcases that looked like they'd been styled for *Architectural Digest*. Colorful books shared shelf space with small sculptures, folk art pottery, and the occasional natural object—a smooth, gnarled piece of driftwood here, a bird's nest there. In the middle of the room stood a large, lacquered desk.

"Was this Betsy's office?" Nell asked.

Don nodded. "It used to be Walt's, but after he died Betsy overhauled it. I guess it used to be all dark wood paneling and old maps on the walls. He collected them."

"Well, she did a beautiful job redecorating." Nell admired the sheer curtains and the window seat topped with ikat throw pillows.

Don walked over to the desk, where he fished around in a drawer and pulled out a sealed, cream-colored envelope and handed it to Nell.

"That's the trust," he said.

"Can I open it?"

"Please," he said. "It's the original, though, so make sure you keep track of it."

Nell slid a finger under the flap of the envelope and, with care, removed the document folded inside. The paper was thick and soft, almost like velvet. She ran her fingers over the bolded letters at the top of the first page: THE ELIZABETH BARRETT TRUST FOR THE FINE ARTS.

"She was constantly calling me about little things she wanted to change. I was worried that she'd pass away before I could finish the next draft so, in the end, I wrote the trust documents as flexibly as I could, just so we'd have something in place." Don nodded at the paper in Nell's hands. "But even after Betsy signed the documents, I know she kept making notes about her ideas. I told her to hang onto everything because it might be helpful later, for whoever ended up running this place. Which reminds me . . ." He pulled a slip of paper out of the pocket of his sport coat. "Keep track of this, too. It's the combination for the safe."

"Where is it?" Nell asked.

"To be honest, I'm not exactly sure. Somewhere in the house, supposedly. I looked around for it, right after she died—checked the closets, the attic, the basement—but couldn't find anything. This was all conveyed to me by a hospice nurse who called me a couple of days before Betsy died. Apparently Betsy was on so much pain medication she could barely remember her name, but she kept repeating the combination numbers." He shrugged. "It was like that at the end. She wanted to make sure she left everything 'just so,' but she ran out of time."

Don walked back over to the desk and opened up another drawer. "Somewhere around here there should be information about all the artists she picked for the program." He fingered past a couple of file folders.

Nell blinked, letting all of this settle in. "Is there anything else I should know?"

Don gave up and shut the drawer. "I wish I could be more helpful. The truth is, I haven't spent much time here except to check the mail and make sure the pipes aren't frozen. I write checks for the insurance and the property taxes, but other than that, I've been saving all the real work for the director." He gave her a sheepish smile. "I'm a lawyer, not an artsy type."

"I'm not really an artsy type, either," Nell said. "I just happened to have studied art."

"Well, that makes you ten times more qualified for this job

than I am," he said, glancing again at his watch. "Look, the college kid should be here soon. You've got the keys, so just make sure to lock up when you leave. As far as I'm concerned, this is your baby now. I mean, it's Betsy's baby, really. Which makes you, what? The nanny? The governess?"

Nell swallowed the sting that rose in her throat at the words "your baby." She didn't want to be the nanny of anyone or anything. She wanted to be a *mother*. Then she chided herself for being so sensitive about a simple figure of speech. Like Josh had said, she needed something else to put her energy toward. And, from the sense she was beginning to get from Don, it looked like the directorship would require all her energy and then some.

Chapter Three

Paige

PIECE: *Dale Chihuly,* Seaform, *circa* 1997. *Blown glass sculpture.*

By the time Paige got off the bus, she was already twenty minutes late for the meeting her advisor had set up. She probably could have walked faster if she hadn't felt so jittery, which, in turn, made her need a cigarette. She fished one out of her pocket, but couldn't find a lighter. A boy at the bus stop stood smoking, so she asked him if he had one.

He nodded and leaned forward, cupping the flame as he lit her cigarette. Paige noticed he was cute in the way she liked best—shy and soulful, all dark hair and skinny angles under his army surplus jacket. She inhaled, then stood back and smiled. "Thanks."

"What's in the folder?" he asked, nodding toward the nylon portfolio that hung against her hip.

Paige didn't usually like small talk, but she made exceptions for men she was attracted to. "Some prints I was working on earlier," she said. "I don't like to leave my stuff in the shared studio up at school. Is that weird?"

He shrugged. "It's your stuff. Are you an art major?"

She exhaled a stream of smoke, savoring the exquisite emptiness within her lungs before answering. "Yeah."

"You sound hesitant about it." He toed a clump of snow with his boot.

"Do I?" she said. "I'm not. I mean, it's the only thing I'm good at."

"I'm sure that's not true." The boy looked up and held her gaze for a fraction of a second before looking back down at his shoes.

Paige saw potential in that tiny opening, a momentary break in the dark clouds that usually muddied her mood. The clouds shifted only when she stood over a canvas or print, or sat with a sketch pad on her lap. Or, like now, when she felt the glow of a boy's attention. They weren't always boys, though. Sometimes they were much older men.

She felt the strap of her portfolio growing heavy on her shoulder, a reminder of just how late she was for her meeting. "Shit," she said. "I've gotta go. Thanks for the light."

She stomped out her cigarette on the sidewalk and, before she left, pulled a pen and scrap of paper out from the side pocket of her portfolio. She scribbled down her number, then stuffed it in the boy's pocket before turning and hurrying down the sidewalk.

The address she'd copied down from her acceptance letter from the residency program matched up with an honest-to-God mansion set back on a deep lakefront lot. Her parents had waterfront property, but it was nothing like this, at least from what Paige remembered.

Going "up north" when she was a kid meant sleeping in a trailer parked on forty acres of swampy woods abutting a river that attracted deer, geese, and all other sorts of hunting prey that kept her dad and older brother busy on fall weekends. She could never get used to firing a gun, so she'd stay back at the trailer with her mother or venture out on hikes with her sketchbook. Once, when she was fourteen, her mom caught her drawing a picture of a buck carcass, shading its bloody, matted fur with a red colored pencil. Her mom tore the page out and showed it to the high school guidance counselor, which set off a slew of meetings, evaluations, and a psychologist referral. Paige hadn't gone up north since.

The white mansion in front of her now was so foreign, it sent Paige searching for another cigarette. The brief reprieve afforded by the one she'd had at the bus stop had already worn off, leaving her nerves as jagged as the icicles hanging from the porch roof. But then she remembered she didn't have a lighter, so she rang the doorbell and picked at the paint underneath her fingernails instead.

The woman who came to the door looked to be in her thirties, maybe, with brown hair pulled into a low ponytail.

"Hi, I'm Nell," she said, extending her hand. "You must be the student from the university."

Paige shook her hand. "Paige Jewell. Nice to meet you."

She noticed that instead of looking her in the eye, Nell seemed to be staring at Paige's hands. Paige looked down and realized that the cuff of her quilted flannel coat had crept up to reveal a pink, puffy mark across her wrist.

Most of the time, she forgot about the scars. They had long since healed over and, now, held no more of her attention than the mole on her left cheek or the closed-up hole where she used to have a belly button ring. She forgot, though, that other people noticed.

Paige pulled her hand back and yanked down her sleeve.

"Sorry I'm late," she said. "I just found out about this meeting today from my advisor. I was in the studio up at school and totally lost track of time. I've been trying to finish this screen print before I leave tomorrow. But I've got five different screens and I can't seem to figure out which order to use them in. Each sequence produces a totally different end result." She stopped, realizing that she'd been rambling.

Nell nodded and said, "It's okay. Come on in."

Paige stepped into the foyer and stomped out of her combat boots, dripping dirty slush on the rug. She tilted her head toward a crystal chandelier hanging from the vaulted ceiling. "Wow," she said. "Do you live here?"

Nell shook her head. "No, I'm just the director of the program. But you and the other artists will stay here. The house was Betsy Barrett's—the woman who set up the residency program. She loved the arts, so she left her home and estate to an arts foundation she set up."

"I bet her kids were pissed." Paige set her portfolio carefully on the ground, leaning upright against the wall.

"I'm told she didn't have any children," Nell said. She gestured toward the living room. "If you want to come have a seat, I can tell you a little more about the program."

Paige shrugged out of her coat. She meant to ask if there was somewhere she should hang it up, but then she got distracted by a pair of glass objects displayed in a wall alcove in the hallway. She dropped her coat onto the rug next to her boots and walked over to inspect the items at closer range. One of them looked, to her eye, to be an ancient Asian vase made from white and blue porcelain. Beside it stood a more modern blown glass bowl that resembled a sea creature—a coral or anemone.

"Huh," Paige said. "I wouldn't have thought to put those two pieces together, but it works." She took out her phone and snapped a picture. Then she realized that Nell was standing behind her, and that what she just did might have seemed weird.

"I hope that's okay," Paige said. "I like to take pictures of things that are beautiful or unusual or unexpected. You never know what might inspire something later."

"It's fine," Nell said. "This will be your home for the next year. Take as many pictures as you'd like."

Paige followed Nell into the living room then. Nell sat down in an armchair and gestured for Paige to have a seat, too, but Paige walked over to the fireplace, where a large abstract painting hung above the mantel. She studied its thick black and gray brushstrokes and the white spaces between them that stared out at her like eyes. And then she felt her phone vibrating in her hand. She looked down at the screen. There was a text from an unknown number: This is Dylan. From the bus stop. What's your name?

Paige felt the sun break through the clouds. She smiled and typed back: Meet me somewhere and I'll tell u. As she hit send, a rush of excitement drowned out the soft, but nagging, voice of caution in the back of her head.

Paige lived for the adrenaline buzz of meeting someone new and, when it came to art, creating something new. These two things made everything else around her seem more interesting and alive. In the throes of a new relationship, her senses heightened. Colors became more saturated, even within winter's limited palette of grays, whites, and blues. She noticed nuances in music she'd never heard before, expanding the range she perceived between the low and high notes. Her artwork, in turn, got a jolt of inspiration. It had become a habit of hers to dive headlong into whatever medium she was working in, just as she dove into a new love interest. And then, when she became bored with a lover (because she always, *always* did), she became tired, too, of whatever type of work she'd been doing.

When she'd been sleeping with a software engineer that spring, she'd been heavy into graphic design work. The graphic design obsession came first, which led to her spending a lot of time in the fancy computer lab at the engineering school, where she hit it off with the only other person who stayed as late as she did. But they parted ways after he made the mistake of introducing her to someone as his girlfriend. Paige was a lot of things, but a girlfriend was not one of them.

She swore off graphic design shortly after that. She told her advisor it was because she didn't want to end up designing corporate logos for a living. Then she moved on quickly to oil pastels after she started having sex with a guy she met at the skate park. She'd been sketching the skateboarders as a study on movement, and he'd had the good luck of missing a landing, sending his board skidding toward where she sat cross-legged near the chain-link fence. She spent a lot of time at the park that summer, and at the boy's apartment nearby, but broke things off in the fall when classes started back up and her focus shifted to watercolor painting and to a shy vet student. She'd since given him up, too, and the break led her to her current obsession with screen printing.

Now, Nell's voice pulled Paige's attention away from her phone.

"Do you have anything you wanted to ask me?" Nell said. "About the program or anything?"

"Sorry," Paige said, stuffing the phone into the back pocket of her jeans. "Um, how many other artists will be here?"

"Just two. I don't have all the details yet, but they should be arriving within the next couple of weeks."

Paige had assumed the woman in charge of the program would know a little more about it. Her advisor had insisted that being chosen for the residency was a big deal, but now Paige wasn't sure what to think. She was grateful, certainly, for the room and board. But she was less excited about the prospect of living with two strangers whom apparently even the director knew next to nothing about.

She felt her phone vibrate again. She ignored it, though it took a lot of willpower to do so. She felt naked, listless without something tactile to occupy her hands—a paintbrush, a cigarette, the prickly stubble on a boy's cheek.

"I know you must have more questions than that," Nell said.

"Can I see my room?" Paige asked.

"Sure, I can take you upstairs. I have to be honest, though. I haven't been up there myself yet." Nell gave her a sheepish smile. "I was just hired this week to replace someone else, and haven't had a chance to, um, settle in yet."

At least that explains some of her cluelessness, thought Paige. She walked behind Nell up the curved staircase, taking the opportunity to pull out her phone and read another message from Dylan: I have to work till 9 tonight. How about tomorrow?

Another girl might have just suggested they get together when she got back from her trip. Another girl might have just let it go altogether. But then again, another girl might not have given her phone number to a stranger at the bus stop in the first place—might not be in the habit of looking for connections whenever and wherever she could.

Paige paused on the landing and responded: Leaving tomorrow for a week. Where do u work? I'll meet u when u get off.

She put the phone back into her pocket and took the last leg of stairs two at a time.

Chapter Four

Nell

PIECE: *Robert Louis Stevenson,* A Child's Garden of Verses, *1942 edition.*

Nell stood at the top of the steps, waiting for Paige to look up from her phone. She couldn't figure out if Paige was arrogant, rude, socially awkward, or some combination of the three. She kept trying to ask the girl questions, to draw her out and learn a little more about her, but nothing Nell said seemed to be as interesting as whatever message or internet meme was on that backlit screen. Nell started down the long hallway, peeking into each doorway she passed. She figured Paige would follow when she was ready.

What a shame, Nell thought, that the couple who lived here had never had any children. The house would have been an incredible place to grow up. She wondered if Betsy had ever felt the weight of all these empty bedrooms, like she did whenever she passed the spare room in her own home, the one Josh had taken over as his office.

Here, the bedrooms all had plush white carpet and furniture that looked like something straight from a museum decorative arts collection. Massive four-poster beds mixed with carved highboy dressers and fainting couches were beautiful for a bed-and-breakfast, Nell thought, but probably not practical for a working artists' colony. She might have to make some changes.

She stepped into the largest bedroom, overlooking the lake. She assumed, from the rose-colored velvet curtains and the damask bedspread, that this had been Betsy's room. An open door revealed a massive walk-in closet, still full of clothing, bags, and shoes.

Nell's first reaction was one of awe. She ran her hand across some of the fine fabrics—a featherlight chiffon dress in dove gray, a cream-colored blazer made from soft woven wool. But her second thought was *What am I going to do with all this stuff?* She had assumed, or maybe just hoped, that the house would be cleaned out and move-in ready for the residents. Now, with every doorway she walked through, her to-do list grew. Remembering the combination Don had given her, Nell pushed aside some of the garments on hangers to see if perhaps the locked safe he'd mentioned was hiding behind the rows of clothing. No such luck.

She heard footsteps somewhere above her, and went back out to the hallway, where she noticed a narrow set of stairs at the far end of it, leading upward.

"Paige?" she said. Nell headed up the steps, which creaked under her feet. At the top, the staircase opened up to the inside of the third-story cupola. The space was small, but bright and empty, illuminated by sunlight from windows on all sides.

Paige stood in the middle of the round room, looking at the exposed ceiling beams and the plank floors, the window seat on the lake side of the room. "I want this space," she said.

Nell blinked, surprised by the girl's boldness after she'd hardly said a word since arriving. "I think we should wait on any room assignments until all the residents are here and we've had a chance to assess everyone's need for space."

"Okay." Paige crossed her arms in front of her chest. "But just so you know, this is the only room in the whole house I'll be able to work in. The light's not right anywhere else."

"I saw that you brought your portfolio with you," Nell said, hoping to change the subject. "Do you mind if we go back downstairs so I can take a look?"

Paige shrugged. "Sure."

Back downstairs in the living room, Paige unzipped her portfolio and spread her screen prints out on the floor. Nell could see immediately that what the girl lacked in social graces she made up for in talent. The pieces ranged in subject matter from abstract patterns to natural objects and landscapes. They employed bold color combinations—crimson layered over orange and turquoise, magenta with emerald and gold. In the midst of January, the saturated hues were a balm to Nell's color-starved soul. Goose bumps crept across her skin.

Nell used to get goose bumps a lot. When she lived in Chicago, she used to view original artwork more frequently than she did her laundry. She would take the bus to the Art Institute at least once a week, just to feel the shivery tingle that ran up her spine when she stood in front of the neon-hued Warhols, the blurred and haunting Toulouse-Lautrec paintings, and Chagall's blue stained-glass windows. Something about the balance of color and space, the dance between precision and imperfection in Paige's prints brought back that shivery feeling for Nell.

The spell broke, though, when Paige pulled out her phone again, in the middle of a question Nell asked about one of the pieces. Instead of responding to the question, Paige began to gather up her artwork before Nell was even done looking at it.

"I've gotta go," Paige said, zipping the last of the prints inside her portfolio. "I'll be back in a week to move in my stuff."

"Let me know if I can help out in any way," Nell said to Paige's back. "Do you want my number?"

But the girl had already put on her coat and was halfway to the front door. "Bye," she yelled, almost as an afterthought and without turning around.

After the front door slammed shut, Nell went into the office, where the trust document still lay open on the desk. Even after she'd read it twice, taking notes, she wasn't certain what, exactly, her work as director was supposed to be. The artists had all been handpicked by Betsy. Nell, on the other hand, had stumbled into her role at the Colony. If it hadn't been for the previous director leaving on short notice and Nell's desperate need to pay down debt, she wouldn't be here it all.

Outside, the sky was going purple and a crescent moon glowed low on the horizon over the frozen lake, even though it was just past five o'clock. Nell opened the desk drawers and found a file folder filled with applications. At the top of the stack were three applications paper clipped together and affixed with a Post-it note that said, simply, "Yes." Paige's application was the first in the bunch. In the section asking the applicant to describe his or her work, Paige had written: "Oil pastel drawings of human subjects in motion."

That's weird, Nell thought. The works Paige had shown her earlier didn't include any pastels *or* human subjects.

Clipped to the application was a typed letter on letterhead from the university.

Dear Betsy,

Thank you for sending word about the residency program you are establishing. I encouraged one of my outstanding students, Paige Jewell, to apply, and I'm writing in support of her application.

Ms. Jewell is a remarkable talent across multiple forms of visual art. She moves brilliantly and effectively from one medium to another. She shows strong aptitude for the technical skills of drawing, painting, and printing, as well as a keen eye for innovation. However, it is my firm belief that she would benefit from focusing, for a longer period of time, on a single medium. The work she produces is consistently excellent, but I fear she is only skimming the surface of her abilities. My hope is that a residency opportunity would provide her with the environment she needs to nurture a drive to go deeper.

Sincerely,
Michael Murray, MFA

Nell turned to the next application, for an artist out of Minneapolis named Odin Sorenson. Stapled to it were professional photographs of stunning metal sculptures—graceful representations of birds, trees, and other natural forms, twisted and molded from steel and burnished copper.

When she picked up the third application and read the name, her hands froze.

"Annie Beck," she said aloud.

Nell had admired the artist's work since studying it in grad school. Ms. Beck was well-known for her public art installations, often with political themes. She'd been a member of the famous Feminist Art Collective in the seventies. Nell had read dozens of interviews the artist had given and watched documentaries about her work. She wondered what the one and only Annie Beck could possibly want with a fledgling residency in a midwestern university town.

The application provided precious little information about Annie's recent work. It said only that she was working on a "groundbreaking photo essay on human pain." Nell pulled her laptop from her handbag and opened it up to Google Ms. Beck. But as soon as she tried to log in to her account, a message popped up on her screen: "You are not connected to the internet."

No Wi-Fi? she thought. She added "set up internet" to her growing mental list of things she'd need to do before the residents arrived.

Nell put her computer back in her bag and picked up the phone instead. She dialed the number written on the application and had to hold in a squeal when she heard the voice mail message: "This is Annie. I'm probably in the studio. Leave me a message."

Nell hoped her voice didn't waver when she said, "Hello, this is Nell Parker. I'm the director of . . ." She paused. She wasn't sure what to call the program. Its legal name, the Barrett Foundation for the Arts, sounded so stiff and impersonal. She thought quickly and blurted out, "I'm with the Mansion Hill Artists' Colony in Madison. I wanted to speak with you further about our residency program and your plans for arrival."

She left her number and then played back the message to make sure she sounded more like a professional program director than a fangirl. When she heard the recording of her voice repeat the impromptu name she'd chosen for the program, she knew it would stick. It pulled in the history of the neighborhood, while also highlighting the community aspect of the residency.

The automated voice on the other end of the line said, "If you're satisfied with your recording, please press one."

Nell pressed one and, just like that, the Mansion Hill Artists' Colony was born.

BEFORE THE ARTISTS arrived, Nell brought a contractor through the mansion to get quotes for setting up Wi-Fi and doing some other updates to better accommodate the house's new use as an artists' colony. The contractor, Grady, came highly recommended by one of Josh's colleagues, so Nell thought nothing of giving him a key so that he could get started.

When she arrived at the mansion on the day Grady was scheduled to start working, Nell followed the sound of tapping and thumping to the living room. There, she saw that the small painting by Wisconsin-born Georgia O'Keeffe that usually hung on the wall had been taken down, as had a larger Lee Krasner piece. The Krasner, an abstract expressionist painting, leaned sideways on the floor, resting against an end table. Had Nell not looked at the piece dozens of times since she first stepped foot in the mansion, she might not have noticed that the painting was positioned on its side. The gray, maroon, and black curves and splotches inside the frame looked almost as interesting from this perspective as they did when the painting was upright.

The O'Keeffe, though, didn't make any sense upside down, which was how it now stood propped against the leg of a chair. Upended, the black hills in the painting looked as though they hung suspended from a smoky lavender sky.

Maybe giving the contractor a key was a mistake, Nell thought.

He stood on a ladder a few feet away, his right arm inserted up to the elbow into a hole in the wall. Plaster dust covered the wood floors beneath him.

"Um, Grady?" Nell said.

At the sound of Nell's voice, Grady twisted his body toward her. "Yeah?"

"So . . . I'm a little concerned about the artwork that's been taken off the walls."

He climbed down from the ladder and wiped his hands on his jeans. "Okay. I won't move anything else without talking to you first."

Nell looked around for a suitable place to put the displaced paintings. She moved a stack of art books from the coffee table to the top of the fireplace mantel to make space. As she did so, a photograph fluttered out of one of the books and down to the floor.

She picked up the small snapshot and recognized the unmistakable image of Andy Warhol, with his shock of white hair and curious, unsmiling expression. Next to him stood Betsy Barrett, beaming. Nell recognized her from the portrait that hung above the mansion's staircase, but she was much younger here. From the dress Betsy was wearing—a ruched black cocktail number with puffed sleeves—Nell surmised the photo was taken in the eighties. She flipped it over, hoping for a date or a notation, but saw none. She tucked the picture back into the book it had fallen out of, which was, appropriately, a hardcover collection of pop art prints.

With utmost care, Nell picked up the O'Keeffe painting and placed it faceup on the now clear coffee table, then followed suit with the Krasner piece.

"It's my fault," she said. "I probably should have hired some art movers to take all the pieces down properly and store them somewhere safe. But I had no idea simply getting the place wired for internet would be such a process. It amazes me that Betsy had the vision to hire someone to put up a website for her art foundation, yet didn't even have internet in her own home."

"It *shouldn't* be very complicated," Grady said. "But . . ."

Nell rubbed her forehead. "What is it?"

Grady shined his flashlight into the hole in the wall, illuminating a labyrinth of black cords and dusty white cylinders that looked like some sort of unstable pulley system.

"Live knob and tube wiring," Grady said. "It's a major fire hazard. And likely a code violation. You'll want to get this replaced."

"Is it something you can take care of?" Nell rubbed her forehead. It had been hard enough to find Grady on short notice. She didn't want to have to start calling other contractors as well. She wished, for the hundredth time, that she'd had a little more time to prepare for the directorship and to get the Colony ready before the residents arrived. As it stood, she still didn't know when they were all showing up. Annie hadn't returned her call, and Odin hadn't responded to the introductory email she'd sent him.

"I know an electrical subcontractor who can probably do

it," Grady said. "But you'll also want to get a plasterer in here to take a look at things. These walls are really thick. And look here." He climbed back onto the ladder and fished around for something in the recesses of the ancient plaster. A moment later he pulled a wad of straw and newspaper out of the wall cavity and handed it to Nell. "Here's your insulation. Guess it explains why the house is so drafty. You'll probably want to have it replaced it with some blown-in insulation if you're gonna open up the walls anyway."

"Okay, so what does all this mean, in terms of time frame? Maybe an extra couple of days?"

"Longer, if you want it done right. I'll make some calls but, depending on the schedules of the guys I want to get in here, it could be weeks before they can come take a look."

Nell rubbed her forehead and looked at the priceless works of art lying on the coffee table as casually as if they were magazines. She brushed a layer of plaster dust off the mantel, then rubbed her temples. She was beginning to feel as if she'd signed up for her own season of *This Old House* instead of an art directorship.

She pictured her own aging home, though much less grand, just a mile away. When she and Josh moved in, they'd made a list of all the things they wanted to tackle, in terms of renovations. They'd envisioned remodeling the bathroom, but saving its classic black-and-white hex tile and claw-foot tub. They'd dreamed of refinishing the basement, which, although a little musty now, could eventually house a playroom or a guest bedroom. But that was all before they, or rather Nell, started funneling all their spare funds toward fertility treatments. But Josh didn't know about all that, and she intended to keep it that way, at least until she had a few paychecks under her belt to put toward the credit card debt.

"Did you get a chance to look at the floors upstairs?" Nell asked.

Grady wiped the plaster dust from his hands onto his jeans. "I pulled up a corner of the carpet in a few of the bedrooms. The hardwood looks to be in good shape, just needs refinishing, so my original quote still stands. I could get started on that while we're waiting to hear from the plaster guys."

"That would be great."

"I'll be back tomorrow, then." Grady picked up his toolbox, tipped his baseball cap, and went out the front door, leaving Nell to contemplate the hole in the wall where artwork had once hung.

She picked up the stack of books she'd placed on top of the mantel and looked for a place to put them on the bookshelves. She paused when she saw a title she recognized in the pile, *Crossing to Safety* by Wallace Stegner. Out of curiosity, she opened its cover and saw that it was signed by the author and inscribed to Betsy, "From one Madisonian to another." Nell slid the book onto a shelf and followed suit with the others. She recognized the names of these books, too, by Joyce Carol Oates, Kurt Vonnegut, and Lorrie Moore. All of them were signed and inscribed with some sort of reference to Madison or to Betsy. Her bookshelves were like a hardbound literary cocktail party.

But one thin, tattered book that had been shelved with the others didn't seem to belong. The title, *A Child's Garden of Verses*, was one Nell had owned as a little girl, though in a later edition with a different cover. This book, too, had writing inside its cover—a handwritten note that said, "Happy Birthday, Elizabeth. 5 already! Love, Mother."

With those simple words, fresh pain welled in Nell's chest. One of the things she'd most looked forward to doing with her own baby was reading aloud. She remembered browsing the children's section of a local bookstore shortly after she found out she was pregnant. There were so many characters and places there she'd completely forgotten about. The Hundred Acre Wood, Madeline and Miss Clavel, Harold and his magical purple crayon.

She swept her palm across the faded cover, removing a layer of dust. Then she traced her finger along the outline of a drawing of a young girl in a white dress, standing in a windswept field of flowers. The girl's fine, tousled hair was tied up with a ribbon. A pink satin ribbon.

Nell had a white box tied with just such a pink ribbon. She knew its contents by heart: a soft flannel blanket, a hospital bracelet, and a silver envelope. As far as she was aware, Josh had never opened the box.

Chapter Five

Betsy

PIECE: *Bill Blass gown, from the fall 1981 collection.*
Black silk taffeta with puffed sleeves.

*B*etsy, *there* you are."

Ingrid Alber, the only person in the room Betsy knew in the sea of tuxedos and winking diamonds, waved at her with a white-gloved hand. Of course, Betsy *recognized* many of the guests at the inaugural reception. Barbara Walters was there, as was an Italian baron. But, other than her husband Walt and a few of his lawyers, Betsy knew the other guests in attendance only from television and the society pages.

Ingrid, though, was a dear friend, and married to one of the partners in the silk-stocking New York law firm that handled all of Walt's business affairs. Betsy saw her only a few times a year, when Walt's business brought him to the city and Betsy would come along for what she called her "tune-ups." On those trips, she would visit museums and galleries, getting her fix for both the old masters and the up-and-coming names in the art world. And she would shop, both for clothing and for art. Ingrid often joined Betsy on these excursions. She'd show up at the hotel at nine thirty with coffee and croissants and say, "Wanna go bummin'?"

"Bummin'" was a term from Betsy's childhood on Milwaukee's South Side. Then, it had meant running errands with her mother. Sometimes it meant dropping shoes off at the cobbler or picking up a meat order at the butcher's. Other times they would board the city bus and go bargain hunting in the basement at Gimbels department store. Where they went or what they did was less important than the chatter and easy laughter that accompanied the errands. Betsy remembered those hours as the rare times she had her mother's attention all to herself. Usually, her mother's focus was fixed on Betsy's brother, younger by eight years, and the three neighbor boys she took care of for extra money.

Ingrid, a lifelong New Yorker, loved the idea of bummin' as soon as she heard it, and began to use the word to describe her and Betsy's few days a year of browsing, lunching, and catching up on one another's lives.

The two women had met through their husbands' orchestrations. The men felt less guilty about being in meetings all day if they knew Betsy wasn't sitting around alone in her hotel room—not that she ever was. Between Jasper Johns at MOMA, Gauguin at the Guggenheim, and Vermeer and Velázquez at the Met, Betsy never felt lonely in New York.

Nonetheless, she was grateful for Ingrid's loud, lively company, and the women developed a fast friendship.

Now, Ingrid made her way through the crowd and embraced her friend. "Bets, look at you! Your dress turned out lovely."

Betsy pulled at the tight bodice of her floor-length black gown. "I'm not used to wearing something quite so unforgiving," she said. "I feel a bit like a ballpark bratwurst bulging out of its casing."

Ingrid laughed. "Now that's an image I don't want to think too hard about."

"You can take the girl out of Wisconsin, but you can't take the Wisconsin out of the girl, I suppose," Betsy said.

Ingrid plucked a Champagne glass from the tray of a passing waiter. "Want one?"

Betsy shook her head. "No thanks. I already had too many canapés. If I consume anything else, I'm afraid I'll split my ruched seams."

"Well, in any event, you look fabulous."

"So do you," Betsy said. She recognized the long, voluminous gold skirt and trim velvet jacket Ingrid had on as something she'd bought at Saks on their most recent bummin' expedition. Betsy wondered what her late mother would say if she could see them now. She'd come a long way from bargain-basement shopping.

"Did you see the protesters on your way over here?" Ingrid asked. "I read some artist got arrested this morning for lighting a TV on fire in Lafayette Square. The article said she'd made models of Ronald and Nancy and stuck them inside the TV in compromising positions."

"Annie Beck." Betsy rolled her eyes. "It was a performance art thing. I read about it, too."

"Do you know her?"

Betsy shook her head. "I used to follow her career early on, when she was with the Feminist Art Collective. Her work seemed really avant-garde back then, but it hasn't evolved at all. Seems like she cares more about the publicity than the art itself."

"I'm no expert, but these days it seems like it's hard to separate the two." Ingrid dropped her voice. "That reminds me. Did you know Andy Warhol is here, too?"

"Really?" Betsy swiveled her neck, scanning the crowd. "Where?"

Ingrid gave an almost imperceptible nod of her head toward the corner of the room. Betsy spotted the artist standing next to a potted palm, holding a Polaroid camera and conversing with two women in sequined gowns.

"I'm surprised they let him bring in his camera," Betsy said.

"He's been snapping pictures of people all night."

"Security made me check mine. 'No press pass, no camera, ma'am.'" Betsy imitated the stern voice of the Secret Service officer who'd greeted her at the door. "I guess they don't want people taking unattractive pictures of the Reagans and then selling them to the *National Enquirer* or something."

"Well, Andy doesn't seem like much of a rules guy," Ingrid said. "Speaking of the Reagans, have they made an appearance here yet? My husband will be absolutely fuming if they don't at least pop in, after what he and his partners spent on this shindig."

"I don't think so. But who cares about the Reagans? *Andy Warhol* is here. That's far more exciting, at least for me."

"Shhh." Ingrid put a gloved finger to her lips. "Don't let Walt hear you say that."

"My husband is all too familiar with my political leanings. I told him that when he dies I'm backing only Democratic candidates, to cancel out all the support he gives to Republicans," Betsy said. She wished she could be more vocal about her political views *now*, but she was realistic enough to know that as the head of a major plastics manufacturer, Walt had business interests that aligned more closely with the politics of conservative candidates. She was smart enough not to bite the hand that fed her affinity for art and travel.

Ingrid laughed. "And what does *he* say about that?"

"He says he'll outlive me just to keep it from happening." Betsy stood on her toes to see over a tall, tuxedoed man now blocking her view of Andy. In doing so, she nearly toppled over in her high-heeled pumps.

Ingrid caught her arm. "Careful there."

"Do you think he'd let me have a picture with him?" Betsy asked.

"On his Polaroid?" Ingrid asked. "I don't know. He seems pretty possessive of it. He hasn't put it down since he got here."

"No, no. I'm not *that* presumptuous. But maybe we could get one of the photographers to take it. They're all over the place."

Ingrid shrugged and took a sip of Champagne. "Can't hurt to ask. You work on Andy and I'll round up one of the photographers."

"I guess I'll have some Champagne after all." Betsy grabbed her friend's glass, took a long swig, and then handed it back. She squared her shoulders and set off in Andy's direction.

He was still engaged in conversation with the sequined ladies, so Betsy hovered nearby, pretending to be absorbed in a painting hanging on the wall. It was an anonymous, hideous attempt at an impressionist landscape. The antique gilded frame encasing it was more interesting than the painting itself. But just when she felt as if her eyes would start bleeding, the two women walked away, leaving Andy momentarily free.

Betsy strode over as casually as she could manage. She was glad, after all, that Ingrid had talked her into buying the Bill Blass gown. It was much flashier and fashion forward than the tailored sheaths she usually wore, and it seemed more fitting, somehow, for meeting one of the most famous artists of her time.

"Pardon me," she said.

Andy looked up from fiddling with his camera. His expression was curious, but not annoyed.

"This is going to sound like an utter cliché, but I love your work," Betsy said. "Of course, I can't *afford* it—"

"And that's saying a lot," said Ingrid, appearing with a photographer in tow.

"Thank you," said Andy. His voice sounded the same as it did in interviews, soft in volume and long on vowels.

Andy looked from one woman to the other, before settling his gaze back on Betsy. "You like art?"

"'Like' is not the word," Betsy said. "I'm a bit obsessed."

"A collector, then?" he asked.

"The woman is an absolute art *hoarder*," Ingrid said. "And she's also a dear friend who would love it so much if you'd be willing to let us get a picture of the two of you."

Andy tilted his head slightly to one side, causing his white hair to fall over his eyes. "Do I know you?"

"I'm nobody." Ingrid gave a dismissive wave. "But *this* is Betsy Barrett."

Betsy held out her hand, and he shook it.

"I'm Andy."

"Delighted to meet you," Betsy said. "It's a true honor."

"As long as we're doing introductions, you should also meet my wife, Sony," Andy said.

"I didn't know you were—" Betsy stopped herself. She was about to say "married," but laughed when Andy held up a tape recorder.

"You haven't answered my question about the picture," Ingrid said. "Is it all right if the photographer here snaps one, pretty please? Then we promise to leave you alone."

"Why not?" Andy said. "But let's use my camera. Then you can have the picture right away."

"Oh no," Betsy said. "We don't want to waste your film."

"I take dozens of pictures every day. What's one more?"

"But you need to be *in* the picture," Ingrid insisted. "None of her midwestern housewife friends will believe she met Andy Warhol unless she has photographic evidence."

"Okay, then." Andy handed his camera to Ingrid. "You take it."

Ingrid raised the viewfinder to her eye. "Smile!"

"For the midwestern housewives," Andy said.

Betsy smiled big, feeling starstruck and flash-blinded.

Andy took back his camera just as it was spitting out the undeveloped photo. He removed it and handed the photo to Betsy.

"Thank you so much," she said. "Really. It means a lot to me. I've followed your work since you first started out."

"Thank *you*," Andy said. "Now if you'll excuse me, I've got to go say hello to Happy."

"Let me guess, Happy is a record player," Betsy said.

Andy shook his head. "No. She's a Rockefeller."

Chapter Six

Annie

PIECE: *Oriental rug with medallion pattern.*
Constructed of hand-knotted wool, 10 x 12 feet.

*A*nnie Beck chained her rental bike to a porch spindle and climbed the mansion's front steps. She rang the bell next to the red door and waited, watching snow swirl around her battered boots.

Annie had been to Madison before, but never in January. Her first visit had been decades earlier, for a protest against the Vietnam War. She remembered the vigorous green of the Capitol lawn in early spring and a humid wind that curled her hair, still long and auburn in those days. In hindsight, maybe it was the hot energy of the crowd that she remembered, and not so much the weather. Today, Madison felt like a place that had never been warm or green, and never would be again.

When no one answered the doorbell, Annie rapped the brass knocker.

A woman opened the door wearing jeans and a University of Chicago sweatshirt speckled with dust. She looked startled at first, but then her brown eyes lit up with recognition. "You must be Annie," she said. "I'm Nell Parker."

"Nice to meet you," Annie said, extending her hand.

Nell wiped her palms on her jeans before shaking Annie's hand. "I hope you weren't waiting long. I was upstairs with a contractor." A mechanical *whir* sounded from inside. "I'm sorry about the noise. He said he should be done with the sander by tomorrow."

"It's no problem," Annie said. "Did you get my email?"

Nell shook her head. "Maybe you sent it to the former director? I was just hired to take her place. I called the number that was written on your application. Did you get my message?"

"That was the number at my old apartment. Maybe you left the message after I moved out?" Annie shifted her backpack from one shoulder to the other. "So this is probably a bit of a surprise, then."

Nell waved a dismissive hand. "Don't worry about it. Come in, it's freezing out there."

Annie stepped into the front hall. She was about to wipe her boots on the throw rug, but stopped when she looked down at the bold bands of orange, blue, and gold running along its borders, framing an intricate design that looked handwoven.

Nell must have caught her looking at it because she said, "It's gorgeous, isn't it? The estate lawyer said Betsy, the Colony's benefactor, bought it in Turkey. That's her, up there." She

pointed to an oil portrait on the wall above the grand staircase, which curved toward the second floor like a fiddlehead
fern. "I like to try to picture her, just like that, navigating a
Turkish bazaar and bargaining with merchants."

The woman in the painting had gray hair, like Annie, but
that was where the similarities ended. Where the portrait subject posed in a suit jacket and diamonds, Annie wore a ther-
mal shirt under faded overalls, paired with dangly turquoise
earrings she'd bought at an art fair in Sedona.

"Seems almost a shame to wipe my shoes on," Annie said.
She stepped out of them and set them onto the tile, which
could at least be cleaned. She wasn't sure as much could be
said for the rug.

"Do you have any other bags?" Nell nodded toward the
backpack Annie was carrying. She had to yell to be heard
above the construction noise coming from upstairs.

Annie shook her head as she shrugged off her winter jacket.
"They're coming later," she shouted. "I had to leave New York
in kind of a hurry. It's a long story."

Nell took Annie's coat and hung it in a closet. "I would take
you up to see your room, but it's pretty dusty up there. The
contractor is taking out the carpet and refinishing the wood
floors."

"No problem," Annie said. "I'm pretty sure I can find a
way to be comfortable in a lakefront mansion, regardless of
what my bedroom looks like. You wouldn't believe some of
the places I've lived. Back in the seventies, I shared an apart-

ment with seven other women. And I'm sure you know how small Manhattan apartments are."

Nell nodded. "The Feminist Art Collective, right?"

"Yes," Annie said, surprised. "For a second there, I was about to be flattered that you knew about me. But then I remembered you probably read my application."

"I did," Nell said. "But I also studied your work when I was in grad school."

Annie felt her cheeks flush with pride. "Well, don't believe everything you read. Some of the press made it seem like the Collective was this urban utopia, all flower power and Indian tapestries on the walls. The truth is that it was teeming with roaches, and I don't just mean the kind leftover when you've smoked down a joint. Our landlord was a total pig, always making lesbian jokes and staring at our chests when he came to collect the rent."

"Well, we won't be charging the residents any rent here," Nell said. "And even if we did, you can be sure you wouldn't get that sort of treatment."

"Oh, I know. And, anyway, anybody staring at my chest these days is likely to be disappointed. Gravity has not been my friend, and I suppose all those years of going braless didn't help." Just as Annie finished her sentence, the sander upstairs switched off, so that she was yelling the part about going braless in an otherwise silent house. She put a hand over her mouth and stifled a chuckle, then let it out when she saw that Nell was laughing, too.

"Your contractor is really getting an earful today," Annie said.

"It's fine," Nell said. "Here, follow me. It's quieter in the back of the house."

Once Nell had closed the office door behind them, she was able to speak at a normal volume. "Please, have a seat. And tell me, what made someone like you interested in coming here?"

Annie eased into the chair across from the desk and set her backpack on the floor. She paused before answering. There were a lot of reasons she'd come to Madison, starting with the fact that she'd been kicked out of her co-op building and blacklisted in dozens of others. But she couldn't say *that*.

She cleared her throat. "I've always thought my best work was from the years I was part of a community. Back when I was involved with the Collective, there was this buzz, you know? This energy that just radiated throughout that dumpy old flat. Listen to me, talking about energy like some sort of burned-out hippie cliché."

There, she thought. *It's not a lie. It's just not the whole truth.*

"No, I know what you're saying," Nell said. "I think that's exactly what Betsy—the one whose portrait you saw—had in mind in setting this place up. She wanted to support the arts with her own resources, but she also wanted the artists to support *each other.*"

Annie tapped her hand against her thigh, brushing her fingers against a hole in the knee of her overalls. "Exactly. I think most artists have this vision of reaching people, of communicating some sort of universal idea. But then we go off into our studios and shut our doors and create in isolation. With the Collective, there was none of that. We commented on each other's work and bounced ideas off one another. I miss that."

"Are you still in touch with any of the other artists?" Nell asked.

"A few. Not as many as I'd like." Annie smiled and shook her head. "I remember this mixed media artist, Luz something . . . I haven't heard anything about her in decades. But she had this giant King Kong statue that she'd made out of all these disposable coffee cups. She wanted to display it in Central Park, but couldn't afford to hire a truck to haul it there for her. So she took it apart and a handful of us took it on the subway up from our place in the Village. One girl held a leg, another held an arm. I got the job of transporting the head. We all had to go in different cars so there'd be enough room to get in and out without smashing the thing to bits. So there I stood on the subway, with this gorilla face straddled between my legs."

"A metaphor for your role in the art world, perhaps?" Nell said.

Annie grinned.

"So what are you working on now?" Nell asked.

"A photo essay," Annie said, giving the answer she'd rehearsed.

"What's your subject?"

"People, of course. It's always people with me. Landscapes, still life—none of that stuff has ever held my interest. So, in terms of work area, I'll need enough space to be able to have multiple people in the studio at a time. I'll need my space to be private, too, with an entrance that's separate from the rest of the house. I'll have subjects coming and going a lot, and I don't want to disrupt everybody else's work."

"Well, the basement has a door that leads to the backyard," Nell said. "But I don't want to stick you all the way down there. The light might not be good enough. Do you want to go down and see?"

"Maybe later." Annie shrugged. "I'm sure it's fine. I'm not picky, and I've got good lighting equipment, so I don't need to be a prima donna about natural light. I've done my artwork in closets, library carrels, and even in the back seat of a bus. I'll be fine as long as there's heat."

And as long as there's no co-op board, she added silently.

"And you're sure you're up for living in Madison?" Nell asked. "You've probably noticed that it's not exactly New York."

"I've been here before," Annie said. "The first time was back in the seventies. This place was *on fire* back then. Seemed like one student protest or another was always making the news."

"You can still find some of that activism, if you're looking," Nell said. "But not on nearly the same level."

"That's okay," Annie said. "The other reason I want to be here is because I need a change of pace. I'm getting older, you know? I love the city, but this old lady could use a bit of peace and quiet now and then. I never thought I'd say it, but there it is."

"Okay. I just needed to make sure we didn't lure you here, only for you to be bored out of your mind."

"I'm never bored," Annie said.

"I believe that."

Annie glanced at her watch. "I hope you won't think I'm rude, but I just came by to introduce myself and drop off my backpack. I've actually got meetings set up all afternoon with some people I hope will be willing to sit as subjects for me. I placed some ads back when I was still in New York and want to meet some of the folks who responded. There's nothing quite like jumping into a new project."

"You're not by any chance making an independent film, are you?" Nell asked.

"No, why?"

"Just something I saw in the classified ads asking for actresses ages eighteen to thirty, no experience needed."

"Oh, *that* kind of film. No, I'll just be doing still photography. And I've already been in touch with the local technical college about using their darkroom." Noticing the strange look Nell gave her when she mentioned that last part, she added, "I'm doing things the old-fashioned way, using film. There's something to be said about developing your own images." Annie stood up. "Anyway, I'm sure the space downstairs will be fine. This is such a beautiful house. How fantastic that it's being used for this purpose."

"It was all Betsy's idea," Nell said. "I'm just the worker bee hired to carry out what she started."

"I never underestimate a worker bee. Visionaries are great,

but a vision isn't worth much without somebody willing to carry out the hard work." Annie moved toward the door. "Sorry to have to run. Will you still be around in a couple of hours?"

"I'll be here," Nell said, walking with Annie toward the front door. "It was so great to meet you."

"Likewise," Annie said.

"Be careful driving out there," Nell said. "The roads are pretty slippery."

"Oh, I didn't drive," Annie said, gesturing toward the fat-tire Schwinn cruiser chained to the porch. "I rented a bike. Heard it's the best way to get around town."

"Biking in the snow? See, you're a true Madisonian already."

It felt strange, Annie thought, to be called anything other than a New Yorker. But for now, at least, she'd have to get used to it.

Chapter Seven

Annie

PIECE: *Lee Krasner,* Hieroglyph, *circa 1969. Oil, collage, and gouache on paper.*

Outside Poughkeepsie, the leaves were still green, but a chill swirled in the air, causing Annie to pull the sleeves of her poor boy sweater down over her thumbs, trying to keep her hands warm. She sat down on a fallen tree trunk and rubbed her palms together. She hadn't been counting on the cold temperature this morning. Back at Vassar, where Annie was a freshman, summer seemed to linger through the first few days of classes, with girls wearing cotton blouses and pulling their hair off their necks in the middle of lectures, securing their buns with crisscrossed pencils. But here, next to the open highway in the early morning, you could smell the promise of the changing season—a damp, earthy coolness on the wind.

Dolores, Annie's traveling companion, who went by just

Dee, stood on the shoulder of the highway just a few feet away. Her long hair flickered like prayer flags around her face. She stuck out her thumb as a Buick blew by them. The dust settled behind it and the road went quiet again.

"Fascists," Dee muttered. She wore a sleeveless top and, as she waved her arm at another passing car, Annie could see fine, dark hair at her armpit.

"Want me to take a turn?" Annie asked. "You've been at it for a while."

Dee flopped her hand to her side and took a step back. "Have at it. You might as well wait until we see a car coming, though. No use tiring out for no reason."

Annie had never hitchhiked before. And, until today, she'd never met Dee. She'd just seen her flyer on the student center bulletin board about going to Atlantic City to protest the 1969 Miss America pageant.

Now, Dee picked up her knapsack and sat down on the log next to Annie. When she set the bag back down on the ground, it made a clanking sound.

"What you got in there?" Annie asked.

"A couple of pots and pans," Dee said. "I've been talking with the group from New York who organized this whole thing, and the plan is to gather on the boardwalk outside the pageant. Someone is making a freedom trash can and we're all gonna throw stuff into it and burn it—you know, symbols of women's oppression and traditional roles. Me and some other girls said we'd bring pots and pans. Some others are bringing mops, makeup. I think one girl is bringing some bras to toss in there. Did you bring anything?"

Annie patted the backpack on her lap. "Straitjacket."

"You serious?"

Annie nodded. "Dead."

A smile spread across Dee's face. "Right on."

Annie had spent a good chunk of her summer at the branch of the New York Public Library in her parents' neighborhood, reading up on feminist theory and the role of art as an agent of social change. Now that she was living away from home, this was her first chance to add to that conversation with her own art. *If* she could get to Atlantic City on time to put together her piece.

"I need to get my hands on a mannequin when we get there," Annie said. "I was thinking I'd have plenty of time before the pageant gets started this evening, but now I'm not so sure."

"You *should* be okay." Dee shaded her eyes from the sun. "If someone picks us up anytime soon."

It was already late morning by the time the next vehicle came into sight. A truck, this time.

Annie sprang to her feet. Her first instinct was to wave her arms like she was hailing a cab, but Dee laughed.

"No, just the thumb out," Dee said. "You gotta look calm."

Annie did as Dee said. She also straightened her miniskirt and smiled her best coed smile.

The truck slowed down and pulled over to the shoulder.

The driver, a deliveryman, leaned across the front seat and greeted them through the open window.

"Where you headed, ladies?" he asked.

"Atlantic City," Annie said.

"Same here," he said. "Go ahead and get in if you'd like."

Annie looked back at Dee, beaming with accomplishment. Dee just gave a nonchalant shrug and picked up her knapsack.

Once they'd pulled back onto the highway, Annie said, "Thank you so much. Can we give you money for gas or anything?"

"Nah," he said. "It's no trouble. I've gotta go there no matter what, so might as well have company. Gotta deliver some rental equipment for the Miss America pageant."

"Oh yeah?" Dee said. "We're headed there, too."

"Y'all are contestants?" The driver turned to look at them. Annie could feel his eyes sliding over her legs, exposed to high thigh on the vinyl seat. She noticed the pause in his gaze as his eyes fell on Dee's chest, where her nipples made two little bumps like marbles under her thin shirt.

Annie snorted. "Hell no. We're going for a—"

Dee shot her a warning look.

"Art program," Annie said. "I'm an art student."

"Oh yeah? Who's your favorite artist?" he asked.

"Living or dead?"

"Let's go with living."

"Then I'd have to say Lee Krasner."

The driver shrugged. "Never heard of him."

"*Her*," Annie said. "She's a woman."

Dee was coloring in a flower she'd drawn on the knee of her jeans with a pen. "Is she the artist who was married to Jackson Pollock?"

Annie rolled her eyes. "Yes. But that's not why I love her. She was a pioneer in abstract expressionism, a field dominated by men. When she married Pollock, *she* was actually better known in the modern art world than he was. If it weren't for her, we'd probably never have heard of Pollock."

"I thought I read that he and his wife both died in a car crash years back," the driver said. "Drunk driving. It was in all the papers."

Annie shook her head. "Pollock died. And there was a woman in the car with him who survived the accident, but it wasn't Krasner. It was his mistress."

"Can we *not* talk about car crashes while we're driving?" Dee asked.

"Fair 'nuff," the driver said.

They kept up small chatter for the rest of the four-hour ride, with the driver talking about his job and the girls talking about the classes they were enrolled in that semester. Dee bitched about how everything was going to change now that the college had started admitting men.

The delivery driver seemed nice enough, mentioning his wife and kids sometimes. Still, Annie was glad when he dropped them off a block from Boardwalk Hall in Atlantic City.

"Good luck with your art project," he said, waving.

After he pulled away, Annie said, "I've gotta get my hands on a mannequin."

Dee laughed. "Right."

"One of the girls from my dorm told me there's a department store just off the boardwalk."

When they found it, they saw that the display windows were decorated for the pageant, with mannequins wearing sashes and dressed according to motifs associated with their states—a dress printed with embroidered stars for Texas, a rainbow-striped miniskirt on Miss Hawaii. Annie pulled at the glass doors, but they wouldn't budge. Dee walked over to a second bank of doors and tried those. No luck.

Inside, Annie saw movement. She shielded her eyes from the late-day glare reflecting off the glass. A woman swayed back and forth, as if dancing. A power cord trailed behind her.

Annie tapped on the glass and waved.

Dee shot Annie a withering look. "She's vacuuming. She can't hear you."

Annie waved her arms higher and wider.

Dee rolled her eyes. "Listen, I'll leave you here with your mission, now that you've found the place. I'm gonna try to get a snack somewhere. Meet you back in front of Boardwalk Hall?"

"Sure," Annie said.

Dee turned and walked back in the direction they'd come, her long hair swishing against her back.

The woman inside the store turned toward the window then, swirling in a circle with the vacuum. As she did, she squinted in Annie's direction, then bent down to flip a switch. She left the vacuum behind her, came over, and unlatched the door.

"May I help you?" the woman asked.

"I'm so sorry to bother you," Annie said. "But I was hoping you could help me with a somewhat unusual request. I'm wondering if I could borrow one of the store's mannequins this evening."

The woman crossed her arms in front of her chest, looking skeptical.

"I'm doing a project, you see. I'll get it back to you tomorrow morning before the store opens. I promise," Annie said, flashing her most innocent smile. She was glad, then, that she had dressed as she did after all. That morning she'd felt square and childish, standing on the side of the highway in her sweater and skirt, next to the much more worldly Dee, braless and bell-bottomed.

Annie studied the woman, noticing the crease in her forehead, the strands of gray winding in and out of the mass of brown hair pinned away from her face. "Listen"—Annie glanced at the name embroidered in red above the pocket of the woman's blue uniform dress—"Mary. I know it's a lot to ask. I bet your boss wouldn't be too happy if he found out."

"My boss isn't happy with pretty much anything." Mary played with her necklace, a small gold cross. "I'd tell him where to go, except that I need this job more than ever now with Bobby off in Vietnam. I used to be able to stay home with my kids, back when he was just in the reserves. Never thought he'd actually get called up. I get checks, but it's not what he made before he left. We used to get two checks, one from his regular job and a smaller one from the reserves."

Annie nodded. "How many kids do you have?"

"Three," Mary said. "After Bobby got called up, I was having a hard time coming up with enough money to pay my kids' Catholic-school tuition. And Bobby's mother won't hear of them being raised as heathens at the local P.S. 'Course she won't spare a dime of her own money to help out, even though I know she's got it. She doesn't know I'm cleaning floors." She stopped then, as if she'd just realized she was telling too much to a complete stranger.

"Nothing wrong with working," Annie said. "Surely your husband must appreciate the extra money coming in."

"At first he didn't want me to work at all. Thinks it reflects badly on him, like he can't provide for us. I say it's just reality. When I explained how much we needed the extra money, he agreed to let me do some interviews. He asked me why I couldn't get a job at a bank or an office or something. And I told him, sure, that sounds great, but nobody at a bank is gonna hire a lady with zero job experience. I can't type, I don't know shorthand. I just married Bobby straight out of high school and started having babies. So that's how I ended up doing cleaning work here."

"Do you like it?"

Mary shrugged. "I don't mind it. I just wish I saw more *people* at work. The girl who got me the job here, she works at the lingerie counter, and that's where I initially wanted to go. Thought it would be nice to be able to work together, and talk with some other women outside of church and the grocery. But Bobby put the brakes on that idea real quick. Said he didn't want me selling women their unmentionables." She put her hands on her hips. "I'm tired of always thinking about what men think and what men want, you know?"

"Oh, I know," Annie said. "That's actually why I'm here."

Mary raised her eyebrows, appearing interested all of a sudden.

"There's a demonstration organized for outside the Miss America pageant today. Protesting traditional women's roles. I'm doing an art piece to go along with it."

Mary looked intrigued, but skeptical. "You think you'll have many people?"

"A few hundred have signed up," Annie said.

"You think anyone will listen?"

"I don't know if it will change anyone's mind about anything, but it will definitely get some attention. All the media will already be there for the pageant. We're just adding to the conversation."

Mary leaned out the door and took a look up and down the sidewalk. "Okay, I can show you where you can find a mannequin that's not being used right now. But you better not let on to anybody where you got it."

"Promise." Annie put a hand to her heart, then followed Mary through the department store.

The overhead lights were off, with just a few service lights illuminated here and there. In the dim light, without all the customers and the piped-in music, the store seemed frozen and eerie. They went down a cement stairwell to a basement storage room. A dozen or so mannequins lay sprawled about, some fully assembled and some limbless like ancient Greek statues.

"I'm not sure what goes with what," Mary said.

"Doesn't matter," Annie said. "I'm putting it in a strait-jacket and I've got lots of glue." She chose a slim, plastic body from a heap in the corner and found a blond head sitting atop a worktable. "You'll do," she said, looking into the manne-quin's painted blue eyes.

Mary grabbed the mannequin's feet and, together, the two women heaved it upstairs and out a back door.

"I can take it from here," Annie said. She stuffed the man-nequin head into her backpack and balanced the stiff body across her shoulders, like a milkmaid carrying a bucket yoke. "Thanks again. I wouldn't be able to create my piece without this."

Mary waved her off. "It's no problem. I'd go with you and watch the whole thing if I didn't have to pick the babies up from my sister's. Just remember not to tell anybody where you got it from, okay?"

Annie nodded. Then she made her way toward the board-walk—a young girl carrying the weight of a plastic one.

Chapter Eight

Odin

PIECE: *Dr. Evermor,* Roost, *circa 2000. Rooster sculpture constructed from scrap metal.*

Odin clipped the padlock on the barn door. He wished he had more to show for all the hours he'd spent inside the barn, his makeshift studio for the past six months. He'd started out with good intentions, rising early every morning to sketch what he wanted to sculpt that day. But as soon as he began to work with his materials—the metal and the welder that shaped it—he lost sight of what he was doing and became discouraged at how pointless it all seemed. Even on the family farm, he hadn't been productive enough. He'd done what he could, helping out with the harvest in the fall. Yet it wasn't enough to keep new creases from cropping up on his father's forehead as he pored over corn prices in the paper.

On rare days, Odin would feel like he was actually getting somewhere with his artwork. For a few golden hours his ideas would translate seamlessly from his head to the hot arc at the tip of the welder to the metal beneath it. But when he stopped working and stepped away, he'd realize that the scale was all wrong. He was making everything much too big and straying from what he was "supposed" to be doing—small-scale sculptures that fit on people's mantels and end tables. The kind that sold well in his girlfriend's Minneapolis art gallery. His late girlfriend.

He turned his back to the barn, with its drafty corners and peeling, rust-colored paint, and surveyed the scene in front of him. The field that separated him from his parents' house sparkled like honed quartz, but he knew the smooth surface was just an illusion of perfection. With each step he took toward the house, his boots cracked the brittle crust of ice atop the snow.

Through a first-story window of the farmhouse, Odin could see his mother in the kitchen, standing at the sink. He'd moved back in with his parents only as a last resort after Sloane died and her older sister swooped in and sold not just the gallery, but the condo loft above it. As was her right. Odin's name wasn't on the deed, nor had he paid the mortgage or even any rent. As far as the sister was concerned, Odin was a freeloader who owed everything to Sloane. And maybe she was right.

Odin had done his best work with Sloane's encouragement. When he thought of her now, he often remembered the early days, back before they'd started dating. She'd seen some of his sculptures on display at a coffee shop on Hennepin, not far from the Walker art museum, and contacted him about selling some pieces at her eponymous gallery. When they spoke on the phone, Odin pictured Sloane to be in her forties or fifties—someone tough and established enough to have her own business in the unforgiving art world.

He had not been expecting Sloane to be thirty-three and blond, with legs for days. Nor had he expected her to fret so much over where to situate each piece. She'd paced around the gallery, waving her freckled arms and apologizing as she asked him to move this one a little to the right and that one a little to the left.

Odin had teased her for being so picky about the placement. "They're just hunks of metal."

Her eyes had gone big. "You know better than anyone that's not true. Like this one." She'd stood next to a sculpture of a tractor made from bent steel, with dismantled computer parts standing in for where the engine should have been. "I think it should go near those wire trees near the windows. They're by an artist from Bemidji. If I put some of your pieces next to his, they become part of a conversation about nature and technology."

"You do a better job of explaining my work than I do," Odin said.

She'd brushed a strand of hair out of her face. "That's why I do what I do. Artists are shit at talking about their own work. They need me to market it. Make people realize why they're drawn to it."

And it was true. Sloane always found a way to articulate

the ideas and emotion that went into his artwork. He'd come to depend on it, so much so that he often wondered, as he sat down to start on a new piece, what Sloane would have to say about it. Now, without that voice in his head, he had a hard time getting a start on anything. And, with the gallery operating under a new name and new owner, his old pieces stopped selling without Sloane to champion them. Not long after the new owner took over, she called to tell Odin that she was terribly sorry, but she could no longer devote precious space to his sculptures. Could he please come pick them up at his earliest convenience?

That call had been the motivation he needed to get up off the couch he'd been surfing on at a buddy's house, toss said buddy the last remnants of the ounce of weed he'd been self-medicating with since Sloane's death, and pack up his belongings. He'd piled his truck bed with his unloved hunks of metal, cushioned by his sleeping bag and a couple of blankets, and moved back in with his parents for a while. He may have been an unemployed, starving artist, but he wasn't going to add homeless to his short list of attributes.

His mom had made for damn sure, over the last six months, that the starving part was no longer true, anyway.

Now, Odin walked into the farmhouse and grabbed the duffel bag he'd left in the front entryway. "I've got all my equipment packed up, so I guess I'd better get going," he said.

His mother came over and hugged him. As she pulled away, she surveyed him with a satisfied smile. "At least we're sending you off to Madison looking healthier than when you came here," she said. "You know I think Sloane was a sweet girl, bless her soul, but all those vegetarian meals . . ."

"Sloane didn't die because she was vegetarian, Mom."

His parents had met Sloane only a handful of times, when Odin had brought her home for the holidays. His parents almost never ventured up to the Twin Cities, since farmwork kept them from going many places. For as long as he could remember, the only times his parents had left the county were for weddings and funerals. Like Sloane's.

"Of course she didn't," his mother said. "All I meant was that you were thin as a beanpole when you first showed up here."

"I wouldn't go that far," Odin said. He was six foot two and "big-boned," as his mom used to phrase it when he was a kid. Far from beanpole status, even at his lightest.

"Well, anyway, you're looking healthier now," she said.

"I've gained fifteen pounds since I got here, Mom. My pants barely fit anymore. I had to drill an extra hole in my belt to let it out."

"You could always stop by Farm & Fleet on your way out of town for some new pants," his father said, coming up from the basement.

"Thanks, Pop," Odin said. "But I don't think I have enough money even for Farm & Fleet. I'll take my chances with the thrift stores in Madison."

"You sure you want to leave?" his mom asked. "You know you're welcome to keep working out in the barn as long as you want."

"Yeah, but I can't afford to lose my fingers to frostbite,"

Odin said, wiggling his hands. "And, in case you haven't noticed, this place isn't exactly teeming with galleries or other opportunities to sell my work. I think I've aged out of being eligible for the 4-H craft bazaar."

"Can't you sell pretty much anything on the internet these days?" his mom asked. "Jane from church has been selling her mom's old Hummel figurines on eBay for years. Makes a small fortune."

"With the sort of work I do, I think people like to be able to see it in person, though," Odin said. "And anyway, I need some new inspiration. I think being around other artists, in a new place, will help."

His mother let out a sigh of resignation and shoved a plate of peanut butter cookies at him. "For your trip."

"Thanks," Odin said. "For everything."

His dad lingered at the door when Odin stepped outside. "You're sure you've got the truck up and running okay?"

"Yeah, Old Gray should make the trip just fine. New battery and everything."

"Okay, then. Make sure you watch for deer."

And that was it. In his pop's words, "watch for deer" was the utmost expression of paternal love.

Odin waved as he climbed into the truck. Before he'd even gotten to the interstate, he'd torn off the plastic wrap cover from the cookies and started in on one. It tasted buttery, still warm from the oven. When he drove by the Pine Tavern at the intersection of County Roads G and T—a locational coincidence that always made him smile—he saw that the parking lot was already half-full at four o'clock. Fridays meant fish fry. Whether the early cocktail hour that went along with it made the winter seem longer or shorter, no one could be sure. Odin suspected he might have ended up bartending there if Sloane hadn't sent in the residency application for him.

He'd been dumbfounded when he got the acceptance letter from the Barrett Foundation. He'd never heard of it, let alone applied for a residency there. But the offer was typed out right there on the letter, and a visit to the foundation's website confirmed that the place was legit. The letter had been addressed to Sloane at the gallery, then appeared to have been forwarded to her sister. Odin got it weeks after it was postmarked, mailed in a big manila envelope along with a couple of photos of him and Sloane and a sticky note from her sister that said, simply, "From the apartment."

The sight of Sloane in those glossy pictures, with the almost imperceptible freckles on her cheekbones and her confident smile, shocked him almost as much as the letter. Sure, he had his own pictures of her, but he was the one who controlled when he looked at them. They never took him by surprise. In the couple of weeks before he got the envelope in the mail, Odin felt like he'd been doing pretty okay. He'd woken up a few days in a row without his first thought being *She's dead*. He'd done some therapeutic hay baling, breaking a sweat in single-digit temperatures. He'd gotten his hands on some high-grade aluminum from the scrapyard, for a sculpture he was planning out. But then the pictures and the letter arrived, and the sight of all he'd lost, reduced to a couple of snapshots, ripped the tenuous scab right off the surface of his grief and stopped his work in its tracks.

The letter from the Barrett Foundation called into question so many things he thought he knew about Sloane and his relationship with her. At first, he was grateful she'd applied for him, since he didn't have a whole lot of other options. And he felt flattered to be accepted. But why had she kept the application a secret? Maybe she hadn't been expecting him to get accepted, and wanted to shield him from the blow of rejection. Then it sunk in that the artists' colony was located in Madison, four hours away from Minneapolis. Had Sloane wanted to send him away? Had she planned to come with him? The latter, he doubted. She'd had a successful gallery to run. All her contacts and customers were in the Twin Cities. Maybe she'd been planning on breaking up with him, and this was her way of easing him along.

With all of these questions rattling around in his head, the idea of the residency lost a bit of its luster, and he'd debated whether he should even go. His inner critic whispered that the offer was nothing more than the final vestiges of his association with Sloane. That he'd never have been chosen if she hadn't been the one to hand in the application. But what other choices did he have? Practicality won out over pride, in the end, which was how he'd ended up packing up his truck in mid-January, to drive south toward Madison.

IT WAS NEARLY nine o'clock by the time Odin could see the dome of the State Capitol building, lit up white at the end of East Washington Avenue, with its strip malls and brake shops changing to high-rise apartment buildings and trendy restaurants the closer he got to downtown. Odin hadn't been to Madison since he was in high school, when he'd ridden a bus down to watch the girls' basketball team in the state tournament. He'd been deep in unrequited love with a redheaded forward who killed him slowly by wearing short skirts and giving him the occasional hallway smile while changing classes.

Odin had to double-check the house number when he pulled up to the address written on the residency paperwork he'd gotten in the mail. The house was massive, and on a lake lot, no less. He noted with approval that there was a sculpture garden. Odin could only imagine what his rusty truck looked like parked in the mansion's circular driveway, with his heap of tools and metal in the back. He grabbed his duffel bag from the seat beside him, went up the walk to the entrance, and rang the bell.

He wasn't sure whom he expected to answer. Maybe a librarian type with pencils stuck in her hair. Or a wizened hermit, perhaps. He'd never set foot anywhere near an artists' colony before. But the woman who came to the door looked normal—no, better than normal. She was cute. Maybe ten years his senior. She had one of those circular scarves wrapped around her neck, but in between some pieces of fringe he caught a glimpse of soft cleavage escaping from her blouse. He flicked his eyes away. *Fucking lizard brain*, he told himself. *Be professional.*

"You must be Odin," the woman said. "I got your email. I'm Nell, the director."

"Sorry it took me so long to get in touch," he said.

"Don't worry about it," she said. "We're glad you're here."

Odin nodded toward his truck. "Where do you want me to put everything? I've got a bunch of equipment out in my truck."

"Why don't you pull it into the garage for now? I'll open up the door for you. Once you've had a chance to look around and see where you want to work, we can find all your things a more permanent place. Unless, of course, you were planning on working tonight."

Odin laughed. "Nah. I mean, I have a lot of goals for while I'm here, but I think I can spare one night."

"Great," Nell said. "Then come on in and meet the other artists."

"Sure," he said. "I'll be right back."

He saw Nell shiver as a gust of wind kicked up a dusting of snow from the porch. She pulled her scarf more tightly around her neck. "I'll open the garage door for you. Feel free to let yourself back into the house. The rest of us are in the kitchen."

Odin thanked her and went out to pull the truck around. Despite the enormity of the house, the garage was tiny, just one stall—a testament to the long-ago days when a car was a rare luxury. Maybe the building even housed a horse and carriage at one point. Either way, the garage had been meticulously maintained and looked far too fancy for the likes of

Old Gray. Brass lamps blinked on either side of the wooden garage door, which went up as he approached.

After he'd secured his stuff in the garage, Odin went into the house and followed the sound of voices to a large kitchen dominated by a massive marble island. Nell sat at the island with two women: one older, one younger. The older woman looked to be in the middle of telling a story. She paused to take a sip from a coffee cup, then looked up and saw Odin. "Our token male is here!" she said.

Odin gave an awkward wave. He didn't know how to take her comment. Was she trying to be funny or trying to insult him?

"Odin, meet Annie Beck," Nell said.

He relaxed and smiled. "Seriously?" he said. "I can't believe it."

"What *I* can't believe is that someone your age—especially a *man* your age—knows who I am. Usually only grad-school types like this one here recognize my name." Annie indicated her thumb toward Nell.

"My girlfriend is—er, was—really into your work," Odin said.

Nell smiled. "Sounds like a smart girl."

She was. Odin felt his stomach sink as all of his mixed emotions about Sloane and the residency resurfaced.

"This is Paige, our youngest artist," Nell said. "She's a senior at the university."

"Hi," said the younger girl. She sat slouching on her stool with both hands circled around a beer bottle. She looked as if she'd been working that day. Her fingers were stained black and she had smudges of what looked like ink on the hooded sweatshirt she wore.

"Would you like something to drink?" Nell asked. "There should be coffee and tea in the cupboards, and a six-pack in the fridge. Well, a four-pack now." She held up her own bottle and nodded toward Paige's.

"A beer sounds great," Odin said.

Nell moved to get up, but he stopped her. "I can get it." He walked over to the built-in refrigerator, took out a bottle, and examined the label. "Pale ale," he said. "This is a treat. Up where I'm from, it's nothing but PBR on tap."

Nell smiled. "My husband's a bit of a beer nerd. I brought these from his stash."

Odin grabbed a bottle opener that was lying on the counter. He popped the cap from the bottle and said, "Well, cheers to your husband, then. Tell him I said thanks."

Annie patted the stool next to her. "Tell us what you're working on."

"Do you want the truth or do you want to know what I *should* be working on?" he asked, glancing at Nell.

Nell held up her hands. "Pretend I'm not here. You've already been accepted, so it's not like I'm going to send you home."

Odin exhaled. "Back in Minneapolis, I'd been doing a lot of small-scale metal sculpture. You know, stuff that fit in the gallery and people could take home easily in the back of their Subarus."

"So you're a practical sort." Annie gave him a little push with the tips of her fingers. "That's no fun."

"Well, that's what I *was* doing. In the last few months, I've been working out of a barn, and every sculpture I start seems to wind up much larger than I intended." What Odin didn't mention was that he hadn't actually *finished* any of the pieces he'd started, or even come close.

Paige looked up now, for the first time since her initial, abbreviated greeting. "Maybe your work is like a goldfish," she said. "It grows as big as its surroundings will allow."

Odin laughed and said, "Maybe."

He knew, though, that it hadn't just been a lack of studio space that had kept his work small in scale when he lived in the city. Sloane, too, had advised him to stick to "more manageable" pieces.

"Save the big stuff for when you get commissioned to do a sculpture to stand in a park or outside a fifty-story office building," she'd said. "For the gallery, we want stuff people can buy on impulse and take away the same day. We want people to fall in love, swipe their credit cards, and take the artwork home without a second thought. Anything that requires setting up a delivery, borrowing a friend's van, that sort of thing . . . there's too much planning that goes into it. Too many opportunities for second-guessing. Art is impulse based. It's about feelings. Joy, passion, awe. We have to capitalize on that."

Now Nell spoke up. "Well, it looks like Betsy, who owned this place, wasn't afraid to buy large pieces of artwork. I'm sure you saw the sculpture garden when you drove in."

Odin nodded. "It was the first thing I noticed, besides how big the house is."

"It *is* big," Nell said. "But none of the rooms are barn-sized, I'm afraid. So I hope you won't be too constrained. There's a pretty large boathouse down by the shore that you could probably use if you really need a bigger space. But it's not heated and pretty run-down. I'm not sure it would be much of a step up from your barn."

"I was actually thinking the garage looked pretty nice," Odin said.

"Sure." Nell laughed.

"What's so funny?" he asked.

"It's just that we've got this whole house to work with and, so far, you guys all seem to want to spread out as far from each other as possible, using the least-finished spaces. We've got Annie working out of the basement, Paige up in the third-floor cupola, and now you'll be out in the garage . . ."

Paige looked up from her phone, which she'd been typing on throughout the conversation. "I always work alone," she said.

"Oh, I'm not saying you have to work together," Nell said. "There are other ways you can collaborate. Betsy, the bene-factor, envisioned the artists doing a joint show at least once during each residency. Maybe as you all get to know one another, you'll be able to see some common themes in your work that we could highlight."

Paige looked doubtful. She turned her attention back to the screen.

"I haven't done a joint show in a long time," Annie said. "I'm not sure my work will be compatible with what everyone else is doing."

Odin glanced at Nell, to see how she was taking the other artists' comments. He thought they were being kind of a pain in the ass, and he raised an eyebrow to show it.

Nell gave a good-natured shrug. "Well, it's a long way off, however we decide to do it. Just something to keep in mind," she said. "But there is one requirement I wanted to mention right away. There aren't many rules around here, but one thing Betsy wrote in her trust was that she wanted the Colony to have a standing communal dinner on the calendar. I was wondering if Sunday nights are a good night for everyone?"

"Every Sunday?" Paige asked, not looking thrilled about the idea.

"I was thinking once a month, maybe," Nell said.

"Works for me," Odin said.

Nell looked at Annie, who gave a quick nod.

"Do you need us to, like, *cook*?" Paige asked.

"I'll take care of the food," Nell said. "I don't want to take you guys away from your work."

Odin realized that between the drive and the conversation in the kitchen, he'd been sitting for hours. He finished his beer, then excused himself to take a closer look at the sculpture garden he'd seen when he pulled in. Outside in the clear night air, it felt good to stretch his legs.

Among the pieces in the garden were a pair of stone figures, a metal sculpture of a flame, and a six-foot-tall rooster made from recycled parts of machinery and musical instruments. Odin bent down to read the plaques at the bottom of each sculpture, squinting in the moonlight to read the names of the artists. He wondered, by reflex, if Sloane had ever heard of any of them. She was so much more tapped into the up-and-comers than he was. He swore he could hear the low whistle of appreciation she always gave when she saw something that swept her off her feet. But then he realized that it was only the sound of the wind, wandering up from the icy lake. And he remembered he was alone.

Chapter Nine

Nell

PIECE: *Oval-shaped Talavera platter with hand-painted blue-and-white floral design.*

It had been a while since Nell planned a meal. Like actually sat down with cookbooks and picked out recipes ahead of time. When she and Josh first got married, meals used to be a source of entertainment in and of themselves, sometimes filling the better part of a day. Josh was a great cook. Nell, not so much, but she *was* good at coming up with concepts for meals. They would spend lazy weekend mornings in bed, paging through cookbooks and poring over internet recipes, letting their whims dictate the day's menu. One winter Sunday, a memory of Nell's junior year in France led them to make a mountain of crepes so large they had to invite neighbors over to help finish them. Another weekend, Josh had become obsessed with the idea of making sushi. They'd driven around to multiple Asian markets to collect the right tools and ingredients. In the end, they'd spent more money and had a worse meal than they would have if they'd just gone out to their favorite Japanese restaurant. But it had been fun.

When Nell was pregnant, her cravings made it tricky for her and Josh to keep up their cooking experiments. She always seemed to crave something specific, like fresh watermelon in the middle of February. But then she'd be repulsed by it when Josh procured it and brought it home. He'd done his best to oblige, though, often calling her multiple times from the grocery store to make sure that the exact brand of potato chips or bagels or sparkling water he had in the cart was consistent with whatever she and the baby needed *right that moment*.

Now, they found it hard to find enough things to talk about to fill an entire meal's worth of time. She and Josh seemed to stonewall one another in the evenings, playing a dinnertime game of chicken until whoever was hungriest relented and started boiling water for pasta or pulling together sandwich fixings. Or, more often than not, one of them called the number on one of the many take-out menus they kept in a kitchen drawer. Given their credit card debt, Nell knew their recent take-out habit was not a great idea, but Josh never said anything. Because he didn't know.

Somewhere over the last year, food had morphed from something they both enjoyed to nothing more than a necessary inconvenience. With this mind-set, Nell found it hard to get motivated to plan the Colony's first communal dinner—especially when she sensed resistance to the idea from the artists. With so much on her mind, between the debt and the divide between her and Josh, not to mention her still-potent sense of grief over their daughter, Nell could barely muster up the energy and desire to eat more than a granola bar, followed by spoonfuls of ice cream straight from the carton, let alone plan an entire meal.

Nell perused the towering bookcases in the office at the mansion, hoping she'd find a few cookbooks in the mix. She pulled out a glossy, oversized book about Provence and the Côte d'Azur and flipped through it for recipes. Seeing none, she replaced the book. As she pushed it to the back of the shelf, she felt it hit something and heard a metallic rattle. She took the book down again and peered into the space where it had been. Something silver winked at her from the back of the shelf. She pulled down more books to reveal a small safe built into the wall.

During her first few days on the job, Nell had peeked inside closets and cabinets, looking for the safe that Betsy had mentioned on her deathbed. She didn't find it, and wasn't even sure it was still in existence. Then, when the artists started arriving, Nell turned her attention to the more immediate task of getting them settled in, and suspended her search.

Now, though, she went to the desk to retrieve the combination that Don had given her. With the numbers in hand, she spun the lock and opened the door. Nell wasn't sure what she had been expecting to find inside—glittering jewelry, maybe, or a priceless Kandinsky drawing. Instead, she found a shoebox.

She placed it on the desk and sifted through its jumbled contents. There were handwritten notes scrawled on letterhead from the hospice facility where Betsy had spent her final days, envelopes postmarked from New York, and catalogs from art galleries across the country. Nothing seemed to fit together in any way that made sense, until she came across a couple of articles torn from magazines. The first one, a piece torn from the pages of *Harper's*, was a feature recalling the literary and art salon that Gertrude Stein ran out of her Paris home in the twenties. The photo that accompanied the text showed Stein, a formidable figure adorned in black, seated on a chaise covered in fussy ruffled fabric. Above Stein's head hung Picasso's decidedly unfussy portrait of her, as well as a couple of the painter's Cubist works. Handwritten in the margin of the article, in slanted script, were the words "Something to strive for."

No problem, Betsy, Nell thought. *I'm sure I'll have no trouble at all re-creating one of the most famous art salons of all time.*

Nell picked up another article clipping, this one cut from a Spanish newspaper. Her Spanish was limited, but she had minored in French in college, and acquired some reading proficiency in Italian in grad school. She deduced that the article was about the famous, long since closed Café Pombo in Madrid. The only reason Nell recognized the name of the café was that it was in the title of a painting by the Spanish artist José Solana.

Solana had immortalized the café by depicting, in his dark expressionist style, one of the weekly *tertulias*, or social gatherings, held there, bringing together writers and intellectuals late into the night. Nell had never seen the painting in person—it was housed at the Reina Sofía art museum in Madrid. But she could picture it, as she'd seen it on slides and in books. She could see, in her mind's eye, the young men gathered around the table, wearing black suit jackets and ties, a testament that they took their time together seriously. She could picture, too, the table cluttered with glasses of all shapes and sizes, bottles of wine and sherry—a sign that the men didn't take themselves *too* seriously.

Though not much else was immediately apparent from the muddled contents of the shoebox, it was clear that Betsy had seen Stein's Paris gatherings and Solana's *tertulia* as a sort of inspiration for the Colony's communal dinners. But Nell didn't feel inspired. Instead, she felt paralyzed. Gertrude Stein had entertained Matisse, Hemingway, and Ezra Pound. Betsy herself had rubbed elbows with Warhol, for God's sake. How could Nell possibly follow in those sorts of footsteps? She had a hard enough time getting the Colony's artists, with their disparate personalities and artistic approaches, in the same room with one another.

Don had emphasized that Betsy's notes—anything outside the typed trust document itself—were not legally binding, but just meant to be used as a guide. But Nell had the sense she'd be letting the dead woman down if she didn't try to follow her vision as best she could. Nell lacked much vision of her own, now that the goal that had driven her for the last year—getting pregnant again—had been taken off the table. Adopting Betsy's vision at least gave her a concrete goal to work toward.

Nell felt pretty certain that Betsy's vision for the communal artists' dinners didn't involve boxed pasta, frozen garlic bread, and salad from a bag. Which was about as far as Nell's cooking skills went when she didn't have Josh around. Of course, she could order in, and maybe in the future, she would. But she felt strongly that this first meal should be something homemade, to make the artists feel like the Colony was, indeed, their home. She'd have to enlist her husband's help.

Lately, she and Josh saw and spoke to one another mostly only in passing. And, in some ways, that made Nell feel relieved. It made it easier to keep the debt a secret. With the semester now in full swing, Josh had been spending a lot of late evenings at his office up on Bascom Hill. And with the all-consuming work of getting the Colony off the ground, Nell often lost track of the amount of hours she spent at the mansion. She hoped that getting Josh involved with planning the dinner would give them something fun to focus on together, after all the stress and seriousness of the last year or so.

"What do you know about Spanish food?" she asked him when he picked up his office line.

"Tapas?" he said. "Cured ham? Why do you ask?"

She held her phone in one hand and, with the other, put the papers she'd scattered on the desk back into the box. "I'm trying to put together a communal dinner for the residents, and I'm going with a Spanish theme. I thought maybe you'd have some ideas. That is, if you're willing to help. Please say yes. You know my cooking only goes as far as coming up with the concept."

"Sure," Josh said. "If you want, I can put in a request at College Library and have them set aside some Spanish cookbooks."

"The perks of being married to a professor," she said.

"We should probably do a little research on what wines we want to serve," he said. "I can pick up a couple of bottles on the way home."

"My favorite kind of research." Nell looked at her watch. It was almost six o'clock. "Do you think you'll be home soon? What are you working on?"

"A law review article," he said. "And it will be here tomorrow morning. Probably with the cursor still blinking in the middle of the same paragraph I've already rewritten six times. So a glass of wine sounds pretty good right now. Meet you at home?"

Nell got home before he did. After a quick run and a shower, she put on some comfy clothes and searched online for Spanish recipes to try out. Many of the classic ones she came across required culinary skills beyond her level and/or called for ingredients she didn't have in her kitchen, like saffron for paella or smoked paprika for lentil stew. One recipe she found, for *tortilla española*, looked easy enough, though. It required only eggs, onions, and potatoes, and looked similar to an omelet, which was one of the few dishes Nell had down pat. She set out the ingredients and got to work. By the time Josh came home, she had the egg dish halfway cooked through and was just about to flip it over to cook the other side.

Josh set two bottles of wine on the counter, one a red Rioja and the other a white wine she didn't recognize. He kissed her and nodded at the egg carton on the counter. "Breakfast for dinner?"

Nell shook her head. "*Tortilla*. I was just about to flip it."

Josh eyed the skillet with suspicion. "Need help?"

Nell shook her head and pointed at the screen of her open laptop. "I've watched this video a bunch of times, and I think I've figured out the trick." She put a plate over the top of the skillet and, with a quick motion, turned the whole apparatus over. But, unlike in the video, the tortilla didn't slide out onto the plate in a single piece. Instead, half-cooked eggs ran out from under the pan and onto the stovetop, where they pooled before dripping onto the floor.

"Shit," she said. She put down the pan and grabbed a kitchen towel.

Josh ripped off a wad of paper towels and bent down to wipe the floor. "You know, you could cater the artists' dinner," he said. "You didn't get hired as a cook."

"I don't know exactly *what* I was hired for, to be honest." Nell turned off the stove and scraped what was left of the *tortilla*—more like a pile of scrambled eggs now—onto the plate with a spatula. "Anyway, I don't know of any Spanish restaurants in Madison."

"You could pick a different theme."

"I feel like that would be giving up." Nell tossed the contents of the plate into the trash and turned back to the counter, where she started cracking more eggs into a bowl.

By the time the day of the first group dinner rolled around,

Nell had made three trips to the grocery store and gone through six dozen eggs, but she'd finally perfected the recipe, producing consistently round, golden-brown, and fully cooked *tortillas españolas* instead of just heaps of scrambled eggs with burned potatoes and onions.

Josh went to the Colony with her that Sunday afternoon to help cook the meal, which had been expanded to include a handful of other Spanish dishes. He turned on the college radio station, which was doing a bluegrass show, and they chopped and sautéed and filled the room with the scent of garlic and peppers while banjo notes kept up a happy, twangy background sound. Nell was enjoying herself, and Josh's company, so much that she almost forgot about the huge secret she was keeping from him, to the tune of thousands of dollars in credit card debt. She put it out of her mind for now, though, and hummed along to the music. The lighthearted moments between them lately had been so few and far between, she wanted to savor this one.

Even with all the windows closed and the music playing, Nell could hear the hiss of a welding torch and, every now and then, the clang of metal being moved around—the sounds of Odin working in the garage. No noise traveled from the basement, where Annie was supposedly working, too. The only sign of life coming from down there was the peaty and unmistakable smell of pot wafting up the stairs.

"Do you think I should say anything?" Nell asked when Josh made a joke about the smell. "About her doing that in the house, I mean."

"What, from like a legal standpoint?"

She nodded.

"Have any of the other artists complained?" he asked.

"No."

"Possession of marijuana's been decriminalized in Madison." He tossed some garlic into a pan on the stove. "As long as she's not bothering anyone, I wouldn't worry too much."

Nell wondered what Betsy would have thought. Would she have cared? Regulars of Gertrude Stein's studio had smoked opium, a much more dangerous drug, but that was a different place and time. Nell could easily ask Annie to stop just by saying there was no smoking of any kind allowed inside the house. It wasn't written anywhere, but it seemed like a reasonable enough rule. But she felt silly telling a woman decades older than her what to do and, like Josh said, as long as Annie wasn't bothering anyone, it probably wasn't a big deal.

A bigger deal, at the moment, was Paige stumbling into the kitchen with a bulky piece of machinery in her arms. She nearly dropped it onto the wood floor, which Grady had just finished restaining the week before.

"Hey, let me help with that," Josh said. He turned off the gas burner and ran over to take the load from Paige. "What is this thing, anyway?"

"It's a tabletop screen printing press," she said. "I bought it on Craigslist."

Josh hoisted the machine into his arms. "Where do you want it?"

"Up in my studio," she said.

"Which is on the third floor," Nell added.

Josh followed Paige up the back stairs, grunting with effort. "How did you even get this here?"

When he came back down a couple of minutes later, he said to Nell, "You owe me." But he was smiling when he said it.

"This is fun, though, right?" she said. "We haven't cooked together in a long time."

He put his arm around her waist and gave her a squeeze before turning the stove back on. "Remember our first Thanksgiving?"

"I remember you cutting your finger to the bone," Nell said.

He shook his head. "There's nothing like going to the emergency room on a holiday to really get an unfiltered glimpse of humanity."

"Your parents saved the day, as usual. Running out to the store and meeting us back at our apartment with a turkey after you got your hand stitched up, since you bled all over the turkey we'd made." Nell took a clean fork from the drawer and plucked a bacon-wrapped date from where Josh had arranged them on a plate. She popped it in her mouth and savored the combination of sweet and salty, crunchy and gooey.

The members of Josh's family never ceased to amaze her with their boundless energy and their easy enjoyment of one another's presence. When she met Josh back when they were both grad students, Nell didn't fall in love at first sight. Introduced by mutual friends, theirs was a relationship that shifted slowly, over dozens of cups of coffee and glasses of wine, study breaks that led to late-night conversations and intimacies. Bit by bit, the balance tipped from acquaintances to friends, from lovers to partners.

With Josh's family, though, it was a different story. Nell fell in love with them immediately. Their house on Chicago's Northwest Side was the sort of place Nell just knew all of Josh's friends probably hung out in high school. The house itself was nothing remarkable, just a modest two-story a few blocks from the Kennedy Expressway. But it was stuffed with three decades' worth of life in a big family, something Nell never had.

If you got chilly and wanted to grab a fleece from one of the pegs in the mudroom, you were sure to find one in your size. There were coats and sweaters in so many sizes and styles that sifting through them was like an archeological dig through the Parker kids' past. Nell had once found a hooded sweatshirt emblazoned with the name of the all-boys Catholic high school Josh attended, hanging beneath a green down vest that smacked of seventies style, a woman's wool dress coat, and a kids' raincoat with whales on it.

The refrigerator was nearly unrecognizable, it was so covered with the grandkids' artwork and sports photos, Save the Date cards for weddings, and flyers for community events. Out in the single-stall garage, bikes in all sizes and states of repair made it impossible to park there, which meant that there were always at least three or four cars in the driveway—the one Josh's parents shared, maybe one of his sisters' minivans, and the car of a visiting friend or two.

Once, she and Josh had been visiting when a big snowstorm hit. After the flakes stopped falling, they went outside to help clear off everyone's vehicles. Josh shook his head as he scraped the windshield of his parents' old wood-paneled wagon.

"If they'd just get rid of something now and then, or at least do a little bit of organizing, maybe they could actually park their car in the garage," he said.

But the things Josh complained about were the very things Nell loved about the Parkers and their home. They had a way of making people feel relaxed and welcome. You never wondered if you should take your shoes off or leave them on. The kitchen always smelled like coffee because they brewed it constantly, one pot after another. If you felt the need to go off and read a book or take a nap, it was okay. It was all okay.

"Whatever makes you comfortable," Josh's mother, Judy, was always saying. And she meant it.

Nell loved the clutter, the chaos, and the constant comings and goings of neighbors and grandkids. It was all so different from how Nell had grown up. And even now, when she and Josh visited her own mother and her stepdad, Nell tread carefully, never quite sure of the way her mother preferred things these days. Because, with her mother, there was always a right way and a wrong way of doing things, but the line was constantly shifting.

WHEN SHE WAS a very young girl, Nell loved to draw. Her sixty-four-count pack of crayons had not just one but seven shades of blue. She knew that the word "blue" had four letters, but the blues in the big box all had longer names, ones she couldn't read. So instead she called them the names of the things they reminded her of. There was bedtime blue, like the color of the sky outside her window when she crawled each night under the cotton quilt she'd had since she was a baby. Aquarium blue, bright like the water in the fish tank in Nell's kindergarten classroom. And disappearing blue, like the color of the faded jeans she remembered her daddy wearing on the last day she saw him.

After he left, Nell's mom starting bringing things home from the drugstore where she worked as a pharmacist. Little presents like a pack of plastic hair barrettes in the shapes of pastel butterflies and lambs, or a bouquet of Tootsie Pops with red tape wrapped around their paper sticks. Her mom would ask if she could have one and Nell would always give her the chocolate ones.

"You're so sweet. You know I love chocolate," her mom would say. She'd sound so proud of her daughter's generous gesture that Nell didn't have the heart to tell her mother that she gave up the chocolate ones because she didn't like them. They were just brown inside of more brown. Nell preferred color.

On the day her mom brought home the crayons—the big box Nell had been coveting since she was four—Nell had been so happy, she'd drawn an immediate picture of two stick figures, one tall and the other short, surrounded by the outline of a big red heart. Then she'd written I LOVE YOU MOMMY across the top, pressing so hard she broke off the tip of two different orange crayons—one bright like sherbet and one light, like the striped fur of the neighbor's tabby cat.

Her mom had thanked her and pulled Nell onto her lap, something she used to do all the time when Nell was smaller, but hardly ever did anymore. "We're going to do just fine on our own, you and me," she said.

Nell thought that was a silly thing to say because *of course* they were going to be fine. Nell's dad had never been around much, and Grandma was always saying how Mom shouldn't have married him anyway.

The pictures Nell drew seemed to make her mom happy, and they made Nell happy, too, because she liked the process of creating something beautiful. She liked selecting the colors, running her hands along the rows of crayons before choosing just the right shade for her latest masterpiece, which her mother would display proudly on the refrigerator, secured by an alphabet magnet.

After a while other daddies as old as Nell's daddy, or maybe even older, started coming over in the evenings. But these daddies didn't bring their kids. Nell wondered if maybe they didn't have any. Or maybe their kids lived with their mommies, like Nell did.

On those nights, Grandma would put Nell to bed and read her stories while Mom curled her hair and dabbed tan-colored paint underneath her eyes. Nell didn't like it. One evening, while they were waiting for Grandma to arrive, Nell clamped her arms around her mother's legs and begged her not to go out. "I thought we were fine, just the two of us. You *said*."

Her mom pried Nell's fingers off her dress. "Honey, I just put this on and you've still got peanut butter on your hands from dinner. I don't have time to change again. I'm already running late. Why don't you go wash your hands and go draw a picture or something until Grandma gets here?"

But Nell didn't feel like coloring. She watched as her mom opened up the top drawer of the bathroom vanity and selected a lipstick from where she kept them, sorted by color, in a special clear container with a spot for each separate tube. It reminded Nell of her crayon box, and how her mom had showed her how to always put each crayon right back where she found it, so that they were tucked in tiered rows like seats in a movie theater.

While her mother was leaning toward the mirror, brushing a fuzzy, clumpy black brush on her eyelashes, Nell got an idea. She grabbed a handful of lipsticks and went downstairs. Her mom liked makeup and also liked Nell's pictures. What if Nell drew a picture *with* her mom's makeup?

Lipsticks in hand, Nell pulled out the bin labeled Paper from the closet, but there wasn't any paper in there. She searched in the bins labeled Barbies and Blocks, but didn't find any paper in there, either. Which shouldn't have surprised her. Her mom liked for things to be in their places, and she liked things to be clean. It was one of the reasons she and Nell's dad used to fight. But since her dad went away, her mom had taken her cleaning and organizing to a new level. She brought home a label maker, like a gun that shot out stickers with words. Now almost everything in the house had a sticker, from the tray for spoons in the silverware drawer to the basket in Nell's room where she kept her stuffed animals.

Nell tried very hard to follow her mom's systems and always put things in their places. But because the systems were constantly changing, becoming more categorized and more complex, sometimes Nell struggled to keep up.

When Nell didn't find any paper in the box labeled Paper, she figured there wasn't any, anywhere. She went to the kitchen and looked at the pictures displayed on the fridge. Maybe she could take one down and draw on the back of it. But then she thought of something even better.

Nell took down *all* of the pictures and the letter magnets. Now the refrigerator looked to her like a vast, white canvas. She took the top off a tube of lipstick and began to draw a house directly on the refrigerator door. When she'd ground down that lipstick to a stub, she set it on the floor and opened up another one, this time drawing a rainbow inside the house. She drew other things inside the house, too. Things she thought would make her mom happy. A vase of fuchsia flowers, a new washing machine so her mom wouldn't have to rattle the knob and say "dammit" every time she threw in a new load of laundry. It felt good to draw on such a big surface, blank and smooth.

Her mother came downstairs just as Nell was finishing her drawing. Her heels clicked on the kitchen tile. But when she saw the streaks of lipstick caked on the refrigerator and the ground-down tubes and caps scattered all over the kitchen floor, the clicking stopped.

"What on earth have you done?" her mom yelled.

Nell had thought her mom would be happy about the picture, but she didn't look happy now. She had on her mad face, with her forehead all wrinkly and her earlobes turning red.

"My date will be here any minute, and now I've got to deal with *this*." Her mother gestured toward the refrigerator, which Nell now saw the way her mom did: a bunch of smudgy lines where they weren't supposed to be.

Nell thought about explaining, but knew it would probably just take up more time and make her mom more angry. So she took the sleeve of her sweater and rubbed it against the fridge to try to wipe the lipstick off.

"No! That will make it worse." Her mom grabbed Nell's wrist so hard it hurt. "Go upstairs and change your clothes. And stay in your room until I can get this cleaned up." She squatted down, balancing on her high heels, and picked up a tube of lipstick.

Nell stood there, watching as her mom picked up another and another, throwing them all away. She wondered if she should get on the floor and help, too, but then her mom yelled, "GO!"

Nell looked at her feet and hurried to the stairs. But she wasn't fast enough to miss what her mother said under her breath as she sprayed down the refrigerator door with disinfectant: "Sometimes I can't even believe you're my daughter."

From then on, Nell redoubled her efforts to keep things orderly and tidy and, in turn, to keep her mother happy. She stopped creating her own drawings and focused instead on coloring, finding comfort in the straightforward task of filling in other people's pictures and staying inside the lines. She hung her clothes by order of color and never left her toys on the floor, not even if she was in the middle of building the most magnificent Lego castle she'd ever created. Her mother was all she had, and Nell couldn't afford to give her any reasons not to love her.

"I THINK THE food is just about ready," Josh said.

The sound of his voice pulled Nell back to the present. She looked at the stovetop, crowded with a pot of chickpea stew, a skillet of fried potatoes simmering in a spicy sauce, and a big pan of shellfish paella.

"Anything I can do?" she asked.

"Maybe set the table?"

"Okay." Nell gave him a quick kiss. "Thank you for all this. You'll stay and join us for dinner, won't you?"

He nodded and wiped his hands on a kitchen towel. "If you're sure I won't be interfering."

She waved off his concern. "I'm sure," she said. "I want you to meet the artists."

Nell went into the dining room and opened up the china cabinet. It was hard to decide which dishes to use because there were so many of them in there: French porcelain, English bone china, and German stoneware. But the formal, matching sets didn't interest Nell much. Instead, an eclectic collection of blue-and-white serving dishes caught her eye. Although all of the platters and bowls shared the same color scheme—a brilliant cobalt blue applied over a glossy white glaze—no two pieces shared the same design. Every bird, petal, leaf, and line had been hand-painted. Nell could see slight imperfections where an artist's hand had shaken a bit, or the glaze had set unevenly in the kiln.

Nell recognized the majolica style of ceramics, and guessed maybe they'd been imported from Italy or Spain. Maybe Mexico. Regardless of their origin, they'd go well with that evening's dinner. She picked up the largest piece, an oval painted with an intricate floral pattern, and flipped it over. The underside bore a maker's mark and a year, 1994. Nell placed the platter in the middle of the table. Under the light of the chandelier, she noticed variations in the shades of blue, where the artist had used more or less pressure or paint. The result was a range of hues on a spectrum from sky to indigo, reminding Nell of all those blue crayons from back when she was a kid, and the feeling of endless possibility that came with them.

Chapter Ten

Betsy

PIECE: *Mosaic made from broken ceramic on wood, crafted by Elizabeth Barrett, age ten.*

I don't care what you say, I'm going." Betsy crossed her arms and sat down on the edge of the bed. Outside, a siren wailed from somewhere beyond the walls of the gated community.

Walt rubbed his forehead. "I'm not sure it's a good idea. Another executive was kidnapped last week. The president of a major Mexican bank this time. I think you should stay in the neighborhood."

"And do what?" Betsy asked. "I've already played all the embassy wives in tennis."

She looked out the window of their rented town house. Mexico City had seemed a grand adventure when they arrived six months earlier—a temporary relocation while Walt opened a new plastics manufacturing facility. Betsy had hoped to travel back and forth to Puebla a few times, just a little over an hour away, to visit a ceramics workshop. The workshop had received a grant from a charity arts organization Betsy was involved with as a board member back in Madison. But a wave of crime and political unrest had kept her, for the most part, *encerrada*. Trapped within the confines of their insular expat community. She hadn't made the trip even once, and already she and Walt were scheduled to go back to Madison at the end of the month.

"The workshop has been there for over a hundred years," Walt said. "It will still be there the next time we come down here. It had better be, anyway, after the size of the donation you made."

"I told the other board members I'd visit," Betsy said. "They're expecting me to come home with some pieces of pottery and pictures of the artists and facility."

"I'm sure they'll understand." Walt straightened his tie. "We'll go check it out in a couple of years, I promise. Hopefully by then things will be more stable."

Betsy shook her head. "I'm going today. I already cleared it with Enrique. He said he can drop you off downtown and then take me to Puebla."

Enrique was the driver-slash-security guard Walt had hired when they arrived. He rarely smiled or said a word.

Walt let out a sigh, but Betsy could tell she'd won. "I should know better than to argue with you," he said. "Just make sure the car's got plenty of gas so you don't need to stop."

Betsy got up and hugged her husband around the middle,

which had grown thick from a steady diet of restaurant dinners and catered lunches.

Walt looked down at her, kissed the top of her head, and
then patted his belly. "Maybe I'm the one who should be making tennis dates," he said.

It was late morning by the time Betsy arrived in Puebla,
and the spring sun blazed uninhibited in a cloudless sky. The
ceramics workshop was located on a historic street lined with
baroque buildings in shades of lemon and coral. The entire
block looked as if it had been crafted by the hand of a master pastry chef, applying ornamentation to the windows and
rooflines like the piping on a cake. The architecture of the
workshop itself, though, was fairly modest—just a white
stucco rectangle that looked squat and plain next to the three-
story confections on either side of it.

Once Betsy entered the courtyard, though, she drew in her
breath. The cool, quiet space was shaded by palms in large white
pots painted with colorful swirls and blooms in blue, yellow,
and green hues. Tiled murals in the same color scheme covered
the walls, sometimes incorporating the other traditional Talavera colors of red, brown, and black. A fountain babbled in the
middle of the space, and the sound washed over Betsy like a
wave of peace, the level of which she hadn't felt even within the
locked gates of their neighborhood in Mexico City.

She rang the bell and waited for what seemed like a long
time. She rang it a second time, with still no answer. She
looked over her shoulder to where Enrique had parked the
car and gone into a café across the street. It had taken her

months to finally make it here, and she wasn't about to give up yet. She knocked, then tried the door handle. It turned and she pushed the door open a crack.

"Hello?" She stepped inside a small front room that looked like it served as a combination office and retail shop. Beautiful pots like the ones she'd seen outside were lined up on the floor, and hand-painted dishes and vases were displayed on shelves. From somewhere deeper inside the building, she could hear a mechanical hum. She waited until the sound stopped, then called out, "Buenos días."

Footsteps thumped on the terra-cotta floors, and then a young woman appeared, smiling and wiping her hands on her jeans. She apologized and asked Betsy if she'd been waiting long.

Betsy replied, in slow Spanish, that it had been only a few minutes.

"You must be Betsy," the woman said in English. "I'm Gabriela. I was in the back mixing some clay so I didn't hear the bell. I'm the only one here today." She turned on the lights in the room and glanced sheepishly at a desk piled with papers. "We weren't sure if you'd be coming, or I would have cleaned up a bit more."

"Don't worry about it," Betsy said, feeling guilty for the previous visits she'd canceled. "Please don't feel like you need to do anything differently because I'm here. I just wanted to see the workshop and learn a little about how you do things."

"A lot of it has been done the same way since the sixteenth century," Gabriela said. "That's part of why our pottery is famous. But we've had a few improvements to make things easier, in part because of the grant your group gave us. Come with me, I'll show you."

Gabriela led Betsy down a hall and into a large workroom. She pointed to a shiny, stainless steel trough filled with milky water. "That's what we bought with the money you sent. It mixes together the white and brown sand used to make the clay, then drains the water through a filter. In the past we had to use three different pieces of equipment to do it. The new machine has made the process a lot easier."

"Probably a little cleaner, too," Betsy said. She took out her camera and snapped a photo of the massive piece of equipment to show to the other board members back home.

"Maybe a little. But we still get pretty dirty." Gabriela smiled and gestured toward her head. Bits of white dust powdered her shiny black hair, held back by a bandanna. She pointed, too, at her feet, which Betsy noticed for the first time were bare and stained orange. "Before you got here, I was kneading out some clay, like this." She walked across the room to where a circle of red-brown clay, five feet in diameter, was stuck to the ground. Gabriela sat down on a wood bench. She cleaned her feet in a bucket of water and dried them before stepping onto the slab of clay. Then she hopped from one foot to the other in a slow, delicate dance, flattening out the lumps beneath her.

Betsy rolled up the bottoms of her linen pants, sat down on the bench, and submerged her own feet in the bucket of cool water. She dried them with a rag, just as Gabriela had done, then looked down at the circle of clay. "May I?" she asked.

Gabriela raised her eyebrows. "Of course. You'll get dirty, though. It's hard to get the color out of your skin, and sometimes it rubs off on your clothes even after you've washed up."

Betsy shrugged. "They're just clothes. This is art." She stepped into the middle of the circle, closing her eyes to focus on the feel of the cool, malleable clay beneath her toes.

After they'd finished kneading the clay, Gabriela showed Betsy the rest of the workshop: the pottery wheels and molds for shaping the clay into its final form, the kiln for firing the pieces and setting the glaze, the paints made from natural, native pigments. At the end of the tour, Betsy selected half a dozen pottery pieces to ship back home. Gabriela offered her a discount, but Betsy insisted on paying full price.

"At least let me send you off with a special gift, then," Gabriela said. She took an oval-shaped platter from a high shelf and handed it to Betsy.

"Thank you," Betsy said, running her hand along the floral pattern in the center of the plate. "It's gorgeous. It actually reminds me of something my mother used to have from Poland."

Gabriela's eyes brightened. "Yes. Lately I've been studying Eastern European pottery, and I find it so interesting because it looks very similar to what we do, with the colors and the floral designs, yet the process is different. Here, I borrowed a Polish technique of sponge stamping the patterns onto the glaze instead of painting them."

Betsy hugged the platter to her chest. "You can't know how much this means to me," she said. "It brings back a bit of my childhood."

She could still picture the pieces of treasured Bolesławiec pottery her mother always used to bring out for holidays. A saltshaker, a small bowl, and a teacup were the last remnants of the half-dozen dishes her parents had received as gifts at their wedding and then, less than a year later, packed inside the single trunk they brought with them from Poland to America. Betsy's mother loved to tell the story.

"Your *tata* said to me, 'Why take up space with things that will only be broken by the time we arrive?'" At this point, she would always pause and ask her husband, "How many were broken when we opened up the trunk in New York?"

Betsy's father would hold up a closed fist. "Zero."

But while the transatlantic voyage did not destroy any of the dishes, family life eventually did. Betsy would never forget the Christmas Eve when her younger brother knocked over the largest piece of pottery, an oblong tray, while reaching for a cookie. Even though she'd only been about ten at the time, Betsy could still picture, with photographic clarity, the tray slipping from the kitchen table. In her memory, the tray fell in slow motion, then shattered as it hit the floor. Her father offered to try gluing it, as he'd glued the handle back onto one of the teacups that experienced a similar fate, but warned that there were so many pieces, it was unlikely to hold together. But her mother simply brushed a tear from her eye, got up, and swept the pieces into a dustpan.

Just before her mother tossed the bits of glass into the wastebasket, Betsy stopped her. "Wait," she said. "Give the pieces to me."

Her mother put a hand on her hip. "You heard your father. There's probably no point in gluing it."

"Please just give it to me. I have another idea."

Her mother gave Betsy a dubious look, but handed over the dustpan.

After her younger brother was in bed that night, Betsy went down to the basement and found a square sheet of wood left over from when her father and his brothers had built the house, putting it together according to plans they ordered from a catalog.

First, Betsy found some sandpaper and smoothed out the surface of the wood, making it soft and even. Then she sat down on the floor and arranged the pieces of ceramic on the board in a swirled pattern, gluing each one down until she'd constructed a colorful mosaic from the jagged shards. When she finished, she sat back on her heels and inspected her work. It wasn't perfect, but it was pretty. Certainly a better option than just throwing away these slivers of her parents' old life.

Seeing the patterns disjointed and rearranged made Betsy notice things she hadn't been able to see when she looked at the dish as a whole. The way the cobalt blue glaze was light in some places and dark in others. The delicate veins on the flower petals, a spotted bug painted at the base of a stem.

Betsy lifted up the board and carried it upstairs, being careful to keep it level so the pieces wouldn't slide around in the wet glue. The house was quiet. She went into the front room, where the air was still smoky from the Christmas tree candles, now extinguished. She lay the mosaic beneath the tree, between packages wrapped in newsprint. She couldn't change what had happened, nor could she replace what her mother had lost. But she could pick up the pieces and create something new.

Chapter Eleven

Paige

PIECE: *Antique map of the City of Madison, 1867.*

The idea of a mandatory monthly dinner at the Colony reminded Paige of when her parents used to drag her to her grandparents' place every Sunday. They'd eat dry baked chicken in the kitchen of their trailer, where the heat was always turned up high and everything took on a yellow tinge from years of cigarette smoke filling the home.

Paige tried to sneak out the back door on the afternoon before the first communal dinner at the mansion, hoping she could stay away and skip it altogether. But Nell saw her, from the kitchen window, when Paige was crossing the snowy lawn. Nell pushed up the sash and said, "Don't forget dinner tonight!" Paige resented feeling like a kid who'd been caught breaking curfew, but she came back that evening in time for the meal.

Fortunately, there were no ashtrays or baked chicken in

sight at that first dinner. The food actually looked really good. Paige didn't know much about Spanish food, but she noticed a bowl of meatballs among the many small dishes lined up on the side table. Meatballs were always a good idea.

Paige's trepidation about the meal returned quickly, though, when Nell asked her to turn her phone off, saying something about the dining room being a "device-free zone" during dinner. Paige stared at her for a few moments. Nell might as well have asked her to sit down at the table and eat naked. But Paige did what she was told, stashing the phone in a drawer in the kitchen so as not to be tempted to try to look at it under the table. A few times during the meal, she found herself patting at the back pocket of her jeans or looking down at her hands, seeking out a digital escape.

For the first Sunday dinner in January, the sky outside had already been pitch-black for an hour by the time the group sat down to eat. By the next month's dinner in mid-February, a Middle Eastern–themed meal, the sun lingered a little longer. They watched it set in sherbet shades of orange and pink while they ate. Still, though, the artists stayed at the table conversing until long after darkness fell.

Paige didn't contribute much to the conversations at those first couple of dinners. Compared with the others, she didn't feel like she'd been anywhere or done anything. But Annie had lived a lot, and talked a lot, too. Paige loved hearing about her life in New York, especially the stories about Greenwich Village in the seventies.

"The guy in the next apartment was an actor," Annie said

as she sipped some tea. "Not like the movie stars who've got pieds-à-terre there now, but the struggling kind. In the summer, when everyone had their windows open, I'd fall asleep to him reciting lines. If he was trying out for a Shakespeare play, it could be quite soothing, with all that rhythmic verse. But a couple of times he must have been trying out for cop dramas and soap operas or something, because I'd doze off only to be woken up by someone saying, 'Put your hands up.'" Annie laughed and shook her head. "Half the time I didn't know if it was coming from my neighbor's place or from down on the sidewalk. The cops were always busting things up on the corner of my block because it was a known spot for solicitation."

"Of drugs or sex?" Paige asked. She was pretty sure she'd never even seen a prostitute. There were no street corners or back alleys where she grew up. Just a lone stoplight on the main highway through town and, past that, houses set back on acres of fields or woods.

Annie shrugged. "Either one. Both. Heroin was at what I *thought* was its heyday back then. But overdose deaths are way back up again, thanks in part to prescription opioids and Big Pharma." Annie sighed and pushed food around her plate with her utensils. "Sorry to bring the conversation down."

Everyone fell silent for a moment. Paige thought about a boy a couple of classes ahead of her from high school whom she heard had just been admitted to rehab after almost dying from a fentanyl overdose. Apparently, despite the fact that her hometown seemed like a place where nothing ever happened, it wasn't exempt from the rest of the world's problems.

Annie held up a ball of falafel she'd stabbed with her fork. "Did you make this, Nell? It's fantastic." Her voice had a forced brightness to it.

"I wish I could take credit, but I ordered it," Nell said. "I'm forbidden from frying anything since I singed off part of my eyebrow once."

"Well, whoever did the frying, I haven't had falafel this good since my kibbutz days," Annie said.

"I didn't know you were Jewish," Odin said, taking a sip from his beer.

"I'm not," Annie said. "But when I was in my twenties, a friend was going to Israel to do volunteer work and invited me along, so I figured, why not?"

"Seems like you've been everywhere," Paige said. "Up until I went to Providence over winter break for that RISD class, I'd never been to a state that didn't border Wisconsin."

"You're still so young," Annie said. "You have plenty of time to remedy that if you start soon."

As if it were that simple, Paige thought. Of course she would love to travel. Wouldn't most people? But with what money? Even with student loans, she could hardly afford to get by, which was why the residency at the Colony had been such a godsend.

"If it makes you feel better, I haven't been many places, either," Odin said. "I've been fishing in Canada, but other than that, I've never been outside the country."

Odin didn't usually say much about how he ended up in Madison. He didn't work inside the house. His tools were too loud and his projects created all kinds of dust and fumes. The communal dinners were the only way Paige started to learn a little bit about him. He talked sometimes about a girlfriend, maybe an ex-girlfriend? Paige wasn't sure what had happened, and she certainly wasn't about to ask him.

Relationships were not Paige's strong suit. She didn't understand what made people stay together, month after month, year after year, without getting bored. Her maternal grandparents, the consistent producers of dry baked chicken, often said they stayed together out of stubbornness. Her dad's parents were another story. They still held hands and called each other sweetie and honey. They'd met in high school—Paige wouldn't be surprised if it was at a soda counter or a goddamn sock hop or whatever people did back then—and they'd been together ever since. The very thought of it made Paige itchy. She could hardly stay with someone more than a couple of months, let alone a lifetime.

At least her own parents had a healthy amount of disdain for each other. They drove each other crazy half the time, between her dad disappearing for deer hunting on major holidays and her mom with her knitting group. As far as Paige could tell, there wasn't a whole lot of stitching that went on at her mom's Stitch 'n Bitch meetings. Mostly it seemed like the members drank boxed wine and complained about their husbands, while maybe passing around a half-finished scarf or two.

Her parents' relationship wasn't exactly something Paige aspired to, but at least she understood it. When they weren't driving each other crazy, they laughed a lot. Their marriage seemed to have just the right amount of dysfunction to be functional, year after year.

Paige guessed Nell knew a thing or two about marriage, seeing as she was the only married one of the group. Her husband, Josh, had come to the first meal, and went around offering people seconds of the Spanish food piled onto platters. He didn't show up to the second dinner, though. When Annie had asked earlier in the evening where the other "token male" was, winking at Odin, Nell had just said, flatly, "He's working," and changed the topic.

Now, Nell started to clear away the dirty dishes and shuttle them back and forth to the kitchen. But Paige noticed that a few times she lingered at the edge of the room, listening to the conversation, especially when the artists turned to the topic of their craft.

"Does it ever happen that you're working on something, maybe you're even halfway done or almost finished, and then you get this idea for something else and that's all you can think about?" Odin asked.

Paige nodded, thinking about all the unpacked boxes in her room upstairs that were full of supplies from love affairs with methods she'd abandoned—paints, pastels, collage papers. "It's the best and the worst," she said. "Because you're really excited about the new idea, but you're also annoyed because now you can barely stand to look at what's in front of you, let alone find the motivation to finish it."

"Well, the garage is beginning to look like a scrapyard,

with all the pieces I've started and stopped." Odin sighed and crossed his arms. "How about you, Annie? Any tips on staying motivated?"

"I'm having trouble with the starting phase," Annie said. "I thought I'd be able to just pick up my photography series where I left off in New York, but with new subjects. It's turning out not to be that easy, though. I'm struggling to find people willing to participate."

Nell set down the platter she'd been carrying. "What sort of subjects are you looking for?" she asked. "Maybe I know someone I could connect you with."

Annie waved away the offer. "I think I just need to be more patient. Being photographed requires a certain level of trust. And that takes time to nurture."

"Well, if you think of anything we can do to help . . ." Nell picked up the heavy platter again.

"Here, give me that," Annie said, getting up. "It's late. I'm sure Josh will be wondering when you're getting home."

"It's okay, really," Nell said. "I was enjoying listening to you guys talk about what you're working on."

But Annie shooed her away. "You've done so much already. We can do the cleanup, right guys?"

Odin rose and began clearing the rest of the table, bringing an effective end to the conversation. Paige followed suit, feeling a small sense of relief, for Annie's sake. She knew what it felt like to not want to talk about her work. When people asked Paige about hers, she often had to curb the impulse to give a truthful answer.

The truth was, if Paige could express with words what her artwork was about, then she would. She'd string together a sentence or two and be done with it. She wouldn't spend hours or days struggling to convey her thoughts, emotions, and perceptions through a work of art. But her mind didn't work in words. It worked in visuals. People didn't ask novelists to paint pictures of what their books were about, so Paige wondered why so many people—professors, art bloggers, and friends—expected her to be able to translate her artwork into language.

After everything had been put away, Paige excused herself and went outside. She lit a cigarette and walked in the direction of downtown, hunching her shoulders against the assault of cold wind coming off the icy lake. A girl from Paige's graduate-level printing class had invited Paige to a party at her apartment. Paige didn't know the girl very well. The address was for one of the fancy high-rise apartment buildings that seemed to be sprouting up on campus in constant succession. Paige usually turned down party invitations from her art school classmates. She always ended up wedged on someone's thrift store couch between people comparing tattoos and artistic influences. She wouldn't mind so much, if it weren't for the fact that those types of conversations usually ended up being a pissing match of pretentiousness, full of words like "juxtapose" and "mélange," as well as lots of calculated adjustments to messy hair buns, sported by the men and the women alike.

Despite being on a campus of over forty thousand students, Paige sometimes felt like her world—especially her program—was very small. If she didn't at least stop by, people would ask her a bunch of annoying questions on Monday, so it was easier just to make a short, obligatory appearance. Plus, with this party, the fact that she wasn't very familiar with the hostess or the building made the invitation more attractive. It meant there would probably be a lot of people there she didn't know. Specifically, a lot of boys she didn't know.

When she reached State Street, the pedestrian mall running from the university campus to the domed State Capitol building, Paige got stuck behind a group of girls dressed nearly identically in leggings and down coats. She could hear them trying to translate the meaning of a text message from some guy. The message couldn't have been more than a line or two long, from the sound of it, but somehow it generated a deeply analytical conversation that lasted for two blocks, until Paige ducked into the glass lobby of the apartment building.

The elevator was mercifully empty. She rode it to the eleventh floor, where she could hear music and loud voices as soon as the doors opened. She followed the sounds to the apartment number on the invitation and knocked on the door. Miraculously, someone heard it. Beth, the classmate who'd invited her, opened the door.

"Paige, you came!" Beth hugged her, even though Paige was pretty sure they'd spoken no more than half a dozen times in class.

"Please, help yourself to whatever." Beth led her into the kitchen, where a group of people mulled around a selection of half-empty liquor bottles on a table. "Everybody, this is

Paige," she said. "She's the one art major I know who actually might make it as an artist after we graduate, instead of going to law school or moving back in with her parents. For the record, I'll be doing both at the same time."

Paige could feel her cheeks burn. "I'm not sure what I'll be doing after graduation. My residency extends a little beyond that, until the end of June, but after that, I don't know . . . do you think your parents have room for one more?"

Beth laughed. "So *you're* the one who got the residency Professor Murray told us about. Good for you. A few of us have been speculating, but hadn't heard anything."

"Thanks," Paige said, feeling even more self-conscious.

"What are the other artists like?" Beth asked. "Anyone we'd know? You could have brought them along, you know."

"I don't think so." Paige shook her head. "They're older. One of them, Annie Beck, is supposedly pretty famous, but I'd never heard of her before. The other, a guy named Odin Sorenson, is a sculptor."

"Huh," Beth said. "Well, I'd love to meet them sometime."

"Yeah, sure. Anytime." Paige sensed that Beth wanted to meet the other residents about as much as Paige wanted to bring her over to the house. Which was to say not at all. But it signaled a good place to end the conversation.

Beth wandered over to another group of arriving guests, freeing Paige to mix herself a weak vodka tonic and survey the space. She must have been concentrating too much on the latter because her plastic cup overflowed, sending sticky fizz all over the table. She looked around for something to wipe it up with.

A tall boy who'd been leaning with his back to the kitchen counter handed her a roll of paper towels.

"Thanks," Paige said, tearing one off. She dabbed at the puddle on the table and noticed that some had spilled to the floor. She maneuvered around a few people who stood talking, oblivious to the waterfall, and ducked down to wipe the tiles. When she got up, she whacked her head on the corner of the table.

"Oooh," said the boy who'd given her the towels. He raised a hand to his own head, which was covered in a knit beanie, and winced. "Are you okay?"

Paige nodded. "Other than my pride, yeah."

"Don't worry about it," he said. "Some drunk girl wandered in here earlier and it took her a full twenty minutes to realize she was supposed to be at a different party on another floor."

"I'm not drunk, though," Paige said. "Just clumsy, apparently. And I *do* know Beth, though I have to admit not all that well."

"Me neither. Just from ski club. Except that I'm not a member anymore, since I dropped out." He took off his hat and shook out a mop of collar-length dark hair.

"Of the club?"

"And school," he said. "It's Paige, right?"

"Yeah."

"I'm Trent."

"Nice to meet you." Paige stared at his hands as he worked them through his hair. She had to resist the urge to reach out and touch one of the wavy strands. Then she realized she was still holding a wad of dirty paper towels. She looked around for a wastebasket.

"Here," Trent said, pulling a trash bin out from under the table.

Paige threw away the wet towels. Before he put the bin back, Trent fished a couple of beer cans out of it. "What the hell is wrong with people," he said, loud enough for a few bystanders to turn their heads. "Blue means recycling. It's not that hard." He tossed the cans into another receptacle a few feet away.

If Paige hadn't been smitten already by his niceness and his smile, Trent's display of environmental conscientiousness would have won her over. The ski club thing was a little too wholesome for her tastes, but she could set that aside.

"So what do you do now?" Paige asked. "That you're not in school, I mean."

"I just got back from Colorado," he said. "I'd been out there since after Thanksgiving, teaching skiing lessons to rich kids. But there's been barely any new snow for the last month, and the conditions have been shitty, so I got let go from my job."

"That sucks," Paige said.

Trent shrugged. "Even if conditions were great, they probably would have only kept me on for another month or so, through the spring break rush."

They inched their way to a corner of the room, standing closer as the night went on. They talked—about music, about Paige's residency, and about Trent's plans to return to school in the summer and, hopefully, pack in enough credits to graduate in December.

"I can't think about December," Paige said. "I've got enough on my plate between my classes and the residency program right now. Besides"—she looked up at him, a flirtatious glint in her eyes—"I'd rather live in the moment."

They found excuses to touch one another in little ways. He brushed her hand when he offered to refill her drink. She declined, but tapped his wrist to look at the time on his watch.

"What would you say if I proposed going somewhere else?" she asked.

The question hung there, a shimmering line cast in his direction. She lived for these moments, when the thrill of risk thumped at her temples.

A slow smile spread across Trent's face. "I'd say yeah. Where did you have in mind? I'd invite you to come home with me, except that my housemates sublet my room when I left, so now I'm sleeping on the living room couch until I find a new place."

A beautiful boy with no place to sleep? she thought. The situation kept getting better.

The mansion was dark when they arrived. Paige's cold hands, in combination with the ancient mortise lockset, made it difficult to get the side door open. She rattled her keys and jimmied the handle back and forth. The door finally swung open when she shoved her hip against it. The momentum threw her across the threshold onto her knees.

Trent burst into laughter.

"Shhh." Paige got up, rubbing her kneecap. "I don't want to wake anyone up."

Trent followed her inside and paused inside the hallway. "I

wouldn't worry too much about that. Someone's already up. Don't you smell that?"

Paige inhaled and caught the smell of pot wafting up from the basement stairs, along with the sound of voices. "Yeah," she said. "It just took a minute for my nose to thaw out." She took a step in the direction of the back staircase that led to her room. "Come on, this way. My room's all the way up on the third floor. In, like, a *turret*."

"Sounds very fairy tale–like," Trent said. "Are you some sort of princess?" He leaned forward and kissed her in a quick, teasing way, then pulled back and gave her a flirtatious half smile.

"Oh no you don't," she said, grabbing him and pulling him in for a longer, wetter kiss. This time, *she* pulled away, and laughed. "I'm the last thing from a princess."

"Damsel in distress?" he asked.

"Maybe," she said. "It's distressing how badly I want to get you upstairs."

"You don't want to check it out down there first? Sounds like they're having fun." Trent nodded toward the basement and the muffled sound of laughter now drifting upward along with the smoke.

Paige shook her head. She didn't have anything against smoking pot. And she didn't have many rules for herself. But a big one was that when she found herself with men she didn't know very well—which was often—she liked to stay relatively sober, sticking with no more than a drink or two and never mixing substances. She relied on her instincts too heavily to dull them. Once, in high school, she'd gotten drunk at the house party of a classmate whose parents weren't home. Paige and a guy she thought was a friend went outside to have a cigarette. It had been a warm summer night, and the moon blinking through the evergreen forest behind the house beckoned them to take a walk. But when Paige didn't want to make out with the guy, he'd gotten angry. The aggressive look in his eyes and the tight way he gripped her arms scared her so much that she ran off in what she thought was the direction of the party. Except that in her state, in the dark and unfamiliar surroundings, she'd gotten lost. She eventually found her way back to the party after a couple of hours of wandering and sobering up a bit, but the experience affected her enough to scare her mostly straight when she was around men she didn't know very well.

Paige slipped her hand into Trent's and led him up the narrow staircase. When they reached the top, she flicked on the light. Trent looked around the circular room with its large windows facing the street on one side and the lake on the other. "Wow. I bet the view is amazing from up here during the day."

"Maybe you'll see it for yourself, if you're lucky and I don't kick you out before then."

"Hey, what's this?" Trent bent down to look at the contents of a cardboard box Paige had found underneath the window seat bench.

"Some old maps that were here when I moved in," she said.

"This has got to be from before World War One." He unfolded a yellowed map of Europe and traced his fingers over the long-since-shifted borders. He unrolled another map. "And look, this one is of Madison, from the 1800s. Someone who lived here must have been a map lover."

"I think someone else must be, too," Paige said, giving him a pointed look.

Trent smiled self-consciously. "Sorry to nerd out on you. I've been interested in maps since I was a kid."

"Let me see if I can find anything else that might interest you." Paige flopped down on the bed and peeled off her layers—scarf, sweater, tee. Trent watched her. She noticed that he had freckles under his brown eyes and over the bridge of his nose.

He dropped the map he'd been holding. "Keep going," he said.

She laughed, and pulled her shirt over her head.

"You know, coming up the stairs in the dark like that, I felt like I was back at the church summer camp I went to as a kid, trying to sneak over to the girls' side. I had the biggest crush on one of the counselors." Trent pulled his wool sweater over his head, revealing a smooth, flat stomach.

"Did you ever make it over to the girls' side?" Paige helped him free his arm from his sweater and threw it on the floor in a heap.

"Nope. We got caught every single time. I swear our own counselor would overhear our plans and rat us out."

"Hmmm," Paige said, placing her hands on his bare chest. She could see black ink under her fingernails. "And what would you have done if you got over there?"

Trent grinned. "The plan was to put frogs in the girls' sleep-ing bags."

Paige pushed him, giggling, and he stumbled backward. He righted himself and closed the distance between them in one big step, scooping her into his arms before settling on the bed.

"Shhh," she said, quieting him with kisses.

Chapter Twelve

Annie

PIECE: *Puzzle box, or secret box, handcrafted from wood in Hakone-Odawara, Japan.*

Annie stood in the center of her basement studio and surveyed the space. In the couple of months since she'd arrived, she'd added pieces of secondhand furniture and knickknacks from around the mansion, trying her best to make the plain, damp space comfortable. Portable heaters placed in strategic corners provided much-needed warmth, as did overlapping rugs strewn on the cement floor. A sheepskin draped over an old couch created a cozy spot to lie down. Above it hung three screen prints she'd found that Paige had tried to discard. Annie had snatched them from the curbside garbage bin before the truck picked it up. They showed the same image of a shed standing among patchwork farm fields, but in varying color schemes of green, yellow, and blue, as if showing the scene in different seasons.

Annie shivered and unlatched a trunk she'd found in an un-used corner of the basement. She brushed a thick layer of dust from the cover, then lifted it open. The smell of cedar crept up from among carefully folded textiles in vivid hues of orange, red, aubergine, and moss. From the varied palette and pat-terns, Annie surmised that Betsy had collected these treasures from far-flung corners of the world. Annie ran a hand along the zigzag embroidery on a wool blanket. She recognized the pattern as an Incan design. On a hitchhiking trip through South America, she'd once seen weavers in Peru work a simi-lar pattern on backstrap looms. Annie had sat alongside them, watching the quick blur of their fingers as they chattered and chewed on *coca* leaves. Annie had brought home a similar but smaller blanket—ever conscious of her limited space, both in her backpack and in her New York apartment.

Just thinking about the four hundred square feet she'd left behind surfaced an ache in Annie's chest that she'd been try-ing, ever since she arrived in Madison, to shove down and shut up. She told herself that losing her apartment was a small price to pay in the name of art. Still, she missed the sounds of the city—the chatter floating in through her open window from the coffee shop below, the sighing sound of the bus stopping at the corner, the constant white noise of hundreds of conversa-tions going on in a single block. She missed how the shadows from the building across the street kept out the morning sun, but flooded her small rooms with light in the afternoon, per-fect for painting or drawing. She missed being able to stop in at a museum or gallery on a whim, whenever she needed rejuvenation. Losing New York, and her tiny foothold in it, felt like losing a family member. But if there was one thing Annie had learned over the years, it was that she had to keep moving.

It's just that she'd always thought of it sort of metaphorically.

Annie never second-guessed herself. Not when she'd been sprayed with teargas while marching for civil rights in Alabama. Not when she'd been hospitalized for heatstroke in DC rallying for the Equal Rights Amendment. And she certainly hadn't flinched when she'd gotten a letter from the co-op board expressing concern over the activities taking place in her apartment. Annie had contacted a lawyer friend at the ACLU, who advised her to obtain a copy of the board meeting minutes. The minutes reflected that Mrs. Van der Woodsen on the fourteenth floor, among others, had voiced worries about "drug addicts" being given access to the building.

For once in her life, Mrs. Van der Woodsen had been right. Annie *was* letting drug addicts into the building. And she was giving them drugs. But not the drugs they were addicted to.

Now, a loud knock brought Annie's thoughts back to the present. She opened the door that led to the basement from the backyard.

"Caroline," Annie said. "I'm glad you came back."

The woman standing on the other side didn't look like someone with chronic pain, and she certainly didn't look like an addict. She looked like a suburban mom, with her yoga pants and short haircut. But Annie had learned, by photographing dozens of people, that not all physical pain was obvious from the outside, and that addictions were easy to hide when a person was determined to do so. Annie knew, though, that the mother of two had become so addicted to prescription opioids after shoulder surgery that she'd once passed out in the bathroom of a dollar store, with both kids in a shopping cart, after buying black-market pills in the parking lot. Annie also knew there were a lot more Carolines out there, and that she couldn't help them all. But maybe if she could document a little bit about a few people's struggles, she'd raise awareness.

"Can I get you anything to eat or drink?" Annie asked as she led Caroline inside.

Caroline shook her head. "No thanks."

"How have you been feeling?"

"Honestly? Like shit. At this point I'm not even sure if the way I'm feeling is related to the surgery or the withdrawal from the drugs. But I haven't had any pills in a month now, so maybe this is just my new normal. I do think the pot helps, though. It at least distracts me from the pain for a little while." Caroline winced as she sat down on an armchair draped with a Turkish kilim tapestry. Annie noticed just how pallid and dull Caroline's skin looked next to the bright diamond pattern on the fabric. It was as if the raspberry and azure tones of the tapestry drew their saturation directly from Caroline, stealing the flush from her cheeks and the color from her eyes.

Annie settled onto an adjustable stool behind the camera she'd set up. "Do you mind if I just start taking pictures while we talk?" she asked.

"Go right ahead." Caroline removed the flats she was wearing and placed them on the rug.

"Just like last time, we don't have to talk about pain, unless you want to," Annie said. "Or about anything, really." *Click click click.*

"Fine with me." Caroline fidgeted and looked around the room.

Annie got up, opened the door of a metal filing cabinet, and produced a lacquered wood box. When Annie first discovered the box in a cabinet in the corner of the basement, along with a set of Japanese language–learning CDs, she couldn't figure out how to open the thing. But after fiddling with it for a bit, she realized it was a puzzle, and became more determined than ever to get it open. When she finally did, she realized it would be the perfect place to store her pot. Now, she jiggled each side of the box in the specific sequence she'd memorized, until the top slid open and revealed various smoking tools and a bag filled with preseeded, high-quality cannabis.

"You're probably looking for this," Annie said, bringing the box to Caroline.

She sat up straighter. "Thank you." Caroline selected a hand-held vaporizer from the box, switched it on, and set it down. While she waited for it to heat up, she picked up a vase from atop an overturned crate being used as an end table. Blown-glass daffodils, tulips, and lilies in translucent shades of yellow, pink, and lavender sprang out from the mouth of the vase on delicate green stems. "This is lovely," she said.

"A friend of mine who's a glass sculptor gave it to me when I left New York. She does mostly large-scale pieces, to install on ceilings and walls and things, but obviously I couldn't move something like that with me, so she made me something small."

Caroline picked up the vaporizer. "I think it's ready. Do you want any?" She held it out toward Annie.

Annie settled back onto her stool, then pressed the shutter release with another click. "No thanks," she said. *Not that I haven't smoked my fair share over the years,* Annie thought. But this was not about her.

Caroline nodded as she inhaled, then blew out a light stream of vapor. "I just didn't know what the etiquette was."

"There is none," Annie said.

To herself, she added, *No etiquette, no rules, no road map.* For someone accustomed to venturing into uncharted territory, Annie wondered why she suddenly felt so nervous.

Chapter Thirteen

Betsy

PIECE: *Yohji Yamamoto, fashion sketch, circa 1990.*

Betsy stuck out in Tokyo. Not only was she blond—well, more gray-blond these days—but she was on the tall side for a woman.

"You know how you always say you like to blend in with the locals?" Walt had said. "That's not going to be possible in Japan."

Despite, or maybe because of Walt's warning, Betsy ordered some language-instruction tapes before their trip, her first ever to Japan. For weeks, she'd walked around the house and the neighborhood with headphones on, repeating phrases about meals and markets, restrooms and taxicabs. Walt had teased her when she nearly crashed into him one evening while rounding the corner from the hallway to their bedroom.

He lifted up one of the earphones. "Before you go to all

this trouble, I should tell you most of the employees at the hotel speak English. I've stayed there before," he said. "Same with the guys I'll be meeting with and their wives. They're a bunch of polyglots. I've heard some of them shift from Japanese to Thai to German with hardly a breath in between."

Betsy paused her lesson. "Well, that's all the more reason for me to at least make an effort. If they speak a handful of languages, there's no reason I can't learn to at least say 'please' and 'thank you.'"

"I admire your dedication. Just don't be embarrassed if you ask a question in Japanese and they respond in English."

"If there's anything I've learned from traveling to other parts of the world, it's that I have to check my pride along with my luggage." Betsy had put her hands on her hips. "And anyway, I'm not worried about when I'm with you or your work people. I want to be able to wander the city . . . to go into neighborhoods that aren't on the usual tourist circuit. I can't do that without at least knowing the word for 'taxi' or 'subway.'"

"I can get a car service to take you wherever you need to go from the hotel."

She'd thrown up her hands. "Where's the adventure in *that*?"

On the evening after they arrived in Tokyo, the Barretts were invited for drinks at the home of a Japanese banker who was assisting Walt's company in its purchase of a Japanese manufacturing business. Mina, the banker's wife, greeted them at the door of their high-rise penthouse. She was decked out in a sculptural black dress that looked familiar to Betsy. Similar to something Calvin sent, probably.

Calvin was Betsy's stylist. He preferred that term to what he considered to be the more crass title of "personal shopper." He and Betsy mailed notes, magazine clips, and catalog photos back and forth all year long, in preparation for Betsy's visits to New York a few times a year. In her younger years, she used to do all her own shopping. Like most people do. Sometimes she missed the days when she and her friend Ingrid would walk miles in a single day, in search of the perfect pieces to wear for whatever galas and globe-trotting adventures the next season had in store for them. But lately Betsy's energy level seemed to be lower, even as she took on more volunteer commitments in Madison. There were the ballet and youth symphony boards. The scholarship committee she steered at the university. Not to mention dinners for Walt's business colleagues and contacts. Calvin, who wore nothing but black T-shirts and black jeans himself, was decisive and opinionated—qualities Betsy had come to appreciate now that her day planner seemed to be booked solid for weeks in advance. As much as Betsy liked fashion, she liked feeling useful a whole lot more.

Now, as Mina ushered her inside, Betsy remembered where she had seen the dress before. Calvin had, indeed, sent her a picture of it. One he'd taken at last season's Fashion Week. He'd sent the photo along with a swatch of black heather flannel and a sketch of an oversized, angular wrap-style jacket. Enclosed with the items had been a handwritten note.

A stunner from Yamamoto's latest collection. Neckline's a little lower than you like, but he designed a coat for one of my other clients to wear over it. Like you, she's of a "certain age" (eye roll here) and concerned about showing too much décolletage. I've enclosed a copy of the sketch for the coat. Something similar might work for you. Tell me what you think. — C

Betsy had ultimately decided against the dress, electing instead to buy a gray Donna Karan surplice-style sheath that Calvin described as "classic and beyond reproach." But the black dress with the deep, plunging V-neck looked perfect on the younger Mina. Betsy told her as much.

"Yohji Yamamoto, right?" she said.

Mina nodded, obviously delighted that Betsy recognized the designer of her garment. "It's more conservative than what I usually wear. When I met Walt last time he was here, he seemed quite . . . traditional? I thought you might be, too."

"Not as much as my husband. Or at least I try not to be." Betsy gave Walt a playful jab with her elbow. "Anyway, I admire your confidence. I told my stylist the dress was too risqué for me. But I'm quite a bit older than you. When you get to be my age, you know what works on you and what doesn't."

"'Invest in quality' is what my mother always said about clothes," Mina said. "It was something I didn't understand until I got older. Probably because I didn't need to. When I was young, I could buy any cheap, trendy thing off the rack and look decent in it. Now, I need tailoring that's intentional. Fabrics that drape in the right places."

"There's nothing worse than fabric that drapes in the *wrong* places," Betsy said.

Mina laughed. "Now, had I known you like fashion, I might have worn something a little more fun. Versace, maybe? I'm absolutely in love with that sequined matador jacket he showed last season."

"Are you women going to talk fashion all night at the front door or are you going to come in and have a drink?" Mina's husband asked.

Walt had been right about the language barrier, or lack thereof. Their host and hostess spoke English so fluently it would have seemed almost ridiculous for Betsy to try to use any of the Japanese phrases she'd learned. She'd have to wait for another opportunity to test out whether she'd actually absorbed anything from all those hours spent saying things like "Where is the bathroom?" and, her favorite, "Do you come here often?" Apparently, whoever created the language-learning series she'd purchased wanted to make sure the listener learned a few pick-up lines in addition to the usual utilitarian phrases.

Mina led the Barretts into a large living room filled with modern leather furniture. She offered them something to drink. The men chose whiskey and quickly became engaged in a conversation about baseball. Betsy followed Mina's lead and sipped warm sake from a small porcelain cup.

"So, if you enjoy fashion, I'm sure you've noticed that we're a bit obsessed with it here," Mina said.

"I've been having fun just seeing what people are wearing. I've only been here a couple of days, but already I've seen some trends we don't have back home. Especially on the younger women."

"Ah, yes, the *kogal*." Mina rolled her eyes. "The schoolgirls. My mother would have wept if I'd tried to leave the house in skirts as short as those girls are wearing now."

"I was a teenager in the sixties, so short skirts don't shock me," Betsy said. "What I've noticed the most is all the unusual makeup—the girls with the white lipstick and dark eyeliner. They were everywhere when I was walking around near Shibuya Station earlier."

"Did they also have fake-tan skin and orange hair?"

Betsy nodded. "Pink hair, too."

"You must mean the *ganguro* gals. I've read some fashion critics say it's all about challenging notions of traditional Japanese feminine beauty—you know, light skin and dark hair. But it seems to me like it's maybe just teenagers having fun. I don't really get it."

"Well, that gives us something in common," Mina's husband piped in. "I don't get any of it. So much of fashion just seems silly to me."

Betsy and Mina exchanged a knowing look.

"Certain trends might *seem* silly," Betsy said. "But fashion can also play a part in social and cultural change. Look at the flapper movement in the twenties. A lot of women bobbed their hair or wore shorter hemlines to get a reaction. Some did it because it was just easier or more comfortable. Others followed suit because it became the thing to do. Eventually those styles were accepted within the norm."

"Well, let's just hope orange hair doesn't become the new norm," Mina said. "Though I'm afraid it already has." She looked across the room to where the men now stood near the windows, returning to their sports talk as the lights of the city sparkled below. "Next time someone tries to tell me that fashion is silly, I'm going to say what you just told me. About cultural shifts. Progress."

Toward the end of the evening, Mina left the room and returned with a small package wrapped in yellow paper. She presented it to Betsy with both hands.

"What's this?" Betsy asked.

"Oh, it's nothing. Just a small gift."

Betsy knew, from seeing the gift-laden suitcases Walt always brought back with him from Japan, that gift giving was an important part of the culture. It was why she'd brought along a box of chocolates that evening from the confectionery in their hotel. The saleswoman had put an uneven number of chocolates in the box, explaining that too many of the even numbers were unlucky (four, in particular, was associated with death).

Walt had told Betsy that it was customary to verbally refuse the gift at first, but accept it in the end. So she and Mina began the dance of "you shouldn't have" and "no, please, it's just a little something" until, finally, Betsy took the package. When she opened it, she drew in her breath.

Inside was a shiny wooden box decorated on all sides with

a mosaic pattern made from inlaid pieces of wood in different shades of brown, red, and black.

"This is gorgeous," Betsy said. "Can you tell me about it?"

"It's a *Himitsu-Bako*," Mina said. "A puzzle box. Legend has it that they were first designed for samurai to exchange secret messages." She paused. "I hope you're not disappointed. Had I known you like fashion so much, I'd have gotten you something to wear."

"Stop," Betsy said, shaking her head. "This is perfect." She tried to remove the cover, but it seemed to be locked shut.

"You have to do it a certain way. Here, I'll show you." Mina walked Betsy through the steps to open the box, first moving this side an inch, then that side, until the cover slid off.

Betsy clapped her hands. "Now, if only I can remember how to do that when you're not around . . ."

Their fussing over the gift had caught their husbands' attention, and Walt came over to see.

"I've noticed boxes like that in some of the shops," Walt said. "Beautiful."

"Probably not like this one." Mina waved a dismissive hand. "Most of the ones in the stores are mass-produced. Just cheap plastic on top of wood. This one was handmade. It's one of a kind."

Betsy ran her hand lightly over the smooth surface of the box, being careful not to leave fingerprints. "It looks like an antique."

"You're right. It's about a hundred years old." Mina smiled and turned to Walt. "Very good eye, this one, no?"

"Sometimes too good," Walt said. "She's very hard to please, but I'd say you've done a great job of it. Maybe I should call you next time I'm trying to pick out a present for her. Her birthday is coming up in a couple of months."

"I'm sure I can think of a few ideas." Mina gave Betsy a wink.

In the taxi on the way home, Betsy chided Walt for not warning her that their hosts might present them with such an extravagant gift.

"I brought them *candy*," she said. "I read somewhere that it's a good hostess gift. But had I known that they'd be giving us a priceless work of art—an antique!—I'd have searched around for something better."

"I've never received something like that before," Walt said. "Usually it's a silk scarf or little cakes or something. I promise."

"Well, you must have gone up in their estimation since then," Betsy said.

"Last time I was here, they asked me about your interests. I said you liked art."

Betsy shook her head. "Why couldn't you have just told them I like chocolate?"

Chapter Fourteen

Nell

PIECE: *Wolfgang Beltracchi, oil painting of a floral bouquet. Purchased at auction as a known forgery of a painting by Moïse Kisling.*

"I finally heard back from Grady, the contractor I hired to do some updates at the mansion," Nell told Josh over takeout from a Laotian restaurant in their neighborhood. "He found some subs available to finish up the wiring and plastering work, so with any luck, we'll have internet by next week. And hopefully no more holes in the walls."

She pushed a floppy rice noodle from one side of her plate to the other. These days, they ate most of their meals in near silence, both scrolling through whatever came up on their phone screens, or sometimes just giving up on conversation altogether and turning on the TV. Today, Nell felt relieved to have something to talk about, even if it was as mundane as renovations.

Josh finished chewing a bite of spring roll. "Maybe you should get the number of the subs. I was thinking we might want to get started on some of the updates around here we've talked about. Now that you're working, we should have a little extra money, right?"

Nell took a sip of water, swallowing the guilt she felt. "I'll get their numbers," she said.

The phone rang. Both Nell and Josh put down their forks and stared at the cordless receiver affixed to the kitchen wall. No one ever called the landline. The only reason they had one was in case of emergency. None of their family or friends had the number. When filling out forms that asked for a home phone number, Nell was usually hard-pressed to remember it.

The thought jogged her memory. Forms. *Shit.* The fertility clinic. Credit applications.

She pushed her chair away from the table, poised to lunge for the phone.

Josh got up and beat her there before she could get up. "Hello?"

Nell watched his face for some sign of who might be on the other end.

Please be a telemarketer, she thought. *A robocall. A political poll. Anything.* Her heart hammered inside her chest.

"I think you must have the wrong number," Josh said.

Nell exhaled. *Sure. Wrong number. That works, too.*

"Yes, she lives here, but I'm sure there's some sort of mistake. I don't think we have a credit card with that bank."

Nell's face felt hot, and her dinner sat uneasily in her stomach.

"Yes, please do send written confirmation," Josh said. "Who can I contact about clearing this up?" He balanced the phone between his ear and shoulder and grabbed a pen from the counter. He scribbled something on the back of an envelope. "Will do. Thanks."

He placed the phone back in its cradle, then turned to look at Nell. "So that was a debt collection agency."

Nell started to sweat. She'd known she would have to tell Josh about the credit card bills at some point, but she'd been hoping to be able to bring it up on her own timeline, once she'd gotten a few more paychecks and had the chance to pay down some of the balances.

"What did they want?" Nell asked. As soon as the words came out of her mouth, she realized how ridiculous they sounded.

"Well, they're debt collectors, so . . . I guess they're trying to collect a debt." Josh dropped his arms to his sides and gave her a pleading look. "Tell me this is a mistake."

Nell put her face in her hands. She couldn't stand the earnest expression on her husband's face as he waited for an explanation. "It's not a mistake," she said through her fingers.

He took a step closer to where she sat at the table. "What? You're mumbling."

Nell looked up at him through tears that had welled up. "I said it's not a mistake."

Josh paced the room—something he did whenever he was stressed out. "They said we owe *forty thousand dollars*, Nell. I don't even understand how that's possible. I don't see a new car parked in the driveway."

"IVF," Nell said, blinking back the tears. "Every single charge was for fertility treatments."

Josh furrowed his brow. "I thought that was covered by our insurance."

"Some of it was covered, for the first round. But not all of it. I put the rest on credit cards—ones we never use." Nell's voice wavered as she choked on the guilt of keeping such a big secret. "You thought the procedures were covered, so I let you believe that."

"We did *three* rounds." He stared at her, arms crossed. "And it never occurred to you to tell me they weren't covered?"

"Of course it occurred to me." Now the tears fell freely, dripping off Nell's face and onto the table. "But I wanted to tell you when I had good news to give you as well—if I got pregnant again, it seemed like the lies would have at least been worth it, on some level. But that never happened."

Josh resumed his pacing, shaking his head. "The treatments took months. So it's not like this was a snap decision on your part. I'm guessing there were multiple times you could have told me about what was going on. Shit, I was just saying something a few minutes ago about doing house renovations." He crossed his arms. "But I guess we don't have the money for that, do we?"

Nell shook her head.

Josh pressed his palms into his temples. "I just . . . I can't believe this."

"I know," Nell said. She was getting angry now, and the anger over everything she'd endured—with nothing to show for it—burned past the sadness. "I can't believe it most of the time, either. I can't believe this is my life. I don't even know how to apologize. I didn't think we would ever be having this conversation without good news to go along with it. I couldn't let myself even think about that possibility."

Josh stopped pacing. "I knew this whole infertility thing had changed you. Had changed *us*. But I had no idea how much, until just now. I feel like I don't even know who you are anymore."

Me neither, Nell thought. But she knew that saying it aloud wouldn't help. After a moment of tense silence, she said, "I know this doesn't fix things, but I've been putting all of my paychecks toward paying off the debt." She reached out and touched his arm. He yanked it away and took a step back from her.

"You know, I was sad, too, about losing the baby," he said. "I'm still sad. But I would never keep a secret like this from you."

"I wasn't thinking straight. It seemed like a baby was the only thing that would even begin to make everything we went through okay—not *okay*, it will never be okay, but just maybe more bearable."

Josh just stared at her, almost looking past her as if he were looking at a stranger, and left the room.

"I'm sorry," she said to his back.

A moment later, she heard the back door slam and the car start up.

She was sorry. And ashamed. But she was also angry. Angry that their daughter had died and no one could tell her why. Angry that what was so hard for them seemed to come so easily to other people.

After giving birth, most people leave the hospital not only with a baby, but also with all kinds of gifts and gear. Receiving blankets, flowers, knit hats, and cards. A car seat carrier swinging off the father's elbow. One couple Nell had seen during a tour of the hospital was so weighed down with baby paraphernalia, they required a double-decker cart to roll everything out to their car.

When Nell was discharged, she and Josh took nothing with them but a white box tied with a pink ribbon. She didn't even take home the clothes she'd been wearing when she checked in. She knew she'd never again want to wear the elastic-waist jeans she'd been wearing on the day she was admitted to labor and delivery, one day shy of twenty-two weeks gestation. The day her body betrayed her. The day she lost her daughter.

NELL'S OBSTETRICIAN HAD been concerned, but not full-on panicked, when she and Josh first arrived at the hospital, with Nell's contractions strong and close together.

"We need to get you to at least twenty-four weeks," he said. "That's when the scale for viability outside the womb tips to the baby's favor."

"But you can stop labor, right?" Nell asked, breathing hard as a fresh ripple of pain clutched at her abdomen.

"We will do everything we can," the doctor said. "More often than not, we have success in stopping or at least significantly delaying labor. But not always. Even with the best medical care, ten percent of women who go into preterm labor give birth within the following seven days."

"What if that's us? What if we're in the ten percent?" Josh asked.

"I've ordered some tests that can give us a pretty good idea of how likely that is," said the obstetrician.

A nurse wrapped an elastic belt around Nell's belly and hooked her up to a fetal monitor. "See there?" she said. "That's your baby's heartbeat."

A line staggered up and down on the screen, a green mountain range against a black abyss. The constant peaks and valleys gave Nell some comfort, but also terrified her. Her baby was alive now. But what if the doctors couldn't keep her inside? What if Nell couldn't keep her safe?

As if he'd read her mind, Josh turned to the doctor and said, in his lawyer voice, calm but firm, "You didn't answer my question. What happens if the baby is born today? Or tomorrow?"

Nell balled up on the bed with the onset of another contraction, clenching every muscle in her body. Even through her pain, she could see the doctor's face change.

"I have the on-call neonatologist on the way here to talk to you about that. But we will do absolutely everything we can to keep the baby inside as long as we can."

The doctor kept his promise. They did try everything. They flooded Nell's veins with IV medications that made her feel even more nauseous than she already was, causing her to vomit between contractions. Nurses elevated Nell's feet above her head to take advantage of gravity and discourage the baby from dropping down into the birth canal. But none of it helped. When the test results came back, her obstetrician's face went from worried to panicked. Nell could see it even through her blurred vision, a side effect of one of the medications. The neonatologist arrived, a woman who looked not much older than Nell, and the two doctors conceded that the baby was coming soon.

In between surges of searing pain, Nell listened as the neonatologist explained the chances of survival for a baby delivered at twenty-one weeks, six days gestation. They were very slim. Even if they took the baby by C-section, which would pose greater risk to Nell's health, the chances that their daughter would survive, even with intensive medical measures, were very slim. And if she did survive, she would most certainly suffer health problems throughout infancy and beyond.

"So what do you recommend?" Josh asked.

"Of course, the decision is up to the two of you. But I can tell you that even with our top-level NICU, no baby this premature has left the hospital alive. So I can't in good conscience recommend that we provide lifesaving measures. Even the tiniest of breathing tubes cannot be inserted without causing organ damage. Are you familiar with the Hippocratic oath?"

"First, do no harm," Josh said, his shoulders shaking.

Nell grabbed his arm with a desperate force. "I don't want to do harm to our baby."

Josh put his hand on top of hers and held her gaze, his eyes brimming with tears. "Neither do I."

"Then in these cases, we recommend comfort care," the neonatologist said. "Swaddling and holding your baby, keeping her warm, and bonding with her as much as you can."

Nell's mind commanded her body to *stop,* but her body would not obey. The uncontrollable urge to push possessed her, and the room filled up with a dozen more medical professionals. One of the nurses came over to Nell's bedside and put a hand on her shoulder.

Nell shook her off. She wanted to feel the physical pain of her baby's birth. Wanted to shift her focus to the tearing, barreling sensations ripping through her torso. Because the physical pain was almost, but not quite, forceful enough to overtake her emotional anguish, if only for a few seconds at a time.

After a particularly intense contraction ended, the nurse spoke to her. "I know you don't want to think about this right now, but I need to let you know about something so that you can make a decision."

Nell looked at the nurse through a hazy film of tears and sweat.

"There's a photographer and her assistant out in the hall," the nurse continued. "They're from a volunteer organization for bereaved parents. If you are willing, they'd like to take some photos of the two of you with your baby after you deliver."

Nell's ears rang as she caught her breath, still recovering from the contraction. The word "bereaved" reverberated in her brain. She still could not believe this was happening, even as she wiped the sweat from her face.

Josh, who had been squeezing Nell's hand, turned to the nurse. "This is the worst day of our lives," he said, his voice shaking with anger. "Why would we want pictures?"

"Many people feel that way at first," the nurse said. "But later, you may be happy to have them. As the doctors explained, we don't know if the baby will survive delivery or, if she does, how long she'll live. Some babies this young live for a few hours, some only for a few minutes. If you do decide you want pictures, we need to let the photographers know now, so they can be ready."

Nell looked up at Josh. His face was white, his eyes large and hollow. "Can we just have them take the pictures and then decide later if we want them?" he asked.

"Of course," the nurse said. "Lots of people do that. That way the pictures are there if you ever want them."

A wave of pain rippled through Nell's back and wrapped around to her abdomen. She writhed on the table, giving herself over to the inevitable.

Through clenched teeth, she told the nurse to let them in.

Nell didn't remember what the photographer looked like. Nell remembered only that she was female and that when Nell came in, she said in a gentle voice, "Pretend we're not here. Or, if you can't do that, pretend we're just one of the medical staff."

Baby Girl Parker came on a tidal wave of pain, followed by

silence. A nurse cut the umbilical cord, and Nell felt instantly helpless and empty. Another nurse whisked the baby away and placed her on a warming table, where she was rubbed clean, weighed, and wrapped in a blanket before being placed in Nell's arms.

At less than a pound, the baby felt lighter than a kitten. She was not red, as Nell had imagined she'd be. Rather, she was translucent, her skin as thin as rice paper. Her eyes were fused shut, two perfect crescent moons underlined by fine, thread-thin lashes. Perfect fingers and toes curled at the ends of skinny arms and legs. Everything about her, actually, was perfect. Just far too small and far too delicate. Her chest and belly rose and fell at an erratic, belabored pace.

Nell took her eyes off her daughter, swaddled in her arms in soft white flannel, for only a second—just long enough to realize that the swarm of people who'd been in the room during the delivery was no longer there. This, Nell knew, was the worst sign of all. She had heard the neonatologist say that medical intervention was not recommended. She and Josh had confirmed that they did not want to take any measures that would cause their baby suffering. But Nell now realized that at the time, with all the doctors and nurses bustling around her, and the machines beeping and the monitors blinking, she'd still been hoping that a miracle might happen. That the baby would come out and somehow be bigger or stronger than anyone had anticipated, and that everyone would swoop in and save her.

Instead, the room had cleared out. Other than Nell, Josh,

and their impossibly tiny baby girl, only one nurse and the two photographers remained.

Josh got up onto the hospital bed, ducked under the IV lines still attached, and positioned himself behind Nell, so that she was leaning against him as she held their daughter. They marveled over her fragile beauty. Cried over her tiny perfection. But even as Nell cradled the limp, almost weightless baby and covered her in tears and kisses, Nell understood that she was slipping away.

Nell tried to stretch each second, but in the end her daughter lived only four minutes.

WHEN NELL WAS finally cleared to go home, a nurse—there had been so many, she could not keep track—gave her and Josh the option of leaving through a back door of the hospital so they wouldn't have to ride in the elevator with people leaving the maternity floor with living babies. It was a merciful offer, and they took it. But riding in the service elevator, with its padded walls and scratched-up stainless steel floor, only made Nell feel more alone. Normal parents left the hospital happy and nervous, checking car seat straps, snapping photos, and saying thank you to the nurses who'd tended to them in their first hours as moms and dads. She and Josh were not normal parents. They left with nothing but the white box, tied with pink ribbon.

NELL KNEW THE contents of the box by heart. The same volunteer organization that had lined up the photographer had given it to her and Josh at the hospital. Before everything they went through, Nell hadn't even known such an organization existed. She, like most people, had never considered what a person did with the tiny keepsakes belonging to a baby that never went home from the hospital. Since then, she'd looked at the contents of the box hundreds of times. As far as she knew, Josh had never once opened it.

Inside, along with the hospital blanket Nell had worn throughout her stay and the flannel blanket the nurses had wrapped around the baby, was a copy of their daughter's Certificate of Live Birth. Because, even though she'd lived only a few minutes, their baby *had* been born alive. The hospital required Nell and Josh to fill it out, for their record-keeping purposes, they'd said. Nell learned later, upon receiving a bill in the mail, that the certificate served the practical, but rather crass, purpose of establishing a separate insurance account for Baby Girl Parker's medical bills, which were substantial, despite her very brief existence. Still, the certificate was important to Nell. It was proof that their baby had lived, even if no one but Josh, Nell, and the few people who'd been in the hospital room ever got to meet her.

They never named their daughter. Back before they'd ever had reason to believe anything could go wrong, they had bantered suggestions back and forth over dinner a few times. They'd come up with a handful of names they both liked, but neither of them thought they'd need to select a name so soon. And then, after the fact, after she was gone, it seemed too heavy a task to name their dead daughter. To call her a name they'd never spoken to her aloud. All Nell had said to her, over and over, in those brief minutes, was "My baby, my baby. I love you so much. My baby girl, I'm so sorry."

And so Baby Girl Parker she remained.

Chapter Fifteen

$\mathscr{P}aige$

PIECE: *Frank Stella,* Polar Coordinates II, *circa 1980.*
Offset lithograph and screen print, Edition: 31/100.

Trent left before daybreak, like he'd been doing whenever he spent the night with Paige, which was often. He'd gotten a job as a barback at one of the hotels downtown, and they met up most evenings when he got off work. Today, when Trent slipped out before the first whisper of morning light made its way through the windows, Paige stretched out under the covers and fell back into a satisfied sleep. As she often did after making love, she dreamed of making art. Colors and lines mingled and intersected until she could see, clearly, a finished work. This morning, she pictured feathers, in various stages of floating and falling, all delicate veins and tufts in various shades of blue.

Based on the complexity, it was something she'd need to create on one of the table presses up at school. She dressed, grabbed her backpack, and went downstairs, hoping no one else was up. A vision this clear was rare, and Paige wanted to get to the studio before the vision faded or got mucked up with the rest of the day's sensory input.

On the first floor, the foyer and living room were still dark. But down the hall she could see the lights on in Nell's office. She heard a muffled sound, like a hiccup, and realized that someone was crying. She had planned to go out the side door, but changed her mind when she realized she'd have to walk past the office. She took a few slow steps in the other direction, but stopped when her foot landed on a creaky floorboard just before she reached the front door.

Nell's voice called out from down the hall. "Hello?"

Paige turned in the direction of the voice and saw that Nell had stuck her head out from the office. Even in the dim light, Paige could see deep-set circles under her eyes.

"It's just me," Paige said. "I didn't mean to scare you."

"It's okay," Nell said. The streaks on her cheeks and the messy ponytail, in place of her usual put-together look, suggested otherwise. Paige felt awkward seeing her this way, both for her own sake and for Nell's. She looked away, focusing instead on a large, framed lithograph print on the hallway wall behind Nell. The print—of bright geometric shapes overlapping in shades of blue, green, and orange, as if drawn with a protractor—was one Paige had noticed before. She'd assumed it was a copy, but now that she was close enough, she could see that the signature of the artist, Frank Stella, was done in pencil.

Nell sniffed and straightened her shoulders. "You're up early.

When I was your age, I don't think I ever got up before ten, unless I had a test or something. Definitely not on a Saturday."

"I need to go up to school to work on something." Paige shifted her backpack from one shoulder to the other. She hoped Nell would catch the urgency in her voice. Already the colors in her head were losing their clarity.

Nell's face brightened. "Yeah? What are you working on?"

"I have an idea for a new series." Paige didn't want to be short with someone who obviously had been crying just a minute earlier. But she also didn't like to talk about her work when she was in the middle of it or, worse, when she hadn't even started it yet. New ideas were too fragile, too susceptible to suggestion. And anyway, she wanted to get to work, now, before the day took on a life of its own.

She knew what would happen if she waited too long. She'd walk down State Street at just the time when people her age were starting to get up and gather for brunch or five-dollar cups of coffee. Her ears would fill with the sound of loud conversations rehashing the events of the night before or the spitting hiss of hydraulic bus brakes. She'd pass homeless people huddled under awnings, asking for spare change or talking to themselves. Even in the short amount of time it took her to walk up to the art school—fifteen minutes, maybe—her head would jam up with images and emotions, occupying the space where beauty and lucidity used to be. She'd go sit in the studio, but the effort to create something would seem immense. Other students would be there already, chatting while they worked or banging around in the supply cabinets.

Paige would dally over setting up her supplies, combining inks to the point where the mixture would take on a brownish hue and she'd have to toss the whole thing and start over. Discouraged at the waste of money and time, she'd redirect her efforts, only to produce something forced and derivative—an inferior shadow of a work she'd already finished and liked. Then, after cleaning up, she'd trudge back over slushy sidewalks to her room, too depressed to study or read or do anything but text her latest lover, craving the tangible reality of skin on skin, the power of pleasure to blunt pain, even momentarily.

This was why Paige rose at dawn. At this hour, the streets were quiet and the pale palette of sunrise complemented, rather than covered, the colors in her head.

"Sorry to interrupt you," Paige said. "I didn't think anyone else was down here."

"I haven't been sleeping well lately," Nell said. "So I figured I might as well work. There's so much to do here. Betsy left behind so many notes with ideas she had for the Colony. Exhibitions, fund-raisers . . . it's sort of overwhelming to try to get everything up and running all at once."

"I bet," Paige said. "Well, I'll let you get back to it then."

"Thanks," Nell said. "Good luck with your project." There was a forced cheerfulness in her voice, as if she were trying to convince Paige, or maybe herself, that everything was okay.

On the way up to school, Paige tried to focus again on the image of the floating feathers. But already the image of Nell's splotchy face and sad eyes had displaced what she'd seen so clearly in her mind just minutes earlier. And maybe Paige could have successfully shifted her thoughts, smoothed them out in the studio as she ran the roller over her screen, again and again. But then she'd gotten a text from Trent, midmorning:

My parents are coming to town this weekend. Want to have lunch?

Oh hell no. Paige shoved her phone into her pocket. She liked Trent. A lot. She'd seen him nearly every day since they met. She'd told him things she'd never told any boy before. About the real reason for the scars on her wrists. He kissed them every time she brought him to bed.

Trent had talked to her a little bit about his family already. How he grew up in Michigan's Upper Peninsula. How his dad was a quarry driller and Trent was the first kid in his family to go to college. How his parents had been so disappointed when he dropped out, even though he insisted it was only for a year. Paige didn't want to add to their disappointment by being the girl he brought to lunch.

When she didn't respond for several hours, Trent sent her another message that afternoon that said, simply: ??? She'd never not responded to him before.

Paige shot back: Sorry, I can't this weekend.

She didn't have plans, yet. But whatever she ended up doing, it would not include meeting anyone's parents.

Trent responded: No big deal. Another time. See you tonight?

Paige felt relieved, for the moment. But as she packed up her supplies to go home that evening, she got the uneasy gut feeling that something had shifted. She looked over at the feather prints she'd spent all day making, now laid out to dry. They suddenly seemed unoriginal, nothing more than flat images on fancy paper.

Before she zipped her phone into the pocket of her backpack, she texted Trent back:

> Really tired and don't think I'll still be up when you
> get off. Coffee tomorrow?

She hesitated before hitting send. For Paige, "coffee" meant only one thing.

TRENT GOT TO the café before she did the next morning. She spotted him sitting at a booth and admired, for a moment, how comfortable he looked being alone. It wasn't a skill that everyone had. Trent didn't check his phone or read the menu on the wall or pretend to be engaged in something other than just sitting there, looking around. He gave a small wave when he saw her. She ordered some tea at the counter.

"For here or to go?" asked the barista.

"To go," Paige said. She waited until the barista handed her the drink in a paper cup, then walked over to Trent's table and slid into the booth across from him.

"Hey." He held her gaze and threw her the sexy half smile she'd come to crave over the last couple of months. "This is about asking you to meet my parents, isn't it?" he asked. "I freaked you out, am I right?"

Paige squirmed a little on the vinyl bench. She took a drink from her tea and gave him a sheepish look over the brim of the cup.

"I knew it." Trent set down his coffee. It was cold brew in a pint glass, and the bottom of the glass clunked against the table. "Let's just forget about it, then. I meant it when I said it was no big deal. I'll admit it was kind of soon for me to bring up, but my parents don't come to town that often, and I like you a lot, so . . ." There he went again, with that half smile.

Before she lost her nerve, Paige took a deep breath and blurted out, "I think we should see other people."

His smile disappeared.

"I need to figure out what I'm doing after graduation," Paige said. "And I don't really want to complicate things any more than I have to."

"It's not that complicated," Trent said. "I like you. And I *know* you like me . . ." He brushed his leg against hers underneath the table, and Paige felt a warm buzz creep up through her body. Then she shifted in the booth again. She needed to keep her focus.

"Okay, I like you, too," she said. "And I don't see any reason we can't keep seeing each other. I just don't want to be, you know, exclusive. Serious."

Trent let out a loud exhale. "I can't do that. If I liked you less, maybe. But I can't be with you and also think about you being with other people, too. It will make me crazy jealous."

"Well, then, that's that, isn't it?" She picked up her paper cup, got up, and kissed him on the cheek.

As she walked out the door, Paige realized that she hadn't really thought the whole thing through. She hadn't thought about the flip side of the equation—how she would feel about *Trent* being with other people. She didn't like the idea very much, either, now that she thought about it. So she resolved just not to think about it.

She walked out into the cool morning air, but somehow she didn't feel quite as free as she'd hoped she would.

Chapter Sixteen

Betsy

PIECE: *Ankle-length mink purchased from Furs by Hershleder in Madison.*

Betsy unzipped the cotton bag containing her mahogany mink coat and paused to rub her cheek against the short, glossy fur. She heaved the weighty garment off its hanger and set it on her bed, then lay her body down next to it, winded from the effort.

The coat was probably too much for a midwestern exhibition opening—too formal, too old-fashioned. Certainly too big to fit in her suitcase. She'd have to bring it on the plane. But Minneapolis was positively glacial in winter, she told herself. And these days, she felt chilled to the bone even when sitting in front of a roaring fire.

Though she never would have admitted it to anyone but herself, Betsy wondered if this would be her last opportunity to wear the coat. It had been a gift from Walt for their thirtieth anniversary, specially fitted for her by a local furrier. Dropping the coat off in March or April for cleaning and storage had become an annual rite of spring, as reliable for Betsy as seeing the first crocus stalks push through the soil in her sculpture garden.

When she arrived in the Twin Cities, Betsy was glad she'd decided to bring the coat, after all. She'd arranged for a car service to take her from the airport to the gallery, but even the two minutes waiting at the curb outside the terminal were enough to make her flip up the tall collar against the wind.

When the driver pulled up in front of the Foster Gallery, Betsy was impressed. She'd been there a couple of times before, when it had been just a small storefront. It had expanded since then, taking over the next-door loft to build a second exhibition space specifically for regional artists. Today was the grand opening of the new space. The floor-to-ceiling windows glowed yellow in the early dusk, with patrons milling around inside—a mix of well-dressed, older people like herself and younger, trendier types.

The driver asked Betsy how long she'd be.

"Depends if I buy any art," she said. But as soon as she walked into the expansion wing, she knew she'd be buying something. It was only a question of narrowing it down.

She used to buy art with a lot of different motives in mind. She had to think about which pieces were likely to acquire value over time, which artists were apt to have long careers because they were doing something new or unusual. She tried to be sure she wouldn't tire of a piece, too, which often meant that it had to have multiple dimensions and meanings. And then there were practical considerations, like would the piece go with the other items she'd acquired? Would a particular artwork even fit in her home or her yard?

Now, though, with a breast cancer relapse that her doctor described as "aggressive," Betsy found herself looking at art with simpler criteria—a single question, really. And that was: Did it bring her joy, or move her in some other way?

Today, the piece that answered that question with the loudest yes was a four-foot-by-four-foot mixed-media piece. The canvas was covered with damask wallpaper in bold coral and white. On top of the wallpaper, in the center of the canvas, was a big green chrysanthemum bloom with the word "forward" printed over it in red capital letters.

But when Betsy got closer to the work, she realized it wasn't a mixed-media piece after all. The entire thing, including the patterned background she thought was wallpaper, had been drawn in oil pastels. What she had guessed was a green flower was actually a ball of frogs, dozens of them, clinging to one another in a scramble of webbed feet and varied shades of green. Even the lettering, which appeared so perfect it could have been typeset, had been hand-rendered and painstakingly colored in. Betsy stood there, marveling at how anyone could achieve such dimension just by drawing on flat paper.

"Amazing, isn't it?" said a voice from behind her.

Betsy turned around and recognized Sloane Foster, the young

gallery owner, standing tall behind her in heeled boots and a short black dress.

"Betsy Barrett, right?" Sloane said. "Thank you so much for coming."

Betsy nodded. "I've followed what you've been doing here. I knew you had a good eye when I was here last time, and I see that hasn't changed." She gestured toward the drawing in front of her, a shock of color against the white wall. "Tell me about this one."

"So, this is by a young artist from St. Paul. She does the initial design in colored pencil, then fills it in with oil pastel."

Betsy removed her reading glasses from the silk-lined pocket of her coat. "*Always Ahead,*" she said, squinting to read the title typed on the information card posted to the wall.

"Because frogs can only jump forward, not backward," Sloane said.

Betsy had already fallen in love with the drawing be-fore Sloane explained the title. It made her think of her late brother, and his childhood nickname, *Zaba*—the Polish word for frog. But once Betsy heard about the concept of moving only forward, she was sold. "I'll take it."

"The artist does commissions, too," Sloane said. "I just saw a piece she did for a client's home. With text, like this one, but bigger. They installed it above their fireplace."

Betsy loved commissions. It gave her a chance to communi-cate with the artist, to go back and forth about ideas and get a glimpse into how the person worked. She had a few commis-sioned pieces in her home and she treasured each of them not just for the finished product but for the process that went into them. But now, she feared she didn't have enough time to see a commissioned project from start to finish.

"No, no, this one's perfect," Betsy said.

"You're sure?"

"Positive." Betsy felt a rush of excitement up her spine, as she always did when she found a new piece for her collection.

Sloane pulled a sheet of stickers from the pocket of her dress and affixed a red dot to the corner of the information card, to indicate that the piece was sold. "It's yours, then. I'll send you the invoice, assuming you haven't moved?"

Betsy shook her head. "Still in the same house." She wasn't sure how long that would be true, though, if her doctor was right about her prognosis. But she didn't want to think about that now, not when she was surrounded by so much beauty. She turned her attention to a group of metal sculptures near the front windows. "I see there are also a lot of red dots for those sculptures over there."

Sloane's face lit up as a smile spread across her lips. "Those are by another local artist, Odin Sorenson. Well, he's from Wisconsin, but he lives here now. That's him there, in the plaid shirt."

Betsy followed Sloane's gaze to a tall young man with broad shoulders and a beard. His head was bent in conversation with a gray-haired couple looking at one of the sculptures. Although Betsy had met Sloane only a couple of times, she'd come to recognize a sort of sharp, exacting element in her facial expressions, an angular scrutiny in her body language. It seemed appropriate for someone who evaluated and sold art—a largely subjective commodity—for a living. Now, though, there was a softness that settled over Sloane when she caught Odin's eye and smiled.

"This is the first time I've shown his work," Sloane said. "I think it's fantastic, but I was a little nervous about it, truth be told. Metal isn't for everyone. I'm so glad to see his stuff is selling. It will be a huge boost of confidence for him. He's insanely talented, but I think the whole art scene intimidates him. He grew up on a farm, where the nearest town had like three hundred people."

"He's lucky to have you," Betsy said.

"No, I'm lucky to have *him*." Sloane pulled at her necklace, a gold tassel on a long chain.

Betsy recognized the mutual admiration that flowed between the young gallerist and the artist across the room. A warm memory stirred in her chest as she remembered how she and Walt used to look at one another through the crowd at a cocktail fête, or from opposite ends of their dining room table during a dinner party. Despite all their differences, Betsy and her husband shared a spark of understanding, a history, and a similar sense of humor. These connections bound them without the need for words. She could see something similar going on with Sloane and Odin, and suddenly Betsy missed her husband desperately.

She'd gotten along fine without him in the years since he'd passed. She sometimes felt guilty, even, at the sense of freedom she now had. She could be vocal about her ideals in a

way she never could be when Walt was alive, still running his
manufacturing business and worried about public perception.
But not a day went by that Betsy didn't miss him. She envied
Sloane, now, for all she had still ahead of her.

THAT WAS THE last time Betsy purchased a work of art in person. She'd planned to have the piece installed somewhere on
the main floor of her house. But by the time the delivery truck
arrived six weeks later and the movers carried it into the house,
Betsy was spending her days in bed, drifting in and out of
drugged sleep. The hospice nurse who'd been tending to her
tapped her on the shoulder just as she was waking up from a
dream in which she was a young woman again, walking down
Mitchell Street to Goldmann's with her mother to buy fabric.

She was confused, then, when she opened her eyes and she
was not on Mitchell Street and it was not, in fact, the forties.
Instead, she was in her room in Madison, in the house she'd
lived in for five decades. She was not wearing stockings and
pumps but, instead, shivered in flannel pajamas underneath a
thick duvet.

"The art movers are here," said the nurse. She was young,
this one. But everyone seemed young, now. It was such a
strange part of growing old. At some point, nearly every face
Betsy encountered was younger than her own.

"They want to know where you want to put it," the nurse
said. Betsy tried to remember her name. Sally? Cindy? She
couldn't keep up with the shift changes.

"Tell them to bring it up here," Betsy said.

"I think it's pretty big," the nurse said. "Are you sure it will fit?"

Betsy pushed off the covers and inched her legs over to the side of the bed. With enormous effort, she rose to a sitting position. A wave of dizziness crashed over her and she had to close her eyes.

"Please, Mrs. Barrett." The nurse grabbed Betsy's arm and put the other hand on her back to hold her steady. "If you just tell me where you want it, I can . . ."

But Betsy pushed the nurse's hands away and got to her feet. She wobbled over to her low dresser and braced herself against its shiny surface for a second, catching her breath. She caught sight of herself in the mirror. Betsy barely recognized the pale, thin face that stared back at her. She'd looked into that same gilt mirror while she dressed for hundreds of dinners, dozens of charity events. She remembered, distinctly, putting on her favorite necklace and looking at her reflection on the morning of her husband's funeral. How heavy the familiar pearls had felt in her fingers that day, how difficult the clasp had been to close.

Now, in a swift movement that surprised her, she reached out and grabbed the mirror, pulling it off the wall and knocking over the perfume bottles that had been arranged in a tray on the top of the dresser.

The nurse rushed over and grabbed the mirror before it toppled Betsy over.

Betsy sat back down on the side of the bed and looked at the now-blank space above the dresser. The wallpaper was dark and unfaded where the mirror had hung for so many years.

"There," she said, pointing. "I want the new artwork there."

Chapter Seventeen

*O*din

PIECE: *Copper weather vane sculpture by unknown artist, reminiscent of the work of Isamu Noguchi.*

Odin turned off the welding machine, pushed up the visor on his helmet, and took a big swallow of black coffee from the thermos he'd brought out to the garage. What he loved most about metal sculpting was that it involved fire. As a kid, he'd always pictured artists as guys sitting around in berets, dabbing bits of paint on canvases, or else madmen having fits and cutting people's ears off.

What he had not expected was that many artists worked with tools and machines—something he had always liked. In high school, his shop instructor had showed him how to use an arc welder his sophomore year and, from then on, Odin was pretty much hooked. He made all kinds of items for his parents that year, ranging from the practical (a wall rack for his parents' mudroom, with hooks that looked like deer antlers) to the whimsical (a two-foot-tall statue of a robot made from old gears and cogs).

Even now, Odin still loved the glow of the arc and the sparks it threw as it made contact with whatever medium he was working with. He loved the way that even the seemingly strongest metals melted into submission with enough power and persistence.

The only downside to his chosen art was that he couldn't really do it indoors. Someday maybe he'd have a proper shop, with heat and worktables and storage for the materials he compiled. His life was a constant search for materials. The cast iron, aluminum, and bronze he liked to use in his sculpting were too costly to purchase raw, so he got them for cheap from junkyards and salvage shops.

For now, though, he was relegated to the garage, which was a step up from the barn at his parents' place. It had a roof that didn't leak, for starters. A beautiful, slate roof topped with a shining copper weather vane that was a work of art in itself, with spheres and ovals that rotated on an asymmetrical axis. On windy days, like today, Odin could hear the weather vane creak as it spun.

The garage also had windows in the back that looked out to the lake, which was still frozen in early April, though starting to thaw. Odin had never lived on a body of water, and it made him notice some things he'd never thought about before. Like how the ice didn't break up in chunks, like he imagined it would, but instead thinned out, became softer. Freestanding water pooled in some places. He noticed, too, the migratory birds that stopped to swim and eat and sing. Just that morning, he had thought he heard the raucous laughter of children out in the yard. He got out of bed and looked out one of the back windows, only to see a raft of loons. He had never seen them this far south before, and realized that they must be on their way back north after spending the summer somewhere with more hospitable weather. The Gulf, maybe. There were no birds out now, though. Rain and ice fell from the sky—a godforsaken combination that local meteorologists referred to as "a wintry mix."

He knew his fixation on the birds and the weather was just a way of distracting himself from the fact that he didn't know what the hell he was doing. He'd been trying to get back into the groove of making the sort of small-scale sculpture work that he'd been so successful with in Minneapolis. He figured the best way to break his creative block was to ease into something he already knew. But he found himself getting bored and frustrated, and abandoning projects at an even faster rate than he had when he'd been working in his parents' barn. He worried that the problem wasn't what he was working on. He worried that all his artistic inspiration had died along with Sloane.

Just as Odin was about to turn the machine on and try to return to work, he felt a burst of cold air. The garage door rose slowly, revealing a pair of feet in red rubber boots. A moment later, Nell ducked under the door. She held up a mittened hand and waved. Odin couldn't help but notice how her dark hair stuck out adorably from the bottom of her wool beanie. Her lips were moving, but he couldn't hear her.

Odin pulled off his helmet and took out his earplugs. "Hi," he said. "Sorry, what were you saying?"

She'd caught him off guard. No one ever came out here. Not that he was complaining. After he'd stared out the window at birds all morning, a good-looking woman was a welcome sight. Even if Nell *was* his boss . . . sort of. Not really. But whatever their relationship was, it was a working one. As if to remind himself of that, Odin cleared his throat.

Nell looked around. "You know, there are plenty of rooms in the house nobody uses, yet you're out here in the garage and Annie is holed up in the basement with space heaters."

"My work is loud." Odin shrugged. "Paige works up in her room sometimes, doesn't she?"

"Who knows? I'm not good at getting information out of her. Or Annie, for that matter." Nell looked at the bench Odin was sitting on. "Mind if I sit down?"

"Please." Odin moved over to make room. Nell sat next to him, and he caught the smell of something floral and soapy.

One of the things that always got him, even months after Sloane died, was the smell of rosemary. She used a rosemary-mint shampoo, one that cost a small fortune at the salon she went to. She insisted it was worth it, and he tended to agree. He used to bury his nose in her blond hair when they lay in bed. For weeks after she died, he didn't wash her pillowcase. Now, even the smallest whiff of rosemary, wafting from a fancy candle or even a loaf of bakery bread, would set a lump in his throat.

Nell's scent was different, though. Less woodsy. Clean, simple, and sweet. If she smelled this good even with a down jacket on, Odin couldn't help but wonder what she smelled like with less on . . . or nothing. He quickly turned his face to the window and the shitty weather outside. He really needed to rein in his imagination.

"Has Annie talked to you much about what she's doing?" Nell asked.

Odin turned back toward her and shook his head, his thoughts diverted for the moment. "I have a Y chromosome," he said. "I think that automatically puts me at the bottom of the list of people Annie wants to talk to."

Nell crossed her arms in front of her chest. "Just because someone is a feminist doesn't mean they hate men." She gave him a scolding look, but the corners of her mouth turned upward. If she weren't married, Odin might have guessed she was flirting with him.

"I just think Annie's kinda secretive," Odin said. "Don't take it personally. A lot of artists don't like to talk about their work."

Nell nodded. "I got the same vibe from Paige. But she doesn't hide out in the basement and invite all sorts of strangers into the house, coming and going at odd hours."

"For the record, I don't mind talking about *my* work," he said. "I'm just not very good at it."

"Your application did a great job of it," Nell said. "Otherwise Betsy never would have chosen you."

Odin wanted to know what *Nell* thought about his application, and about him. But instead he said, "I'm not sure if I should admit this, but I never actually saw my application. My girlfriend sent it in for me."

A crease appeared on her forehead. "I didn't know you had a girlfriend."

Was she disappointed? he wondered. Then he thought, *Don't be ridiculous*. He really needed to get out more.

"I don't have a girlfriend," he said. "Anymore, anyway. She died. It's been almost a year now." The words came out before Odin really had a chance to think about them. There was something about Nell that made her easy to talk to. "Her name was Sloane. She had her own gallery."

Nell put a hand over her mouth. "Oh my God. I'm so sorry."

"Don't be. I actually don't mind talking about her. I mean, her death—I don't like talking about that part. It was terrible. But I do like to talk about *her*. The person she was. I like to remember, you know? I just don't bring her up very much because it makes other people feel uncomfortable."

Nell nodded—an emphatic gesture that sent her bangs, which had been pushed to the side, flopping down into her eyes. She brushed them away. "I know what you mean," she said. "For the person who's grieving, the grief is everything. It's all you can think about. You feel like it's written on your forehead. But everyone else keeps interacting with you like nothing's wrong. And that's what's so hard. Because you want to scream, 'I'm not okay. Things are not okay.'" Now her face was flushed, her eyes glassy. She looked down at her mittens and took a deep breath.

"I think people mean well, but they don't know what to say," Odin said. "God, if I had a dollar for every time someone told me time heals all wounds or how everything happens for a reason or some bullshit."

"'Everything happens for a reason' is the *worst*," Nell said, her voice heated. "Really? There's a reason my daughter died? Because if you know what it is, then I'd really like to know, too."

Odin blinked. His mouth fell open. "I didn't know."

"Of course not," Nell said. "I actually can't believe I just told you."

"I'm glad you did."

Nell pulled off her mittens and played with them in her lap.

"Do you want to talk about it?" Odin asked.

"You don't want to hear my sob story."

"I just told you mine."

She tilted her head and looked at him, as if trying to assess whether telling him would be crossing some sort of line. Odin wondered what the line was. Was it a professional one, since she was the director and not an artist, like he was? Or perhaps the line was a personal one. Maybe she felt hesitant to open up to a man who wasn't her husband.

Regardless, Nell set her jaw and started talking. She told him about her baby. How much she missed her. How her husband seemed to be able to move on, but she was stuck.

"Every time I see a baby, I think about all the moments and milestones that were ripped out from under me," she said. "And it's not just babies. Kids, too. I'm afraid that for the rest of my life, I'm going to walk around looking at kids who are the age she would have been and wonder what she'd be like, what she'd be doing."

"You might," Odin said. "But what's wrong with that? Losing a kid goes against the way things are supposed to be, you know? There's nothing wrong with thinking about her."

"People make me feel like there is. I can see it in their faces."

"That's because they're uncomfortable," Odin said. "I know that look. But guess what? It's not your job to make them feel comfortable. This happened to you, and it's what you have to deal with. If people can't handle hearing about it, that's their problem, not yours."

Nell nodded, as if considering this.

"And anyway, everything happens for a reason." Odin glanced at her sidelong.

Nell cracked a smile and gave him a shove. Due to his size, though, Odin didn't budge. Instead, the impact sent Nell toppling backward. He reached out and righted her, grabbing hold of her arm through her puffy coat. Even through all the layers, the physical contact sent an electric buzz of attraction through his body.

Nell looked down at his hand, then up at his eyes. Odin became acutely aware of how close their faces were. If she weren't the director of the program, and if she were single, he would kiss her right now. Tension hummed between them and, for a moment, he could have sworn *she* was going to kiss *him*. But he realized it was probably wishful thinking, and he pulled back his hand.

"I should let you get back to work," Nell said. She got up and pulled her mittens on. "Thanks for listening. There aren't many people I can talk to about this—Josh is the only one, really. It's good to have a friend."

"Yeah," Odin said. "Anytime."

He needed friends, too, he thought. But as he watched her go, he noticed the way her hips curved underneath her jeans and how her body swayed slightly when she walked. He fired up his torch, letting the flame distract him from going any further in his thoughts.

His current project was one he'd been struggling with for a couple of weeks—a sculpture of a blue heron, inspired by one he'd seen perched on the retaining wall down by the water. His goal with this piece was to capture the way the bird looked just as it was taking off for flight. He used repurposed steel rebar for the trailing legs and hammered sheets of stainless steel for the wings. But the wings were tripping him up. He really wanted to make the sculpture life-size, but the wingspan of the real bird he'd seen had to be five, maybe six feet. Perhaps if he folded the wings in a certain way, the sculpture wouldn't take up so much space.

He worked through dinner, pausing only to eat a granola bar he'd stuffed in his pocket. By the time he finished for the day, it was almost midnight. When he went inside, a slant of light glowed under the basement door. Annie must be working late, too. He considered going down to say hello, but remembered Nell saying earlier how difficult it had been lately to get Annie to talk about much of anything. He was too tired for that sort of effort tonight, so he hung up his jacket and made his way toward the main stairs.

Odin stopped near the open office door because something inside the room caught his eye—a dark figure balled up on the couch. He took a few cautious steps closer and saw that it was Nell. She'd fallen asleep there with a scattered stack of papers and an open shoebox on the cushion beside her, and her boots kicked off on the floor next to the couch. The end table lamp was on. Odin switched it off, then went upstairs to his room and grabbed a blanket from his own bed. He brought it back down and covered Nell with it, tucking the ends around her wool-stockinged feet. She stirred slightly, then snuggled the blanket to her face, buried her nose in it, and let out a contented sigh. Odin wished he were under the blanket with her, curled around her, but he turned away and walked toward the door.

There was a rustling sound behind him and then Nell said, "Hey, you."

Odin looked back toward the couch, where Nell was now sitting up, stretching.

"Sorry if I woke you," he said.

"No, I needed to get up anyway. I can't believe I fell asleep here."

Odin noticed that her hair was matted to her face on one side—bedhead. An image flashed through his mind of being in bed with her, her dark hair splayed across the pillow, the sheets playing peekaboo with her soft curves. He blinked hard to get the image out of his head.

Nell rubbed her eyes and riffled through the papers next to her. "I was going through some of Betsy's things, so I pulled your application out for you," she said. "Thought you might want to see it."

Nell held out a packet of papers to him. He took it and said, "Thanks. Is it okay if I read it later?"

"Sure. I should probably get home." Nell pushed the blanket off her legs, gathered it in her arms, and got up from the sofa. "It was really good to talk with you earlier."

"I was thinking the same thing. There aren't many people I can talk to like that."

"Anytime." She held out the blanket to give it back to him. As he reached for it, their hands touched inside the folds of the soft cotton fabric. Nell looked at him with still sleepy, heavy-lidded eyes. He closed his hands, callused from the long day's work, over her smaller ones. He felt the same jolt of attraction he'd felt when they'd touched earlier that day, sitting side by side on the bench. Except that this time, it was stronger. She was closer.

A voice inside his head told him he'd probably crossed the line. He tried to silence it, but the voice only became more persistent. Reluctantly, he loosened his grip on her hands.

But she tightened hers. "It's okay . . ."

This time, Odin couldn't stop himself from bending his face down toward hers. She leaned closer to him, tilting her chin up. Then, just as their lips were about to touch, Nell looked down, and his mouth landed awkwardly on her forehead, at her hairline. Instead of the wet press of her lips, he got a whiff of flowery shampoo.

Nell covered her face with her hands.

"I'm sorry," he said, taking a step back. "I thought you were trying to . . ."

Nell dropped her arms to her sides, and he could see that her cheeks were bright red. "I don't know *what* I was doing." She shook her head. "I wasn't thinking. I'm so embarrassed."

"You don't have to be embarrassed," Odin said. "It was stupid of me. I think I've been spending way too much time alone. It's messing up my judgment and I misread—"

Nell hoisted her bag onto her shoulder. "You didn't misread anything." She looked him directly in the eye, her expression earnest. "But my judgment has been screwed up lately, too. I should really get home."

She left the room, and her footsteps clicked on the tile floor of the hallway. The sound stopped suddenly and, for a few quiet seconds, Odin wondered if Nell had changed her mind about leaving. His heart pounded with desire and anticipation.

But then the sound of a siren at close range broke the silence.

Chapter Eighteen

Nell

PIECE: *Erté (Romain de Tirtoff), Justice. Bronze art deco sculpture. Edition: 15/1200.*

Nell would never forget the flash of red and blue lights reflected on the marble floor of the mansion's foyer, or the sight of Annie running barefoot down the wet driveway while paramedics loaded a woman into an ambulance on a stretcher. A policeman shouted questions over his shoulder as he climbed into the back of the ambulance.

"Are you sure you don't know what she took?" he yelled. "Or how much?"

By the time Nell and Odin reached Annie, she was standing in the middle of the street, shaking her head and staring after the ambulance as it sped away, followed by a squad car that had been parked behind it.

Nell put an arm around her. "What happened?"

Annie turned and gave her a bewildered look before saying, "Caroline—one of my subjects—was acting strange and having trouble breathing." She choked back a sob. "I called 911. I wanted to go with her to the hospital, but they wouldn't let me in the ambulance."

"Put some shoes on," Odin said. "I'll drive you there."

Annie shook her head. "The paramedics said we should stay here. More police are on their way to investigate. They have to with overdoses."

Nell thought she must have heard wrong. Or maybe she was still asleep on the couch and this was all a nightmare. She opened her mouth to ask questions, but Odin started talking first.

"Let's go inside," he said. "It's freezing out here."

In the house, Odin led Annie to the living room couch. He left and came back with the same blanket that had been covering Nell just a few minutes earlier. Those moments in the office, alone with Odin, now seemed fuzzy and unreal in Nell's head.

Odin gave the blanket to Annie and she draped it around her shoulders, shuddering.

Paige came running downstairs just then, followed by a guy with a shaved head and a goatee.

"Who's that?" Odin whispered.

Nell shrugged. She had never seen the guy before.

"What's going on?" Paige asked.

When Nell explained that someone had been taken away by ambulance and the police were on their way, Paige's friend said quickly, "I'd better go."

Paige raised an eyebrow. "What, do you have an outstanding warrant or something?"

"Something like that." He gave Paige a kiss on the cheek and practically ran out the door.

Nell had the sick sense that she was way out of her depth. But now, with the three residents staring at her as if they expected her to know what to do, she snapped out of her shock and found her voice.

"Annie," Nell said. "What do we need to know before more police get here?"

Annie hugged the blanket tighter around her shoulders. "Caroline is an addict." She shivered. "I've been working on a photo essay about addiction and recovery. That's why she was here."

Nell tried to remember how Annie had described her project on her application. "I thought you were working on a series about human pain."

Annie waved a hand. "It's all related, don't you see? Pain, pain relief, addiction. All part of the same cycle. Caroline was addicted to prescription painkillers, but she'd been clean for a little while now." Annie's forehead contorted with worry. "As soon as she showed up tonight, I knew something was wrong. She was hours late. Her pupils were tiny and she was barely speaking coherently. The paramedics said it looked like opioid overdose."

Nell took a deep breath, trying not to let on to the others how panicked she was. "Okay," she said. "Here's what we're going to do. I'm going to get in touch with Josh—he's a lawyer and can help us figure how to handle things when the police get here."

She stepped into the office and, with shaking hands, called Josh. The phone rang several times, and she wondered if he'd even pick up. She couldn't exactly claim her marriage was in a good place. She and Josh had hardly spoken in the last couple of weeks. Since the night the debt collector called, he had been sleeping in the nursery-made-office. And tonight Nell had almost kissed Odin. She rubbed her forehead, remembering just how badly she'd wanted to. How close she'd come. Josh had every reason not to pick up the phone. But he did pick up, on the fourth ring.

"Nell?" he said. "Where are you?"

"I'm at the Colony," she said. "I could really use your help."

"What's going on?" Alarm sounded in his voice.

"I don't know all the details, but it looks like one of Annie's photography subjects overdosed. The paramedics said they suspect opioids. There were already a couple of police officers here, but they went with the woman to the hospital. More police are on their way to ask some questions."

"Okay, okay," Josh said. Nell could practically see him bolting up to a sitting position. "I'll be there as soon as I can. Whatever you do, don't answer any questions until I get there, got it?"

The police arrived shortly after Nell hung up. One male officer and one female officer came to the door.

"Evening, ma'am," the policeman said to Nell. "I'm Officer Schultz with the Madison PD. This here is my partner, Officer Green. May we come in? We've had a call that a woman was taken from here by ambulance and we need to ask some questions."

"Of course." Nell said. She took a deep breath to try to slow her racing heart and stepped aside to let them in.

"Which one of you is Annie Beck, the one who placed the 911 call?" Schultz asked.

"I am." Annie got up from the couch and came into the foyer.

"Do you live here?"

Annie nodded. "Is Caroline okay?"

The two officers looked at each other. Schultz nodded at Green, who said, "I'm sorry, but we've been authorized to tell you that she passed away en route to the hospital. We just found out from the officers who accompanied her there. The paramedics administered several rounds of naloxone, but their attempts to reverse the effects of the overdose were unsuccessful."

Annie sunk to the ground and hugged her knees to her chest. Nell clapped her hand to her mouth.

"The cause of death is respiratory arrest from suspected opioid overdose and, with all these types of cases, we're required to treat the place of overdose as a crime scene," Green said.

Annie got up. "No," she said, her voice insistent. "She didn't overdose here. She was with me the whole time. She was already acting strange when she showed up."

"So if we search the premises, we're not going to find any controlled substances?" Green asked.

Annie paused. "You'll probably find some pot," she said.

"Caroline liked to smoke pot to relax when I photographed her. But you won't find anything else."

"I wouldn't be so sure about that," Green said. "Preliminary observations from the medical team who treated the deceased indicate that she was probably under the influence of heroin, given the existence of an injection site on the body. Overdose by IV tends to happen very quickly, so it's likely she shot up here or somewhere very close by. So you can understand why we have some questions."

Nell had spent many hours watching Josh practice lectures about constitutional law. She remembered a thing or two now, and she spoke up. "We're happy to cooperate and give you whatever information you need, but if you don't mind, we'll wait until our lawyer gets here. He's on the way."

Green nodded. "Do you live here, too?" she asked Nell.

"No," she said. "Everyone else does, but this is an artists' colony. I'm the director, so I work here." She cleared her throat, trying to think of how she might stall until Josh got there, or if saying anything would just make the whole situation worse. She decided she had to do something, anything, so she said, "Maybe you've heard of the woman who used to live here . . . Betsy Barrett? She was the founder of this artists' colony. If you hold on a moment, I can show you the legal documents if you'd like. The house is actually owned by her trust."

Nell went to the office. The serene, organized space suddenly seemed completely out of context with what had just happened elsewhere in the house. She heard footsteps behind her and turned around. Officer Green stood in the doorway of the office.

"I have to accompany you, since we haven't done a protective sweep of the house yet," she explained.

While the officer watched, Nell bent over to scoop up the papers from where she'd left them on the couch and put them back in the shoebox. Her hands were trembling, and when she stood up straight again, a bronze figurine on one of the bookshelves caught her eye. She'd noticed it before, this small statue of a woman draped in a gold shawl. But she hadn't looked at it closely enough to realize, as she did now, that the objects the woman held in her hands were, on one side, a scepter and, on the other, the scales of justice. Nell shook her head and tucked the shoebox under her arm.

"Everything's in here," she said. She realized she probably looked like a crazy person, with her jumbled papers and cardboard box, but if it bought them some time until Josh arrived, she could live with it.

Green followed her back to the foyer where, to her relief, the others were still standing around, but not talking. Nell plucked the envelope containing the trust from the box and held it up. "Here's the legal document for the Colony, if you need to take a look," she said.

"Thanks, but I'm not sure that will be necessary," Schultz said. He was peering over her shoulder. "I was wondering if we might take a look around."

"Do you have a warrant?" Nell asked. She felt suddenly, fiercely protective of the Colony. She looked up at the portrait of Betsy Barrett over the stair landing. She couldn't decide if the woman in the painting was judging her or silently sending strength.

"These are exigent circumstances," Schultz said. "No warrant needed. So if you don't mind stepping aside, we'd like to get started." He held up his badge. "First, I'm going to ask you all to stay in one room, like the living room over there, while we do a quick walk-through to make sure the premises are safe. Then we'll come back and let you know before we start the search."

"Is it okay if we wait outside?" Paige asked.

"That's fine," Schultz replied. "Just don't leave the property."

Paige gave the others an apologetic look. "Sorry, I could really use a cigarette."

"No, it's okay," Annie said. "I could use some fresh air, too."

Nell and the artists grabbed their coats and went outside to wait while the officers walked through each room of the house. Paige sat smoking on the front porch, and Odin and Annie sat down on the steps next to her. Nell, though, couldn't sit still. She walked around the house and down to the shore. The sleet had stopped, but a frigid wind whipped across the lake, still mostly frozen. Against the retaining wall, jagged ice heaves stuck up like sheets of broken glass. The moonlight filtered through them and cast shadows on the rocks that lined the bank. Local folks were saying it was the latest thaw Lake Mendota had had in years. Given the events of the night, Nell was grateful, for once, for the numbing cold.

With the shoebox still clutched in her hands, Nell stared

up at the white, waxing moon. *Betsy*, she said silently, *what do we do now?*

Nell wandered back to the front porch and, after a few minutes, Officer Green opened the door and gave them the all clear to go back inside. The cops began their search in the basement while Nell and the artists stood in the foyer, unsure of what to do. There was still no sign of Josh, and Nell began to worry that maybe he'd had second thoughts about helping out.

Officer Schultz emerged from the basement a few minutes later holding Annie's camera in one hand. In the other, he clutched a shiny wooden box covered in a mosaic pattern.

Annie pressed her hands together in a prayer position. "Not the camera, please. My work is on there, on film. I don't have another copy."

"So the camera's yours?" Schultz asked.

"Yes."

"And how about the box? Is this yours, too?"

Annie's eyes drifted to the wooden box in his hands.

"Technically, the box isn't mine," Annie said. "I found it. In the basement."

Schultz cleared his throat and nodded at Annie. "Would you mind opening up the container for me?"

"If you could just wait," Nell said. "I think it would be better if she has a lawyer present."

"It's okay, I've already caused enough trouble." Annie took the box from the officer and moved each side slightly and deliberately. "It's a puzzle," she said. "It only opens if you do it a certain way." She slid off the top and handed the box back to

Officer Schultz, who reached inside and held up a clear baggie full of marijuana.

Just then, Josh walked in. Nell felt an immense sense of relief. She knew Josh didn't have to come as soon as she called, but she was grateful he did. Josh took off his glasses, which had fogged up from coming in from the cold. He rubbed them against the sleeve of his duffel coat, then put them back on. He looked from the drugs to Annie and then shot Nell a look that said, *What the hell have you gotten yourself into?* Nell wished she knew the answer.

"You must be the attorney," Officer Schultz said.

Josh extended his hand. "Joshua Parker."

"I was just about to tell Ms. Beck that we need to take her to the station for some further questioning. You're welcome to join her if you'd like." Schultz looked over at Green, who nodded. Then he looked back at Annie and said, "At this point I have to advise you that you have the right to remain silent . . ."

Josh waited until the officer had finished reciting the Miranda warning, then asked, "Just so I'm clear on what's happening here, since I obviously missed quite a bit before I arrived, are you *arresting* her?"

"Not just yet," Schultz said. "But we do need her to come in for questioning."

"On what basis? Possession of marijuana is an ordinance violation in Madison, not a crime," Josh said. "I'm not sure a little container of marijuana for personal use warrants taking an elderly woman to the police station."

"I don't see anyone elderly here," Annie said. She understood that Josh was just trying to be persuasive, but the descriptor still stung.

"I'm well aware that simple possession is not a punishable crime," Schultz said. "But that's not what we're dealing with here. Ms. Beck has admitted that the marijuana we found in the basement was hers, and that the deceased smoked marijuana on the premises. The DA's office is under direction from the attorney general to investigate all opioid overdose cases with the utmost diligence, to ferret out the source of the drug. We have reason to believe that Ms. Beck not only provided the deceased with marijuana, but also may have information on where she obtained the opioids."

"No," Annie said. "Heroin? You've got to be kidding me. In addition to having no idea where a person would even get something like that, it goes against the whole point of my project, which is to bring awareness to—"

Josh cut Annie off with a sharp look. To the officers, he said, "That's quite a leap, don't you think?"

Schultz shrugged. "It's what we have to do. We'll leave it to Ms. Beck to tell us the whole story." He handed the baggie to Officer Green, who put it inside an evidence bag and slapped a label on it. She was about to do the same with the camera, but Annie begged her not to.

"You can go ahead and take the box and what was in it," Annie said. "But not the camera. I'll tell you whatever you want about it. I'll even show you the pictures that are on there, but please don't take it away."

"You said you took pictures of the deceased," Green said as

she placed the camera in another evidence bag. "So we really don't have a choice but to take this."

Josh gave Annie a gentle nudge with his elbow. "Leave the talking to me, okay? You'll have a chance to say whatever you need to, but please wait until you and I have had a chance to talk privately."

Josh went over to Nell and said quietly, "I've got this. I'll go with her."

"Thank you," she said, touching his arm. Josh nodded in acknowledgment, but didn't make eye contact with Nell.

To the police, Josh said, "Since you haven't arrested her, I'm assuming you'll have no problem with Annie riding with me to the police station? I'd like to have a chance to speak with my client privately before she's interviewed there."

Green waved a hand. "Go ahead. We'll meet you there."

After they'd left, Paige sat down on the stairs and said, "What the fuck just happened?"

"I have absolutely no idea," Nell said.

Chapter Nineteen

Annie

PIECE: *Catalog for Annie Beck's* Elysium *exhibition,*
New York.

The drive to the police station wasn't very long. When Josh parked the car, Annie grabbed the door handle, ready to get out, but Josh stopped her.

"I still have some questions for you," he said. "We could talk inside, but it's more private here. Let them wait a little while. You still haven't told me how you and Caroline met."

Annie sat back in the passenger seat. "It was Craigslist," she said. "I placed an ad."

Josh pulled out his phone and gave it to Annie. "Is the ad still posted? Can you find it?"

Annie tried to type on the tiny screen, but her hands were still shaking from the shock of the last few hours. Josh noticed her struggling and took the phone back. "Here, I can do it if you tell me where to look," he said.

"Thanks," Annie said. "It should be under Creative Services. I haven't had very many responses, so I've kept it up, in the hopes of getting more participants."

"Is this it?" he asked. He read from the screen:

I am a visual artist with four decades of experience documenting social and political issues. I'm working on a photo essay about the opioid epidemic, for display at a gallery exhibition in New York City. If you are interested in sharing your story of addiction and recovery, please contact me.

"That's it," Annie said. She remembered typing up the ad just a few days before she left New York to come to Madison.

"How many people have you photographed?" Josh asked.

"In New York, more than a dozen. But in Madison, just a few. But Caroline was the only one who was consistent about coming to our scheduled sittings. I think she saw it as part of her recovery process, telling her story." She looked down at her hands. "Her kids were taken away, you know. They live with her ex now. She knew she needed to get clean if she was going to have a chance of getting them back."

Josh grabbed his briefcase from the back seat and scribbled some notes on a yellow legal pad. When he stopped, he looked up and gave Annie a puzzled look. "So explain to me how pot came into the equation."

Annie hesitated, unsure of how much she should tell Josh. Sure, he was acting as her lawyer, which made what she told him confidential. But he was also married to Nell, and Annie wasn't sure how realistic it was to expect that he wouldn't tell her whatever they talked about. And Annie wasn't sure how Nell would feel about what she'd been devoting her time to since arriving at the Colony. On a personal level, Annie got the impression that Nell was pretty open-minded. But it was also Nell's job to direct the Colony and, given how new it was, to establish its reputation in the public sphere. A police search and criminal charges were probably not the sort of thing Nell had in mind for getting things off to a good start.

As if he'd read her thoughts, Josh said, "I'm ethically prohibited from sharing with anyone else what you tell me. Even my wife. But if you don't feel comfortable with me helping you, you're entitled to find a different lawyer. No hard feelings whatsoever."

"It's okay. There's nothing I'm going to say now that Nell and the others wouldn't have found out eventually. I was just hoping to keep my project under wraps until after the residency was over, so that I didn't have to pull the Colony into any sort of controversy."

She had never been worried about controversy before, but that had been when she hadn't been close enough to anyone who might get hurt by her actions. Her mother, when she was still alive, had long since accepted what she called her daughter's "nonconformist" tendencies, and didn't ask too many questions about how she went about exercising them. Annie had had lovers throughout the years, both men and women, but she always chose them from a circle of like-minded individuals. When tensions arose, Annie just moved on. Now, she worried—albeit too late—about how the risk she'd taken would affect Odin and Paige, who were so much younger and had more to lose. She also worried about how it might affect Nell's ability to attract other artists to the Colony in the future. And she realized she was having these thoughts too late.

Annie shifted in her seat. "It's a long story," she said. "The pot was a way to keep people coming. Because I realized that if I was going to get addicts to show up and sit with me and let me take their pictures, I had to give something to them, too. I offered some of my first subjects pot as one of many things I thought might make them feel comfortable—a cigarette, a coffee, a snack. But then I heard back from people that they thought it really helped with some of the lingering detox symptoms, like nausea and anxiety and insomnia. So I started making sure I had it available, and people told their friends about it, so word got around and I got more subjects that way. At least, that's how it worked in New York. Here, it's been harder because I don't know that many people."

"Did you pay money to any of your subjects for sitting?" Josh asked.

Annie shook her head.

"So, it was pot for pictures."

Annie bristled. "I've never looked at it that way. Not everyone who sat for me smoked. But many did."

"Look," Josh said in a softer tone of voice. "I'm on your side. But I'm just trying to ask you the same sort of questions you're going to get when we go into the interview room. Along those lines, did it ever occur to you that it might be dangerous to provide *any* sort of drug to an addict, even if it's not the drug they're addicted to?"

"There's quite a bit of evidence out there that marijuana helps with the opioid withdrawal process. You can Google it," Annie said. "I'm not a doctor, though. I'm just an artist, so my job is to see things. And make other people see things. I promise you I had nothing to do with whatever it was that Caroline took."

"What about where she got it from? Do you have any idea?"

Annie shook her head. She thought about the conversations she'd had with Caroline over the handful of sittings they'd done. "Caroline mostly talked about her life *before* addiction, and how badly she wanted to get it back."

"She never asked you about obtaining anything else? Anything stronger than pot?"

"Never."

Josh nodded and looked down again at the ad on his phone screen. "What's the 'gallery exhibition' you mention here?"

"It's with one of the galleries that used to show my work in New York," Annie said. "They've been waiting for something new from me for years. I submitted a few projects, only to keep getting rejected. The feedback was always the same. The curator wanted something more current. More 'now,' he said."

"Well, opioid addiction is definitely a 'now' topic," Josh said. "Unfortunately."

Annie nodded. "Yeah, but I didn't start off photographing addicts. I started by photographing sick people. Dying people."

She told Josh about how she stopped making art for almost a year to care for her mother after she was diagnosed with pancreatic cancer. She had never been so close to another person's physical pain before. After her mother passed away, Annie got back to work. She started taking pictures—something she hadn't done much of since art school. She made it her passion to document the raw humanity that accompanied terminal illness and chronic pain. She also wanted to help ease suffering in a way that hadn't been available for her mother.

"New York had just launched its medicinal marijuana program," Annie said. "But it was still in the early stages. Finding a doctor to prescribe the drug was hard enough, and then you had to navigate all these rules just to fill the prescription. You could only fill it at a state-approved dispensary, and there weren't many around. The people I photographed complained about it all the time. They didn't have time to fill out a bunch of forms and travel all over the city and wait in lines while the state program got its shit together. They were dying."

"I think I know where this is going," Josh said, scribbling furiously on his notepad to keep up with her story. "But go on."

Annie explained how, in exchange for her subjects' consent to be photographed, she provided free pot for those who wanted it, organically grown by a farmer friend of hers upstate. Her one condition was that people had to smoke it there, at her apartment. She didn't want word getting out that she was dealing drugs, because that wasn't the way she saw it.

When Annie showed a few of the early pictures in her death series, *Elysium*, to the gallery's curator, he loved them.

He put together a small, invitation-only showing of the photos for his longtime customers. Not to sell them—neither he nor Annie felt right about selling the photographs—but to raise awareness of topics that were often taboo: death and pain. At the same time, they'd be getting people into the door of the gallery, thereby raising its profile and bringing Annie's name back into relevancy in the art world.

"I thought it went well, though some of the reviewers disagreed," Annie said. "The curator told me that if I could deliver another series along those lines, but with a new theme, we'd do a big, public retrospective of my work. We'd show the photos, which wouldn't be for sale, but we'd also show some of my earlier works, including some pieces that the gallery had previously rejected because the curator didn't think they could 'stand on their own.' The gallery and I would take a portion of the proceeds from the sales, and then donate the rest to a national nonprofit for addiction and recovery research.

"My project was going well, and I'd built up trust with some subjects who were willing to sit for me and have their photos included in the show. But then I got kicked out of my apartment and the project came to a standstill. Until I moved here."

"Why did you choose addiction to focus on?" Josh asked. "Or, I guess, why didn't you just stick with photographing dying people?"

"Addiction seemed like a natural spin-off from my series on death and pain management," Annie said. "And on a personal level, I've known more than a few people in the art community who've been lost to heroin overdoses." She paused and took a deep breath. "If I'm being completely honest, though, it's because addiction was what the gallery wanted. Robbie— he's the owner—thought addiction was a more controversial topic and, therefore, more like the sort of thing people were used to seeing from me. Death was, as he put it, too 'boring.'"

Josh exhaled and set down his pen. "I'm sure you don't need me to tell you that what you've been doing is not exactly all aboveboard. I can see that your initial intentions were good, but there are a lot of details here that the DA might not view quite as sympathetically."

"What do you think we're looking at, for charges?" Annie asked. She'd been arrested and charged before. She'd been in court and in jail before, too. Those things didn't scare her. But the thought of being kicked out of the residency program— and losing whatever chance she had left of making a come-back in the art world—did.

"The drug charges are what I'm most concerned about," he said. "There's a Good Samaritan law that prevents you from being prosecuted for drug possession, since you're the one who called 911 to get help. And, like I mentioned before, the DA doesn't prosecute simple possession cases anyway. But the law doesn't protect someone who gives or sells drugs to another person. So that's likely what you'll be charged with— possession with intent to deliver THC. It's a felony."

The tears Annie had been holding back started to seep out of the corners of her eyes as she thought about Caroline and her children, now motherless.

Annie had known she was treading in gray territory. She'd known that what she was doing could be seen as endangering, enabling, and worse. But taking pictures of people was deeply personal, and required trust. In order to gain that trust, Annie had had to risk something. She'd had to venture closer than ever before to the line where her comfort zone ended.

"I'll admit to everything I've done," Annie said. "But you have to believe that I had nothing to do with whatever killed Caroline."

"Okay. I believe you." Josh rubbed his temples and said, "The question is, will anyone else?"

Chapter Twenty

Nell

PIECE: *Catalog for first Art Basel Miami international art show, canceled due to the September 11 terrorist attacks.*

At first, on the day after Annie's arrest, everyone sat around in the living room with the fireplace lit, as if holding vigil. Paige sat in a leather wingback chair, scrolling the screen of her phone and biting on her lip. Odin leafed through art books, pulling one after another from the shelf. Nell made every effort *not* to check her own phone, instead pacing the floor from the kitchen and back, bringing plates of crackers no one ate and cups of coffee that grew cold.

Eventually, Paige excused herself. "I'm gonna go upstairs and try to work. You'll let me know if you hear anything?"

Nell promised she would, and Paige went up, leaving Nell and Odin alone. A charged silence grew between them. The last time they'd been alone, they'd almost kissed. Nell had wanted to, so badly. Even now, with everything that was going on, she felt a strong, pure pull of attraction to him, even though he was across the room. It was such a different sensation than what she felt with Josh.

With Josh, everything was . . . complicated. Even before their recent fight about the credit card debt, Nell had felt like she and Josh were on completely different pages, in the lengths they were willing to go to have a child, and in the way they mourned the one they lost. Josh mistrusted her now, and rightly so.

The mistrust went both ways, though. Since Josh seemed to have moved on from their loss more easily than Nell, she had stopped revealing her deepest emotions to him. She didn't trust Josh to understand without judging her, without thinking she was somehow broken. As a result, it had been a long time since Nell felt like anyone had really listened to her. But Odin had. And Nell had been so starved for connection that for a few moments late last night, she'd contemplated cheating on her husband. She wasn't sure what that said about her marriage, or about her. She'd have to answer those questions at some point, but at the moment, she had much bigger worries to deal with.

Now, Odin got up from the couch and cleared his throat. "I think I'm gonna get back to work, too," he said. "I need to get my mind off things."

By "things," Nell guessed he meant Caroline and Annie. But she wondered if he was thinking, too, about what had transpired, or not transpired, in the office last night.

Nell envied the fact that Odin and Paige had their work to distract them. Sitting alone in the big living room, Nell stared at the hole in the wall above the fireplace. It occurred to her that, based on his last phone call to her, Grady and his subcontractors should have been out to the house by now to finish the wiring. She was beginning to wonder if the hole would ever be patched up. It seemed symbolic of the rift that the events of the previous night had torn through the balance of work and life at the Colony. She couldn't stand to look at it.

She went out to her car and got her running clothes. She usually waited until after work to run, but she needed to clear her head. She changed and set out along the sidewalks, winding her way down Gorham, past James Madison Park and toward the university campus. She wondered what was taking Josh and Annie so long at the station, and decided it couldn't be a good sign.

She ran until she could strip away, at least for a couple of miles, the shock of the last day, the marital stress of the last few weeks, and the grief that had clung to her heart for months. She knew it would return, all of it. But for a little while at least, she focused on the soft thump of her shoes on the sidewalk and the quick, simple cadence of her breath.

When Nell got back to the mansion, she went into the office. She normally wouldn't hang around at work in her running clothes, but if the events of the previous night had taught her anything, it was that this was far from a regular job. A little bit of sweat and some sneakers were the least of her worries.

She picked up the shoebox she'd taken out of the safe the

night before and left on the desk. She remembered seeing some exhibition catalogs rubber-banded together among the other papers, and she dug through the contents of the box until she found them. She sat down on the office floor and spread them out around her, sorting them by date. It was a soothing task that took a bit of the edge off her anxiety. There were thick catalogs from various years of the international Art Basel exhibition in Miami, skinnier pamphlets from Wisconsin galleries, and dozens of publications from shows in Chicago and New York. Some of the catalogs were yellowed and curled at the edges, others were slick and new.

Among the newer items was a small one from an art gallery in New York. The cover read *Annie Beck: Elysium*. Now that she saw it, Nell remembered having read on an art blog that Annie had done a small, private show that didn't get very good reviews from the handful of press members who were invited. Here, though, was a catalog that seemed to indicate that Betsy had been there.

The cover of the catalog bore a note handwritten in blue ink: "No. 2?" Nell flipped to the inside, where reproductions of black-and-white photographs had been printed on thick matte paper. She located the image labeled No. 2. The picture was a close-up image of a pair of eyes, dark and bright and framed by laugh lines at the sides. From the way the lashes spread out like spokes, thick with mascara, the subject appeared to be a woman, and not a young one. The rest of her face was obscured by a veil of smoke, but the angle of the woman's long, graceful neck could be seen at the bottom of the frame. There was something haunting, yet beautiful, about the image, and Nell could see why Betsy had made note of it.

Nell flipped through the rest of the catalog for more hand-writing, or for some indication as to whether Betsy had purchased the photograph. She didn't find anything that gave her an answer, but she did find a folded newspaper clipping tucked into the pages. The article read much like the blog piece Nell had seen.

> Beck brings her keen eye for social commentary to her latest project, a potentially groundbreaking photo essay on death and pain management. However, her technical skills fall short of the level required for her ambitious subject matter. Though fans of Beck's earlier work will no doubt flock to view the full series when it opens in earnest at a later (still unannounced) date, they will likely leave disappointed. Bottom line: Beck should stick to the large-scale, abstract work and performance pieces on which she built her reputation.

In blue ink, a handwritten note had been scrawled in the margin of the article: "How *dare* an old lady try something new?" Nell smiled. Betsy's slanted script hinted at her insight and humor. Nell wondered how much Betsy had known about this project when she chose Annie for the residency. Annie's application said only that she was working on a "ground-breaking photo essay on human pain." It didn't say anything about death, like the article mentioned, and certainly didn't say anything about addiction. If Betsy had traveled to New York to see the exhibition, it was likely she'd met Annie in person. How much had Annie disclosed?

Nell set aside the catalog and sifted through the other scraps, hoping to find anything else that might give her some insight.

"Hello?" At the sound of Josh's voice in the foyer, she placed the papers back into the box and went out to greet him.

Before Josh even said anything, Nell could tell he didn't have good news. His shoulders slouched under his rumpled button-down shirt, and one clasp of his thick leather briefcase hung undone. A sense of gratitude washed over her. Josh had spent the entire day at the police station, canceling his lectures to field questions with Annie, simply because he knew it was important to Nell. For a moment, everything else that had happened between them faded, and she went over and hugged him. Josh must not have felt the same warm feeling, though, because he startled at the physical contact from her.

Nell stepped back. "What happened at the police station?" she asked.

He shook his head. "I made every argument I could think of, but they wouldn't let Annie go. They're holding her in jail until they can get her into court for an initial appearance tomorrow. Then hopefully they'll let her out, at least on bond, until the next court date."

From the earnest expression on his face, Nell could tell that he truly felt terrible about not being able to do more. Josh did not like to fail, and she was certain he saw this as a failure.

"Give yourself a break," Nell said. "Annie didn't exactly make it easy for you to defend her. You literally walked in as the cops were holding up a bag full of pot. And, anyway, Annie's a pretty strong woman."

Josh cracked a small smile. "I overheard someone say at the police station that a guy was arrested at the Capitol today for disorderly conduct during the Solidarity Sing Along. Perhaps he and Annie can lead a rendition of 'Have You Been to Jail for Justice?'"

"Did you eat anything?" Nell asked.

Josh shook his head.

"Well, come on, you must be starving." She brought him to the kitchen, where the untouched plate of cheese and crackers she'd made hours earlier was still sitting on the counter. "I can offer you some cheese that's been sitting out all day. Or . . ." She opened the cabinets. "A bowl of cereal? Sorry there's not much else. Except for the monthly dinners, the artists are in charge of their own food."

Josh grabbed a cereal box from the open cabinet and read the label. "Granola, huh?"

"I know, it's exactly what you'd picture an artists' colony having in the cupboard."

Nell opened the fridge, then shut it. "Sorry, there's no milk or yogurt or anything." She handed him a spoon. "Guess grocery shopping hasn't been a priority."

Josh sat down at the table, poured the granola into a bowl and ate it dry, with his fingers. When he'd finished one bowl, he poured himself another.

"Did you talk to your friend in the prosecutor's office? The one who used to teach at the law school?" When Josh didn't answer right away, she added, "Sorry, I guess maybe you can't talk to me about Annie's case."

"No, I was just chewing," he said in between bites. "She said it was fine for me to talk to you about it. Anyway, my friend said the DA's office will likely put together a plea deal."

"Do you think I should come to court tomorrow?"

Josh shook his head. "Tomorrow she won't even be in front of a judge, just a court commissioner. It's pretty short and routine. But eventually, yeah, it might be good for you and the others to show up for some of the court dates, so the judge can see that the residency thing is real and not just some sort of cover for running pot out of the basement."

Nell shook her head. "It's ridiculous, right? I mean, that we're even having this conversation."

"Yeah. When you got your PhD I can't say this was a career scenario I ever would have pictured for you."

"Which part, directing an artists' colony or defending it from criminal charges?" she asked.

"Both—I mean, neither. I pictured you lecturing alongside slide shows of old paintings. Maybe working for a museum. Definitely something more . . . I don't know, removed?" He put his spoon down. "Today I realized just how removed *my* job is. I like teaching and research, but I realized I've never represented an actual client. Depending on how far Annie's case goes, I may need to refer her to an experienced criminal attorney to take over things. I'm a little out of my depth."

"I don't think she can afford to pay a private attorney," Nell said.

"She filled out the paperwork to see if she qualifies for a public defender," he said. "But I can help her out in the mean-time."

Nell listened as he explained what was likely to happen when Annie went in front of the court commissioner the next day. She noticed the fire in his voice as he talked—she hadn't seen him get this animated over anything in a long time. So much of their lives in the last several months had been mundane at best, a struggle at worst. It was good to see him get excited about something. It was sexy, even.

He caught her watching him and said, "What?"

Nell smiled. "Nothing. I just really appreciate what you're doing for Annie, and for the Colony. You would have had every right just to tell me to figure it out for myself, after the mess I made of everything with you and me and the money . . ."

Josh set his lips in a firm line. "This doesn't have anything to do with that. I'm still angry. Like really, really angry."

And there they were, completely out of sync again. Just as she'd started to feel a spark of attraction for Josh again, he'd snuffed it out by reminding her of just what a mess their marriage had become. Nell looked down at her hands. She noticed that she'd been fidgeting, unconsciously, with the cereal box on the counter, tearing the corners of the cardboard top into little shreds.

"But," Josh said, "even though I'm still mad at you, I don't see that as a good reason not to help out."

A warm feeling expanded inside Nell's chest. One of the main reasons she loved Josh was that he was a good person, a generous person. He was lending a hand, despite being pissed off on a personal level, because it was the right thing to do.

"Thank you," she said. "And I'm sorry. Again."

Josh nodded in acknowledgment. "Anyway, we really can't afford for you to lose your job right now, so we might as well manage this the best we can."

Nell cracked a smile in spite of everything and reached out to touch Josh's hand. Hearing him say "we," even if he was still angry, was a great comfort.

Odin walked in at that moment and saw them. He looked away, as if it was something he wasn't supposed to see, or didn't want to see.

Nell immediately thought of holding Odin's hands the night before. Guilt churned in her stomach. She had liked the way her hands had felt in Odin's. His hands were larger and rougher than Josh's, callused from working with metal. Contact with Odin had sent a tingly thrill all over Nell's body. It had made her forget, for a moment, about all of her grief and emotional exhaustion.

But the hand Nell held now was her husband's hand, and he'd just spent an entire night and day at the police station with Annie, without being paid for it, just because she'd asked him to. Josh's touch didn't set off the same sort of chemical fireworks now that it once had. But it did give her the solid, reassuring sense that everything would be okay. And, at this moment, it was exactly what she needed. She gave Josh's palm a squeeze, then stood up straight, slipping her hand out of his.

Josh nodded in Odin's direction and said, "Hey."

"Hey." Odin grabbed a glass from the cupboard and filled it with water. He swallowed a sip and asked, "Any news?"

"Annie has to stay in jail until her court appearance," Nell said.

"That's too bad," he said. "But something tells me she's probably rounding up all the other people in jail as we speak, giving them a lecture about speaking truth to power."

"I was just saying something along those lines," Josh said, smiling.

Nell forced herself to smile, too, but she was relieved when Odin went back out to the garage.

Chapter Twenty-one

Annie

PIECE: *Flyer promoting the Equal Rights Amendment, from an Inauguration Day 1981 demonstration in Washington, DC.*

Annie noticed the woman in the red dress right away. Aside from the bold color of her garment, the woman gave off an air of confidence and timeless elegance. Her short gray hair was stylishly cut and a large diamond necklace glittered on her collarbone. She looked older than Annie, in her seventies maybe, though it was so hard to tell. Age seemed more and more irrelevant to Annie. Either you connected with someone or you didn't. Either you had something to offer to them, or them to you, preferably both, or you moved along. Annie supposed she could have saved her younger self a lot of unnecessary angst had she accepted those basic truths about human interactions decades earlier.

Betsy Barrett was the woman's name. At least, that's what

Robbie, the curator of the gallery, whispered to Annie as the woman made her way across the room.

"She *always* buys something when she comes to New York. Always," Robbie said, resting one elbow on the opposite hand. "Sometimes it's here, sometimes other galleries. But she comes like she's got money burning a hole in her pocket. And those are my favorite kind of customers." Robbie stepped forward and shook Betsy's hand.

"Betsy, meet Annie Beck," Robbie said. "She's our featured artist."

Betsy smiled at Annie, a genuine smile that brought color to her face, which looked rather pale, now that Annie saw her up close.

"I believe we've met once before," Betsy said.

Annie tilted her head, trying to place the woman. It had been such a long time since she'd shown new work. And exhibition openings were the only type of event where Annie would expect to cross paths with someone like Betsy. The opera-going, gala-attending, diamond-wearing crowd wasn't exactly Annie's scene.

"It's okay if you don't remember," Betsy said. "It was ages ago, and only for a moment, at Reagan's inauguration," Betsy said. "I was on my way to one of the parties and you stopped me and handed me a flyer about the ERA."

"Ah," Annie said. "I could probably print up the same flyer today and it would still be relevant. Just swap in the name of the current president."

"Unfortunately, I think you're right," Betsy said. "I kept the flyer. Back then, I'd already heard of you—the work you did with the Feminist Art Collective."

"Well, my new project is a big departure from what I've done in the past." Annie waved her hand toward the large black-and-white photographs framed on the gallery walls. "So if you're looking for that sort of thing again, then you've come to the wrong place."

"I'm not," Betsy said. "I'm actually much more interested in what you're doing now."

"Tell that to the reviewers. I can't seem to escape the shadow of what I used to create." Annie shook her head. "Not that I want to. I'm proud of what I did back then. But I didn't know that that's all I'd be allowed to do. Ever."

"Forget the reviews," Betsy said. "Somehow I don't think you've ever cared much about what critics think. Or what anyone thinks, for that matter."

"No," Annie said. "But I do want people to pay attention to what I'm doing. It's quieter than my past work. More intimate. But I still have a lot to say." She pointed to a picture that hung on the wall behind Betsy. A woman lay in a four-poster bed with an IV attached to her arm and a collection of prescription bottles scattered on the nightstand. She was propped up against her pillows, a flowered scarf wrapped around her hairless head. And she was reading Proust in French.

"Geraldine," Annie said. "She was a retired literature professor at Columbia. She spoke three languages. Lived in Paris in the summer of sixty-eight when all the student protests were going on. Bone cancer had her bedridden at the end.

Her granddaughters would bring her magazines and movies to keep her occupied, and the magazines just piled up on the dresser, unopened. She said she wanted to spend her last days rereading some of 'her early loves.' And so she did. Goethe and Kafka in German, Camus in French."

"I envy her," Betsy said. "I've tried to pick up a few foreign phrases here and there for travel, but I'm not proficient enough to read much more than a menu or a road sign in any language."

Annie nodded. "I envied her a little, too. And that's what I wanted to portray here. That this woman was not someone to be pitied. She'd be the first to tell you that. She led an incredible life. Sharp right up until she passed away in her sleep."

"The picture says all of that," Betsy said.

"Good," Annie said. "Because if I took the Proust novel and the silk scarf out of the picture, a lot of people would just see a sick old lady. And even with everything I've tried to get across in these photos, by surrounding people with the things they love and trying to capture little bits of their lives as they're forced to look back on them . . . some people still don't seem to get the message. They see my name and come in here expecting, I don't know, performance art against the patriarchy or something. And, yes, I had a lot to say about that, once. And I still do. But it's not the conversation I'm most interested in now. I have other things to say. But no one seems to be able to hear me because the past me is so much louder."

"*I* hear you," Betsy said.

Chapter Twenty-two

Odin

PIECE: *Letter from Sloane Foster of Foster Gallery, Minneapolis, to Elizabeth Barrett.*

For Odin, all the focus on Caroline's death, and the investigation surrounding it, brought memories of the first few days after Sloane died. Those memories intensified when the dates on the calendar crept toward the one-year anniversary of her death, in mid-April. He'd been dreading the day and, when it finally arrived, he woke early and went out to the garage. He hoped his work would, if not help him forget, at least turn down the intensity of his recollections. But even his noise-canceling headphones couldn't silence the clamor in his head. As he worked, the memories hit him like waves. Sometimes he'd go for an hour or more of ebb time, where he thought of nothing but the piece in front of him, coaxing something smooth and identifiable out of twisted, sharp metal. And then, without warning, the "what ifs" and "whys" would crash over him, nearly suffocating him.

When Sloane died, it had been the first warm day of the year. A rare and glorious seventy degrees in early spring. The type of day when everyone in the Twin Cities, from school kids to stockbrokers, heads outside to play in the parks, dine alfresco, and blink in the long-forgotten sunlight. Never mind the fact that winter is certain to bring down its wrath even harder after the tease, and that spring won't settle in solidly until May. The first warm day brings out the type of selective amnesia that is required for living through midwestern winters.

Sloane had closed the gallery early and asked Odin if he could help her get her bike from the attic. He'd carried the bike down to the street and put air in the tires.

"Want to join me?" she'd asked.

But Odin had been close to finishing a sculpture he was working on at the time—a complicated piece with three different kinds of metal twisted into the form of a running horse. It was the hardest thing he'd ever worked on. Getting the metal to mimic movement was tricky, and he wanted to get it right. So he told Sloane he'd join her next time.

Next time . . .

Those words still haunted him.

He remembered watching Sloane bike down the alley. How her tires sloshed through a puddle of melting snow, saturating her socks and leggings.

He should have gone with her. He always biked behind her when they rode together. Surely he would have seen the SUV when it veered into the bike lane. Drivers in other cars had seen it happen. If Odin had been there, he could have shouted to her. Maybe he could have warned her. Maybe he could have saved her.

What if he'd told Sloane he wanted to finish what he was working on before going up to the attic to get her bike? Even five minutes could have made a difference. The distracted driver would already have been ahead of her on the road. What if he'd taken just a little more time tuning up her bike before letting her go? He should have greased the chain and tightened the brakes, as well as put air in the tires. And— always, this thought lingered even after the "what-ifs" had washed back out to sea—why hadn't he at least told Sloane he loved her that day, before she rode off?

Odin sat down on the bench. From the front pocket of his flannel shirt, he pulled out a copy he'd made of a letter typed on letterhead from the Foster Gallery and signed in Sloane's loopy handwriting. It had been attached to the application Nell gave him.

Odin had been carrying the copy of the letter around with him, so that he could look at it when, like today, he needed a reminder. The letter, addressed to Betsy Barrett, contained the usual words of praise you'd expect from a recommendation: "talented," "full of potential," and so on. But it also said the following:

As you so quickly deduced when you saw us to-
gether, Odin and I are in a relationship. You might be
wondering if that is the only reason I'm submitting this
recommendation on his behalf. On the contrary, I'm
submitting it in spite of our relationship. On a selfish
level, I want to keep him near me. But in the interest
of his career, I cannot let him pass up an opportunity to
focus on his work and explore directions that he might
not otherwise pursue. I fear that if he stays here, I'll be
holding him back.

The letter jarred something loose that had been keeping
Odin from finishing anything he'd started, ever since Sloane
died. It was the license he needed to let go of what he thought
she would have wanted. Already he'd been playing with the
limits of what he could create. Freed from his doubts about
whether he was worthy of the residency or whether he'd only
been admitted as a favor to Sloane, he dove into his work in
a way he hadn't since before she died. Or, rather, in a way he
never had. Today, on the anniversary of her passing, he finished his blue heron sculpture, stretching its hammered steel
wings out to the full five-foot wingspan he'd envisioned when
he first saw the real bird tuck up its legs and take flight over
the lake.

As Odin stepped back to look at his work, his stomach
growled, and he realized he hadn't consumed anything but
coffee since breakfast. It was nearly dinnertime now. He went
inside to get something to eat, and almost ran smack into

Paige in the kitchen. She had her coat and backpack on, plus a large duffel bag slung over her shoulder.

Paige noticed him eyeing the bag and said, "I'm going to stay with a friend."

"That guy who was here the other night, who took off when the cops showed up?" Odin asked. He hoped the answer was no.

Paige shook her head. "Nah, he was just someone I met at a bar. I'm going to stay with this other guy, Jay, who I met online. He's a guitarist in a geek metal band."

"Geek metal?"

"Yeah. They write songs based on, like, *Star Wars* and *Dungeons & Dragons* and stuff."

Odin raised his eyebrows, amused. "I didn't know you were into that sort of thing."

"What, because I don't do fan art of dragons and wizards and shit?" The strap of Paige's bag slid down her arm and she hoisted it back onto her shoulder.

"Well . . . yeah."

"Trust me. My sketchbooks from when I was a teenager are filled with, like, drows and mind flayers."

"What about Trent?" Odin asked. For a while there, it had seemed like he came home with Paige every night.

"Trent and I are done."

Odin wasn't about to judge how quickly somebody else moved from one relationship to the next. Before he met Sloane, he'd certainly had his share of one-night stands and casual, friends-with-benefits arrangements. But he could see in the way

Paige looked away and bit her lip after she said Trent's name, that she still had feelings for him.

"I know it's none of my business," he said. "But can I ask what happened?"

Paige shrugged. "He didn't want to see other people, but I did. So I am."

"Okay," Odin said. After a long pause, he added, "But for what it's worth, the right relationship can actually be pretty great. Take it from someone who had one and lost it, but not by choice."

"Noted," Paige said. There was an annoyed edge to her voice.

"Sorry, it's the anniversary of when my girlfriend died, so I guess I'm all about the unsolicited advice today."

Paige's tone softened. "I didn't know. I'm sorry about your girlfriend."

"Me, too."

Paige switched her duffel bag from one shoulder to the other.

Even if Odin couldn't stop Paige from running off to someone new, he did still worry about her safety, going to stay with a stranger she'd met online. "Hey, why don't you leave Jay's contact info, just in case?" he said. "I'm pretty sure Nell will want to know where you are. Seems like this whole thing really has her—I guess all of us—on edge."

Paige shrugged. "Sure." She set down her bag and rooted around for a pen. When she found one, she scribbled something down on a scrap of paper and gave it to Odin.

He looked at the address she'd written. "I don't know Madison all that well, but isn't this way out on the west side? Do you need a ride?"

"No, he's picking me up." Her phone dinged and she pulled it out of the back pocket of her jeans and glanced at the screen. "This is him. I've gotta go."

She went out the side door, and, after she was gone, it occurred to Odin that if Paige, a pure original, could find people she connected with online, Odin was pretty sure he could meet people that way, too. But meeting people, even online, meant having to go through the small-talk stage. And Odin hated small talk. It was why he and Nell seemed to click so well. She didn't hold back what was really on her mind and, in turn, neither did he.

Odin made himself a grilled cheese and went out to eat it at his workbench. When he was done, he put on his helmet and headphones. But he'd only just started to get to work when Nell came in, ducking under the garage door. It was as if she'd read his mind and knew he'd been thinking of her.

"Hi," he said, pulling off his gear. He slung the headphones around his neck.

"Hey," she said. Odin was surprised to see that Nell was wearing sneakers and running clothes. She usually wore professional-looking attire around the Colony. He tried to keep his gaze on her face and not let it wander down to her butt in the tight leggings.

"What's up?" he asked.

"We need to talk about the other night in the office."

Odin nodded.

"Before the paramedics came," she added.

She didn't need to be so specific, though. Odin knew exactly what she was referring to.

"Sure," he said. "I figured we'd talk eventually. I thought about bringing it up, but you've been dealing with so much lately, I didn't want to add to your stress level."

Nell took a deep breath. "I want to start by saying that I hope you know I respect you and your work," she said. "And I enjoy your company . . . maybe almost a little too much." She cracked a sheepish smile, and Odin returned it, which cut through a little of the uneasy tension.

"But . . . ," he prompted her.

"I know nothing ended up happening between us. But it needs to stay that way." Nell shifted her weight from one foot to the other. "I know I wasn't clear about it the other night, but I've had some time to think since then. And I really need to work on my marriage right now." Nell looked relieved after she'd gotten the words out.

As much as he would have loved to try to convince her otherwise, Odin knew she was right. "I get it. And I wish you the best with that, I really do. You have a chance to fix things, and you should take it," he said, thinking of how he'd give anything to have a second chance with Sloane.

"Thanks. I figured if anyone could understand, it would be you." Nell held out her hand and said, "So we're friends, then? Colleagues? Some awkward combination of all of the above?"

Odin laughed and shook her hand. "Friends," he said.

He was still a guy, though. Which was why he couldn't help but sneak a glance at her backside in her running tights as she turned and went back to the house.

Chapter Twenty-three

Paige

PIECE: *Watercolor painting of Sagrada Família church, Barcelona.*

*P*aige was freaking out. She was the only one of the residents who had never laid eyes on Caroline, but the sirens and the cops and the fact that *someone had died* had her so shaken up, she couldn't stand the thought of sleeping at the Colony. A part of her wanted to call Trent. She knew she would find comfort if she could curl up against him and rest her head on his chest—even if it meant she had to share space with him on his friends' couch. But pride and fear kept her from contacting him. To go to Trent in such a vulnerable state would only launch them back in the direction they'd been going, which, in Paige's opinion, had been too serious, too fast. Paige found another escape, though, in the form of a musician named Jay whom she'd met while playing the online version of *Magic: The Gathering.*

Back in high school, she'd been deep into role-playing games. She got into them after her parents figured out that the cuts on her wrists were not, as Paige claimed, "burns from taking a pizza out of the oven."

She hadn't been trying to kill herself. Just trying to *feel* something. Because pain, even the type of physical pain that came from taking a hunting knife to her wrists, was better than the big hole of nothingness that seemed to live in her chest.

Her parents came from the sort of stock that said things like "chin up" and "you'll feel better in the morning." Paige never felt better in the fucking morning. Not in those days, at least. The thought that depression could be a disease and not just an attitude problem never crossed her parents' minds, until her high school guidance counselor told them that Paige should probably "see someone." Paige hated that phrase. It could just as easily mean "I'm dating someone" instead of "I'm meeting with a mental health professional." Was it, like, supposed to be polite? Because, to Paige, it just seemed shaming and secretive.

A few things saved her from herself, and none of them was the drowsy, cliché-spouting psychologist her mother used to drive her an hour each way to see. The first was gaming. Battling fictional monsters on the board was a hell of a lot easier than battling the ones in her head. When Paige sat down for a campaign, she could block out, for a few hours anyway, how out of place she felt in every other aspect of her life. School was okay—well, the class part anyway. At least there was an art room, even if it was forever running out of supplies because of budget cuts.

Between classes, though, Paige knew girls whispered behind her back. Called her things like "freak" and "slut." Because apparently having no-strings-attached sex in high school made you a whore. At least if you were a girl it did. But sex, like gaming, got her out of her head. Art did, too, sometimes. But art also could backfire, and push her deeper in. And deep in her head was a very unpleasant place to be.

Since she'd been at college, though, art had expanded to take up the time and headspace that gaming used to. With deadlines and final projects, Paige didn't have ten hours to spend sitting at a table in some strip-mall game shop, rolling twelve- and twenty-sided dice and drinking Red Bull.

When she and Trent split, though, a couple of weeks earlier, she'd been shaken up in a way she'd never been before. And she didn't like it. Even though she was the one who had cut things off, the breakup made her feel out of control, emotionally. And she'd worked very, very hard so far, in these few, nascent years of adulthood, to keep her thoughts and emotions under control. So she tiptoed back into gaming because it was an excellent escape. So was sex with someone new. All the better that with Jay, she got the prospect of both in one.

As a lover, Jay was just okay. Paige was pretty sure he hadn't been with many girls. But he and his friends were a lot of fun to game with. That Saturday night, she stayed up with them until dawn to finish an epic *D&D* campaign—something Paige hadn't done since high school.

But after a few days, Paige grew tired of being stuck without a car on the outskirts of Madison. Jay lived on several acres of land, which made sense as soon as Paige met his bandmates. His gaming friends were harmless enough, drinking microbrews while immersing themselves in fictional battles and expeditions. His bandmates were another story. They were like nerds on steroids. Or—more accurately—nerds on some sort of strong mind-altering drugs. When they came over to practice one night, the whole house shook. And their music was awful. So loud and awful that Paige was only able to fall asleep after she put earplugs in. She'd gotten in the habit of carrying them in her backpack for when she needed to tune people out in the studio at school.

She went into the spare bedroom so as not to be woken up when Jay eventually came to bed, and she fell asleep to the *whooshing* sound of the blood in her own eardrums. She woke up when she felt hands against the skin of her back, underneath the T-shirt she'd worn to bed. She swatted the hands away, still half-asleep. "Knock it off, Jay, I'm tired."

But he didn't back off. Instead, he reached around to her waist and pulled her into him. Paige felt the rough texture of denim against her legs, and his hard-on jabbing into her back. Now she was pissed. She pulled out the earplugs, shoved him off, and turned around, now sitting up. "What the *fuck*? I said back off."

But the glassy-eyed, laughing face she saw wasn't Jay's. It was one of his stupid bandmates, reeking of booze and who knew what else. Paige got out of bed, shaking with anger, and pointed to the door. When he didn't move, she yelled, "Go!"

As soon as he left, Paige locked the bedroom door, grabbed her phone, and called Odin. When he picked up and said hello, it sounded as if he, too, had been asleep.

"Hey, it's Paige," she said, still shaking. "Sorry to be calling so late, but could you come pick me up? I think you have the address."

"Yeah, sure, I'll leave right now."

Paige didn't say good-bye to Jay or his friends before she left. She waited inside the locked room, looking out the window until she saw Odin's truck pull into the driveway. Then she slipped out the front door, unheard over the sound of screamed lyrics about wizards and rogue warriors.

"Thanks for picking me up," she said as she got into the passenger seat of the truck.

"Don't worry about it," Odin said. "Everything okay?"

Paige nodded. "You were right, though. It wasn't a good idea for me to go." As they pulled out of the driveway, she sent Jay a text: Your drummer's an asshole. Ask him why.

"Annie's home," Odin said. "They let her out on bond a couple of days ago."

Paige felt bad that she hadn't checked in at all while she'd been gone. She realized how much she'd been holding herself at a distance from the Colony, not just by being at Jay's, but before that, too.

When they got home, Paige was happy to be back in her room, with the sound of the wind whistling over the lake and the old house creaking, instead of the aggressive wail of a guitar in its death throes. Before she went to bed, though, she opened up the closet to look for the old maps she'd stashed in there after Trent stopped coming around. She pulled what she thought were the rolled-up maps from a cardboard box. When she unfurled them, though, Paige saw that they were watercolor paintings of famous sites in Europe that Paige had never been to, but still recognized—the Colosseum in Rome, London's Tower Bridge, the Sagrada Família church in Barcelona. The paintings were yellowed at the edges, all done by different artists, and probably weren't worth much. It made Paige smile, though, to think of Betsy buying them. Apparently the old lady's love of art and the people who created it encompassed a range wide enough for both Georgia O'Keeffe and a sidewalk artist selling paintings on a tourist drag—and, somewhere in that range, people like Annie, Odin, and Paige, too.

Paige finally found the maps, tucked into the bottom of the box. In putting them away, she'd done a good job of making sure she wouldn't stumble across them and, in turn, have to think about Trent and all the time they'd spent together up here, in her room. Her tactic hadn't worked, though. Neither had hiding at Jay's house for a few days. Since she hadn't succeeded in getting over Trent, either with physical distance or sex with someone else, Paige figured she'd have to try to get over him the only other way she knew how: with her art. And his fascination with old maps gave her an idea.

The next morning, she went to one of the rare book rooms on campus, where she donned white gloves to pore over sixteenth- and seventeenth-century atlases. In the margins of the yellowed maps, giant serpents coiled around ships, and lions with scaly tails salivated over stranded sailors.

The reference librarian, a middle-aged woman with a round, pleasant face, looked over Paige's shoulder and said, "Intriguing, aren't they? 'Here be dragons.'"

"What?" Paige turned around.

"Cartographers used to draw monsters and mythical creatures on areas of the map that were beyond charted territories," the librarian said. "'As if to say, 'Who knows what's out there? Venture at your own risk.'"

It was how Paige felt about so many things in her life—about getting too close to someone, about sticking with a single art medium for too long, about graduating in a few weeks. She had no clue what she was going to do for work after the residency ended in June, let alone what she'd do about studio space and equipment.

All the old maps at the library, and in her room back at the Colony, gave Paige the idea for a new series she titled *Maps and Monsters*, for which she tried out a new technique, woodblock printing. Usually, Paige moved from one medium to something completely different. Now, though, she'd still be doing printmaking, but just adding a different skill to her arsenal. If she got good enough at different types of printing, maybe she could combine several of them into one project.

From the library, Paige went to a used bookstore on State Street, where she purchased some old atlases for next to nothing. Then she went to an art supply store on Gorham Street and bought blocks of tight-grained maple and a graver, or chisel. She planned to carve images into the wood of mythical sea creatures like the ones she'd seen in the rare book room, then stamp those images onto torn-out pages of the atlases.

When Paige got back to the Colony with her new supplies, Nell was in the kitchen, pouring herself a coffee.

"Hey, welcome back," she said, sliding the carafe back into the coffee maker with a clatter. "Odin said you were staying with a friend?"

"For a few days, yeah," Paige said. "Where's Annie? Odin said she was let out."

"She was, but she had to go back to court today for a status conference. She's there with Josh right now." Nell held both hands around her mug and leaned her back against the counter. "It's been so quiet around here."

Quiet sounded just fine to Paige, after geek metal. But she had really been hoping that Annie's case would have been dismissed by now. "I can't believe they're actually following through on the charges," she said. "Have you, like, called the papers or anything to see if they'd want to do a story about Annie's case?"

Nell shook her head. "Usually Annie is all about drawing attention to her causes, but Josh told me she asked that we not talk to the papers. Something about Caroline's family not necessarily wanting word to get out about how she died."

Paige sat down on a counter stool. "Is there anything we can do to help?"

Nell put her mug down on the counter. "Do you remember me mentioning a group show? It's one of the few requirements for the Colony that Betsy actually wrote out in the trust."

Paige nodded. "I didn't think much about it at the time be-cause I didn't have enough pieces to show. But I do now, with all my screen prints. And I'm starting up a new series, too, of woodblock prints."

"Madison does a citywide Gallery Night on the first Fri-day of every month. What if we opened our doors to show some work and raise money for Annie's case? Josh is handling it right now pro bono, but she might end up needing more help than he can give her. And I guess she's already racked up court costs, and had to post money for bond. I called the orga-nization that does the planning for Gallery Night. They print up a map ahead of time with a listing of all the places that are participating. The April one already happened, but it's not too late to get added for May, if you and Odin are willing to do it. And Annie, of course."

"I love the idea," Paige said. "But aren't you worried about, I don't know, the Colony's reputation or whatever?"

"I want the Colony's reputation to be that it stands behind its residents. I've been doing a lot of thinking, and I think Betsy would have agreed. She went to Annie's most recent show in New York. I checked the date of the show and the date on Annie's application. Annie applied for this residency after her show. I just have this feeling they met. And that Betsy knew at least something about what Annie was doing."

"But what if she ends up actually getting convicted of some-thing?" Paige asked.

"I thought about that, too," Nell said. "Because I think we have to be prepared for that possibility. But everyone is entitled to a legal defense. And Annie doesn't have any family or know many people in town who could help her out."

"We're the closest thing she has to family," Paige said, nodding. "Count me in. What does Odin say about it?"

"I haven't talked to him yet. But he probably has a few pieces he could show, don't you think?"

"He'd better," Paige said. "He's out in the garage *all* the time."

Chapter Twenty-four

Nell

PIECE: *Gucci shoulder bag in brown coated canvas,*
trimmed in iconic green-and-red stripes, with
monogram.

The upcoming Gallery Night gave Nell an excuse to follow up with Grady and finally get the wiring finished
and the hole in the living room wall repaired. With everything patched and painted, she was finally able to rehang
the Krasner and O'Keeffe paintings. They now occupied
their rightful spots above the fireplace again, in their bright,
contrasting beauty, instead of in the dark recesses of Betsy's
bedroom closet, which was where Nell had placed them for
safekeeping.

Venturing back into the cavernous master bedroom closet
motivated Nell to accomplish another long overdue task.
Betsy's will made clear that when she died, her home and estate were to be placed in trust and used to establish an artists'

colony—with one exception. The contents of her bedroom closet were supposed to go to a secondhand shop called Hourglass Vintage. According to the address written in the will, the shop was only a few blocks away. Still, Nell had been putting off the task because of the sheer number of items in Betsy's closet. Inside hung not one but three fur coats—one ankle-length, one calf-length, and one that hit at the hip. Nell tried all of them on, running her hands along the soft hides. She was pretty sure Betsy wouldn't have minded. There were purses arranged in rows on shelves, each contained in a protective flannel bag stamped with the designer's logo. Nell had never been much into fashion, but even she recognized the name stamps: Fendi. Tod's. Balenciaga. The closet contained a sizable fortune in handbags alone, not to mention a range of dresses and separates that from their styles looked like they dated back to at least the sixties.

As an art historian, Nell knew that such a well-curated collection deserved to be packed up properly and transported with care. She folded slacks and sweaters carefully into large plastic bins and hung the coats and dresses in garment bags, making a note of each item. She remembered, back when she first started, that Don had impressed upon her that she needed to keep track of all of the estate's bequests, for tax purposes.

Nell loaded what she could into her car, knowing she'd have to make more than one trip, and drove the few blocks over to Johnson Street. When she saw the green bungalow with a sign that said Hourglass Vintage affixed to the front porch, she slowed and parked on the street. She hoisted one of the bins out of the trunk and made her way to the shop entrance, being careful not to slip on the slushy sidewalks under the awkward bulk of the container.

She couldn't see very well over the top of the bin as she pushed open the front door, and she nearly knocked over a toddler with blond pigtails. A man in hospital scrubs scooped the child up and kissed her on the cheek, saying, "Watch where you're going, big girl." Then he called over his shoulder to someone inside the store. "Are you sure it's okay if I bring her here tomorrow for a couple of hours again? I've got lab and April has an exam."

"Of course," replied a woman's voice. "Amithi gets back from India tomorrow. I'm sure she'd love to see little Katie."

Nell stepped back from the door and let the man and the toddler pass. The little girl looked directly at Nell and waved bye-bye. Her dad set her down on the sidewalk and she splashed her feet in a puddle. Nell felt a pang of longing, but it was quickly followed by a reflexive smile. She said bye-bye back. The fact that she hadn't dropped the plastic bin or burst into tears felt like a small measure of progress.

Nell went inside, setting off a chime above the door. In the front room, a woman with black hair and tortoiseshell glasses stood bent over the counter, arranging costume jewelry on a rack made from a curly piece of driftwood. Despite the sleet and wind outside, the woman had on a sleeveless black maxi dress and her cheeks were flushed. She had a starfish tattoo on her bicep.

At the sound of the door, the woman at the counter stood up straight. Nell could now see that she was very pregnant. For some reason, the sight didn't trigger the sharp stab of sadness and jealousy that it usually did. Nell didn't know if it was because so much had happened in the past couple of weeks or because the woman looked to be about forty or so, and Nell knew all too well that pregnancy didn't always come easy for women of "advanced maternal age." Whatever the reason, this too felt like progress.

"That cold air feels good," the woman said.

Nell paused, resting the bin against one leg. "Do you want me to leave the door open?"

The woman shook her head. "Probably not a good idea, in terms of the heating bill. I'll just have to sweat it out."

Nell didn't think it was hot inside the shop. If anything, it was a little drafty.

"What can I do for you?" the woman asked.

"I'm Nell. I'm the director of the artists' colony that's run out of Betsy Barrett's old home. She left some things to the shop in her will." Nell made her way to the counter and set the bin down on the floor.

"Oh!" the woman said, obviously delighted, but with a hint of sadness in her voice. "I'm Violet. We miss Betsy around here. Her lawyer told me back when she passed away that she left her clothing to us, but said it might take some time until we got it. Something about the administration of the estate being kind of complicated. I meant to get in touch with him to follow up and ask him about it but"—she looked down at her belly—"I've been kind of busy."

"I see that. Congratulations," Nell said. And she meant it. "I've got more things out in the car. I'll go get them in a minute. But first, would you mind telling me a little bit about Betsy?"

Chapter Twenty-five

Betsy

PIECE: *Miniature globe made from Venetian blown glass, acquired in 1958.*

When Betsy was younger, people were nice to her because of her looks. They saw her pink cheeks, honeyed curls, and high cheekbones and projected onto her a bright, kind disposition to match. Her mother noticed, early in Betsy's adolescence, the way the world laid itself at her daughter's feet. She warned her not to get used to it.

"*This* is where pretty gets you," she'd said once while standing at the stove. She'd gestured then, with a wooden spoon, toward her sagging breasts and thick ankles. "Before I had children, I used to look just like you do now, you know."

At that moment, Betsy's younger brother came barreling into the room, along with the three neighbor boys from next door. The boys chased each other noisily around the table, shedding chunks of dirty snow from their hand-me-down boots, until Betsy's brother slipped and whacked his head on the edge of a chair. He began to wail and reached up to his mother, but at that moment she was removing a hot pot from the stove, so she shooed him away with a swish of her hip in Betsy's direction.

Betsy scooped up her brother and smoothed her hand over his hair. "There, there, Zaba, you're all right."

No one called her brother by his given name, Xavier. Instead he went by the nickname Zaba, or frog, because of the way he was constantly hopping from one activity to the next. Betsy's father insisted it was a term of endearment back in the old country, but the neighbor boys sometimes used it against him. All they had to do was call him Toad in front of his grammar-school friends if they wanted to get back at him for something.

Older than her brother by eight years, Betsy kept out of that sort of conflict for the most part. Instead she picked up, quite literally, where her mother's exhaustion left off. She tidied and tended as needed, which was often. Betsy had wiped so many sticky cheeks and played so many hours of monotonous make-believe games in her teenage years that by the time she met Walt at the age of twenty, she already knew that motherhood was not for her. And she told Walt so, the same night he proposed to her.

It had been a magical evening. A magical trip, really—Betsy's first one abroad—and it had whetted in her an appetite to see so much more. Walt had needed to go for work, and Betsy jumped at his invitation to go along, despite her mother's very vocal reservations.

At thirty-four, Walt was quite a bit older than Betsy, but still the youngest executive at the Madison plastics manufacturer where he worked. Even so, he was the natural choice to send to Italy to negotiate contracts, having picked up the language when he was stationed there during the war. While Walt toured industrial plants scattered throughout the countryside, Betsy visited the many rural churches along their route.

At the end of a dirt road she found a fourth-century chapel with exquisite floor mosaics depicting scenes from the Stations of the Cross. Gold tiles gleamed from the halos and crowns adorning the saints beneath her feet. Though much of her Catholic upbringing had been lost on her, despite her parents' best intentions, Betsy found herself kneeling on the floor of the chapel and running her hands over the smooth, timeworn tiles, not out of any sense of piety, but out of humility in the face of peerless human talent and skill.

An elderly priest came out of the sanctuary and, seeing her on her knees, said something in Italian. She caught nothing but *"Cristo"* from his fast, fluid words, but understood the smile behind his white beard, and the gesture he made toward the ceiling, where a Renaissance fresco stretched over the nave, depicting Mary being assumed into Heaven on a beam of light that seemed almost to glow from inside the plaster, despite the painting's cracks and faded colors. Later, from talking at dinner with one of the Italian executives who was courting Walt's business, Betsy learned that the painting was added in the sixteenth century by a student of Tintoretto. Such masterpieces, it seemed, were commonplace in this country.

At night, she and Walt would sit on the patio of the simple but elegant *pensione* his colleagues had recommended, sipping Barolo from small, stemless glasses and gazing over the tiled roofs of the village. In the mornings, they'd linger over a breakfast of espresso and crescent-shaped *cornetto* pastries in a nearby café. Betsy felt as if a whole new world had opened up for her. If just one small corner of Italy held so many treasures, how many, then, did the rest of the world contain?

After Walt had finished with his schedule of meetings, they spent a weekend in Venice. On their final day in Italy, Walt proposed to Betsy at twilight on a narrow bridge that arched over a quiet canal. Swept up in the romance of it all, she had pulled him up onto his feet and kissed him, long and slow. But then a church bell rang from a brick tower above them, and the weight of his question sank in.

She had only just discovered this world. He'd shown it to her, really. Never could she have afforded on her own to go to Italy. Walt had given her a glimpse into the possibility of what the world held, but then, with his surprise proposal, he'd yanked it away. Marriage, from what Betsy had seen in her own South Side neighborhood, meant pregnancy and children. It meant women never veering far from the circuit of supermarket and school, drugstore and church. It meant being tethered to home by the timer running on a roast in the oven and the pull of tiny hands on her skirt hem.

The lap of a gondolier's pole underscored the silence that followed Walt's question. As a boat slipped by beneath them, carrying another set of lovers, Walt squeezed Betsy's hand.

"You haven't answered my question," he said. "Look, I know we haven't known each other that long, but it's long enough for me. I know it's you I want to spend my life with. If you need a little time to make sure you feel the same way . . ."

"I *do* feel the same way." She touched his cheek. "It's not that. It's just . . ."

Betsy broke his gaze. She studied the red flowers spilling out of a planter box built into the railing of the bridge, and she thumbed a rope of ivy that had wound its way around a lamppost. Suddenly, being here with Walt no longer felt like an adventure. The iconic beauty surrounding her seemed like an elaborate set. If Betsy accepted his proposal and the diamond ring that sparkled from the blue velvet box in his palm, the curtain would soon close on the wanderlust that had only just been awakened in her.

"Okay, forget the ring," Walt said. "For now." He stuffed the box back into the pocket of his sport coat. "Let's go for a walk."

They climbed down the steps of the pedestrian bridge and onto the sidewalk. The sidewalk was more of a ledge, really, crammed at a precarious slant between the sheer bank of the canal and the cavalry of ancient row houses casting shadows over the water. Walt reached out to take Betsy's hand but, realizing there was no room, he gestured for her to step in front of him.

Betsy led the way through labyrinthine streets that opened at intervals into piazzas and parks. She didn't know where she was going, but that was sort of the point. Since she and Walt first arrived in Venice, she'd teased him every time he took out his guidebook to study the map.

"Don't you just want to get *lost?*" she'd asked him outside the door of St. Mark's Basilica. "I feel like this city is begging for it."

Walt had replied, "Is that your way of trying to throw me over? Telling me I need to get lost?"

"Never," she'd said, standing on tiptoe to kiss him.

Tonight, though, Betsy led him through cobbled streets, turning wherever she pleased. She followed the babble of water to a small fountain shooting straight from the side of a building. She dipped her fingers into the stone cistern below it, thinking of how many hands had been washed, how many vessels had been filled over the centuries in this very spot. In a tiny square, crisscrossed overhead by clotheslines, she paused to listen to a man plucking at a guitar. All the while, Walt walked beside her or, when required, behind.

Finally, Betsy stopped and sat on the steps of what looked like a school, emptied out for the evening. The construction-paper stars and crayoned drawings taped inside the windows struck a stark contrast to the building's formal, ancient exterior, which consisted of grand arched doorways and marble carvings.

Walt sat next to her and nudged her knee with his own. "What is it?"

Betsy let out a long exhale. "I'm scared," she finally said.

He furrowed his brow. The concern in his expression filled her heart with affection for him all over again. She really did love this man. But . . .

"Look, I'll just say it. I've seen so many of the girls I grew up with get married and live identical lives. Dinner on the table. Diapers in the wash. Not that there's anything wrong with any of that. It's important, if that's the life you want. But it's not the life *I* want. So if you do, then I'm not the right girl for you."

Walt put his arm around Betsy's shoulders and squeezed them. "You're exactly the right girl for me. You think I haven't noticed that you're not just like everyone else? It's what I love about you. You want something different, something more. So do I."

"What about college? I still have a year left at Mount Mary." Betsy thought about how several of her classmates had dropped out after they got engaged or married. And how she had worked so hard to get a scholarship from her neighborhood parish.

"Finish your degree," Walt said. "There's no reason you have to choose one or the other."

Betsy tilted her head to look at this man, whom she'd met on the train from Milwaukee to Chicago just a few months earlier and seen every day since. He had boundless energy. For ideas, experiences, and, most especially, people. He listened to people. Figured out what made them tick. Remembered details no one else would notice. These traits crossed cultural barriers, too, to the point where he could have dinner with a group of Milanese executives who spoke minimal English and have everyone laughing and lingering at the table long after they'd finished their espressos.

"I have something else to admit to you," Betsy said.

"What's that?"

She gave him a sheepish smile. "I'm afraid I've gotten us hopelessly lost."

"Congratulations," he said. "You've accomplished your goal." He got up and pulled Betsy to her feet. "Look, I don't want a *wife*, if by that you mean someone to iron my shirts and make dinner. There are half a dozen perfectly good restaurants within a mile of my house in Madison and, as for the shirts, I send them out. I don't want a wife, and I don't need kids, either. Let other people have them. I want *you*. Your smarts. Your style. Your sense of adventure. Not every woman would hop a plane to Italy with the likes of me on short notice, you know. Or toss back grappa without so much as a grimace at a union tavern."

Betsy recalled the disapproval on her mother's face when she told her mother about the trip. "A man taking a girl your age clear overseas is going to have a lot of expectations, you know." She'd put her hands on her hips and looked heavenward. "Your father must be rolling in his grave."

But to the extent her mother had been talking about sex, she needn't have been worried. Walt was a perfect gentleman, booking Betsy her own room wherever they went. And now he'd proposed marriage. Her mother would have been thrilled, but here Betsy was, hemming and hawing over her answer.

They started back in what Betsy thought was the direction of the hotel. "I'm not sure this is right," she said as they turned onto a street of small retail shops, each selling a different specialty—watches, leather goods, lace. One store sold exquisite jewelry and figurines made from Venetian glass. In the window, a parade of tiny animals twirled on an automated carousel made from orange and yellow glass and adorned with ribbons. Betsy stopped to marvel at the exquisite detail of the translucent zebras, ostriches, and tigers that danced in delicate poses under the display lights, no one animal exactly like the other.

The shopkeeper, a middle-aged man in a starched shirt and wool trousers, stood outside the door with keys in hand, about to close for the day. Walt waved and said, *"Aspetta!"*

The shopkeeper paused and, after an exchange in rapid Italian, he opened the door.

"Wait here," Walt said to Betsy, and he ducked inside the shop. She watched through the window as Walt pointed to something in the window display, something she hadn't seen a moment earlier because she'd been so fixated on the moving carousel.

Nearly hidden behind a display of gold-plated goblets stood a small globe fashioned from blown glass. The continents, each a different color, looked like puzzle pieces stretched with care over swirling seas in variegated shades of blue. The shopkeeper went over to the window and picked up the globe from the marble pedestal on which it sat. Betsy watched as Walt paid for the item and the shopkeeper packaged it inside a red cardboard box.

Walt came back out holding the box in his hands. He waited until the shopkeeper had locked up and walked away before saying, "I take back my earlier proposal."

"What?" Betsy's heart pounded. Once again, she'd mucked

things up with too much *thinking*. Now, the way her head went hot and her vision went blurry at the thought of losing him, she knew her answer. "You don't have to—"

But Walt interrupted her. "It was all wrong."

"No." Betsy shook her head. "A bridge in Venice? I don't think a girl could dream up anything better."

"Maybe that would do for other girls, but not for you. Forget the ring. You can have it later if you want, but this is what I should have done."

He got to one knee now, for the second time that evening, and held out the red box.

Betsy said yes first this time, and then opened the box.

There, nestled among crinkly folds of gold tissue paper, was the world.

Chapter Twenty-six

Nell

PIECE: *Tiffany silver frame engraved with the monogram WBE.*

By the time Nell finished her trips to and from the second-hand shop, she was exhausted from hauling the heavy plastic bins and bundles of garment bags. When she returned to the mansion after her final run to the shop, she went upstairs and stood inside Betsy's now empty closet, feeling a sense of accomplishment but also a twinge of sadness. There had been something comforting about having all those clothes hanging there, their textures and colors and patterns providing a glimpse into the personality of the woman who wore them.

Nell shut the closet door, turning to look around the large master bedroom. With a little bit of work, it could easily serve as a bedroom or studio for someone from the next group of artists, whoever they might be. Applications had already begun to arrive in the mail.

Nell had done enough for one day, though. She'd tackle this room another time. For now, she just collected a few items from the top of the dresser and placed them into a drawer—a crystal ring holder, a mother-of-pearl hand mirror, and a tarnished silver frame holding a black-and-white photo of the Barretts on their wedding day. Betsy, in a full-skirted gown with lace sleeves, had her gaze turned on Walt instead of the camera. In turn, Walt, tall and handsome in a white jacket and black bow tie, looked down at Betsy with a glint in his eye and an openmouthed smile, as if he'd been caught laughing at something she'd said when the shutter went off. The photo reminded Nell of the conversation she'd had earlier with Violet at Hourglass Vintage about the Barretts.

"I can't help taking a peek at a few of these items right away," Violet had said, unfolding a tweed Chanel jacket from one of the boxes. "Betsy had such fantastic taste."

A woman who'd been browsing the racks near the register stopped to gape at the handbags, coats, and glittering costume jewelry that Violet was piling up on the counter.

"Where did all that come from?" the customer asked.

"A dear friend who died," Violet said. "She was so generous to leave all these things to the shop."

The woman's eyes widened. "She didn't have a daughter or granddaughter who would have wanted them?"

"She didn't have any children," Violet said.

The woman clucked her tongue. "Such a shame. To have all those beautiful things and no one to pass them on to."

Violet shook her head. "Betsy didn't think so. She never wanted children."

Those words stuck with Nell. Back when she first accepted the directorship, she'd assumed that for one reason or another, the Barretts weren't *able* to have children. It was uncommon for a couple of their generation not to have a family. But the more she learned about Betsy, the more Nell had begun to suspect that the Colony's benefactor chose the life she had. And today Violet had confirmed it.

Now, as she left Betsy's room and let herself out of the house, Nell thought about the legacy of the woman who had lived there. Betsy didn't have a human heir out there in the world, carrying on her name or the particular slant of her nose. But she'd lived a rich life, crossing continents and meeting fascinating people. She'd left behind a collection of artwork that would continue to touch people's lives with beauty, introspection, and joy. And, through the Colony, Betsy had made sure that—at least in one house, on the shores of one lake—a handful of artists would continue to cultivate and create more of the same.

When Nell arrived home, she was startled to find Josh sitting on the floor on the living room rug. As she came closer, she saw that their baby's memory box had been taken down from the mantel where Nell kept it. The box lay open on the coffee table, its pink ribbon untied and cast aside. Josh sat in the middle of a circle of items—a hospital bracelet, tiny footprints cast in plaster, a copy of a blessing read at the memorial service held in the hospital's chapel.

Nell knew the items by heart. If Josh had suddenly grabbed an item without her looking, and hidden it behind his back, she could have described the missing keepsake in seconds. It was like that game played sometimes at kids' birthday parties, where a grown-up brings in a tray with a random assortment of items—a pencil, an orange, a penny, a plastic army guy, and a paper cup—and then the tray is taken out of the room and one item removed. When the grown-up returns, the kids have to guess what's missing.

It was that way with the box.

Josh sat clutching something in his closed palm. He startled when he saw Nell standing in the room, and slowly opened up his hand.

"I didn't know we had this," he said, revealing a wisp of hair so short and fine it was held together with a piece of thread. He nodded toward the other items spread out on the table and floor. "I didn't know we had any of this." He picked up the white knit hat a nurse had placed on their daughter's head. "Do you remember how perfectly round her head was? It's a weird thing to remember, I guess, but people are always talking about how newborns' heads are misshapen. But not hers. It was perfect."

Nell began to cry. Fat tears fell onto the rug and sank into the tufted wool.

"I'm sorry," Josh said. "I didn't want to upset you." He moved to get up from the floor, but Nell stopped him.

"No," she said, blinking. "I'm okay. Spend as much time looking as you'd like. These aren't sad tears. Well, maybe a little. I'm relieved. I thought you just wanted to put this all behind us. That there was something wrong with me for wanting to remember. It's good to see that you want to, too."

"Of course I want to remember." The words came out terse, and he looked away for a second.

"What is it?" she asked.

Josh exhaled, loud and long. "This didn't just happen to you, you know," he said. "I've been here the whole time. Maybe I've handled it differently than you have, but . . ." He set his jaw, as if fighting back tears. "She was my daughter, too."

Nell bent down and sat next to him on the floor. She put a hand on his back as his shoulders shook. The last, and only, time she'd seen him shed tears before this was at the hospital, after the nurse took their daughter's body out of the room, and away from them forever. Josh had shuddered and put his face in his hands. He'd been silent as the tears pooled in his palms and spilled onto the floor. The only sound Nell recalled hearing was the wail, muffled through the walls, of other people's babies in other rooms.

Nell realized now just how much she'd been clinging to the kernel of grief inside her, protecting it as if it belonged to her and her alone. Nell had been the one who carried their daughter. She'd felt her baby's fluttering. Every night of her pregnancy, she'd fallen asleep with her arms cradled over her belly. She'd even been the only one to hold their daughter in the few minutes she was alive. It wasn't until her little body began to go cold that Nell handed the baby to Josh. She could see now that she'd been possessive in her pain. It was how she'd felt justified in forging ahead with fertility treatments while keeping the cost a secret.

But what would it cost to share some of her pain? To feel it together with Josh instead of letting it drive them apart? It would cost her nothing. Nothing except opening herself up wide and letting go a little.

Nell looked at her husband. "I'm sorry," she said.

Josh furrowed his brow. "I've told you a hundred times. There's nothing you could have done to save her. You heard the doctors."

"No, not that." Nell scooted closer to her husband, so that their legs were touching on the carpet. "I'm sorry you didn't get to hold her until she was gone. I wish you could have."

Josh's lips formed a straight line, as if he were weighing what to say. "I wish that, too," he said. "But there's no way you could have known she'd go so quickly."

"I was so unaware of anything else but holding onto her for as long as I could," Nell said.

Josh put a hand on her knee. "I know."

They sat there like that for several minutes, until Josh's breathing slowed back to normal and he wiped his face with the back of his hand.

"What made you think about this today?" Nell asked.

"The investigation into Caroline's death, I guess. It got me thinking about loss."

Nell reached over and picked up a silver envelope. She remembered the day it came in the mail, a few weeks after they came home from the hospital. At first Nell had thought it was a wedding invitation. But inside she had found a thumb drive and a handwritten letter from the photographer. She had mentioned it to Josh, but he'd said he wasn't ready to see the pictures, so Nell kept them—and the letter—to herself, looking at them often, whenever she felt the need.

Now, though, she unfolded the letter and leaned against Josh's shoulder so they could read it together.

Dear Nell and Josh,

Enclosed are the photos I took of your beautiful daughter. Thank you for the opportunity to document her life. These pictures are yours to use in whatever way you wish, whenever you feel ready.

I know the pain you are going through because I also lost a baby, two years ago. A boy, Nathan Andrew, stillborn at 38 weeks. I didn't tell you this at the hospital because I didn't want to interfere in any way with your precious few moments with your baby.

When I got the call about coming to the hospital to take these pictures, I wasn't sure if I should do it. I had made some progress in my own healing, and I worried about the emotions the experience would bring up for me. But, deep down, I knew I didn't have a choice. I had to do it. A photographer came and took pictures after I delivered Nathan, and I look at my favorite picture of him every single day. I knew I had to make the same thing possible for you.

Dana B.

The first time Nell read the letter, Nell had looked up Dana B.'s photography website and bookmarked it. The pictures posted there were very different from the ones she'd sent to Nell and Josh. There were senior portraits of smiling teenagers, lifestyle shots of families playing at the beach and walking on wooded trails. There were baby portraits, too, so many of them. Bald, plump babies. Babies with full heads of hair. Black babies and white babies. Crawling and walking and sleeping babies. But nowhere on Dana B.'s site were there pictures of any babies as small as Baby Girl Parker. Nor nearly as beautiful.

Josh opened the envelope wider and looked inside. "There aren't any photos in here."

"She sent them on a thumb drive, so I loaded them onto my computer. I've never had prints made because . . . Well, because I knew you hadn't seen them and it seemed wrong to, like, force you to look at them. I didn't want to print them out only to stick them in a drawer somewhere. So I just kept them on there."

"Maybe I needed to be forced." He got up and left the room. Nell didn't know whether she should follow him. Maybe he was upset and just needed a moment to himself.

He came back a few seconds later, though, holding Nell's laptop. He settled back down on the floor, cross-legged next to Nell, and opened it.

Nell studied his face. "You sure?" she asked. But she already knew the answer from the way he'd set his jaw and fixed his eyes on the screen. Still, she waited for his nod before she leaned over and clicked open the folder that contained the pictures.

Josh looked through the pictures slowly. At first, he sat silent. Then the memories started to flow out of him.

"Remember when she reached up and touched your arm?" he asked. "She couldn't even see us, we were probably just shadows and light. But she knew we were there."

Seeing Josh finally go through the pictures, Nell felt grateful, for the hundredth time, that the photographer, Dana, had been there. That she had not let her grief and her fear of reopening the wounds of losing her own son stop her from taking the pictures. And it occurred to Nell all of a sudden—she was surprised she hadn't realized it before—that what Dana had done for her and Josh was similar to what Annie had done for Caroline, and for all the dying people she'd photographed when she was in New York. Annie, too, had stepped past her own emotions and hesitations in order to record something that she thought was important.

Nell looked down at the screen, where Josh had paused on a black-and-white photo of their daughter. In the picture, the baby's lips were pursed and slightly parted, as if waiting for a kiss.

"We should print this one out and frame it," he said.

"I'd like that," Nell said.

Josh touched the screen with a finger, as if touching their daughter's cheek.

"Do you think she knew we loved her?" Josh asked.

Nell shook her head. "I *know* she knew."

Josh looked so vulnerable just then that Nell took a risk and followed her instinct to kiss him. She knew he very well might inch away from her. It had been a long time since they'd been close, either emotionally or physically, and Nell guessed that at least a part of him was still angry about the debt and the lies. But, in this moment at least, she felt more drawn to Josh than she ever had, because of all they'd been through together.

Nell put her hands on either side of her husband's face, feeling the soft prickle of his beard beneath her fingers. She pressed her lips to his, gently at first, as if to ask, *is this okay?* Or maybe, *are we okay?*

He wrapped her in his arms and kissed her back, saying yes without saying yes.

That night, Josh stopped sleeping in the office and moved back into the bedroom.

Chapter Twenty-seven

Annie

PIECE: *Bill Curry,* Giant Jack *bookends. Chrome-coated cast iron. Purchased in 1967.*

"I met with the assistant DA today," Josh said. "And I've got some good news."

He and Annie were sitting inside the office at the Colony, which Nell had offered to let them use for their meeting.

"It's about damn time," Annie said. Then, realizing that her comment may have sounded harsh, she added, "I didn't mean that as a reflection on you. Just on everything that's happened."

"It's okay, I get it." Josh pulled some papers out of a file folder. "So here's the deal: the DA's office is willing to amend the charge of 'possession with intent to deliver' to 'keeping a drug house,' which is still a felony, but a less serious one. You'd have to plead guilty to the amended charge, and then the DA would recommend that the court withhold sentence and give you probation only. No jail time unless you violate the terms of your probation."

Annie didn't say anything. Josh had been so patient over the last several weeks of interviews, filings, and hearings. After he helped her out on the day of her arrest, Annie had planned to find a different lawyer. It wasn't that she didn't like Josh—she did, actually, and more importantly, she trusted him. But it felt like too much to ask him to take on her entire case. When she started looking around for someone else to represent her, she realized quickly that she couldn't afford the retainers and hourly rates quoted by the private attorneys she contacted. Yet, when she applied for appointment of a public defender, her application was denied because her monthly stipend, room, and board at the Colony bumped her just above the eligibility threshold. Her friends back at the ACLU in the city couldn't help her, either. They only took on New York cases. So, despite Annie's best efforts to the contrary, Josh was stuck with her. And now she was going to act against his advice.

She took a deep breath and crossed her arms. "I can't do it."

"Is it the idea of admitting guilt? Because if that doesn't sit right with you, you could always plead 'no contest.' It would have the same effect as a guilty plea, but you wouldn't actually have to say the word 'guilty.'"

"It's not the word 'guilty' I'm worried about," Annie said. "It's the words 'drug house.'"

Josh nodded. "Look, I know it *sounds* bad, but it's a much less serious charge than what you're facing now, and carries a lesser penalty."

"But it's going to reflect really poorly on the Colony, don't you think?" Annie asked.

Josh got up and started pacing the room. Annie had noticed it was a habit of his when he was thinking. "If it would make you feel better, you could talk to Nell about it and make sure she's on board with the idea of the plea," he said. "I think she will be."

"Yeah, but the drug dealing charge reflects only on me. If I plead to 'keeping a drug house,' I'm afraid it will look bad for everyone who lives here. Because this isn't just a house." Annie waved her hand toward the office door and the rest of the mansion on the other side of it. She looked around the room at all of the lovely books and art prints and antiques. Then she pictured Betsy, the woman who had owned this house and carefully curated everything in it, right down to the artists who now lived here. Annie felt like she had done enough damage already, and didn't want to do anything that might further jeopardize the Colony and Betsy's vision for it.

As for Annie's own vision, she felt like she'd been blinded. She'd been so consumed with her project, so obsessed with making a statement that would launch her back into relevancy, that she hadn't fully anticipated the risks inherent in what she was doing.

She remembered, on the night she called 911, watching as one of the paramedics injected Caroline's unresponsive body with a shot.

"Naloxone," the paramedic had said when Annie asked what it was. "It can reverse the effects of an overdose, if administered in time. You should consider having it around if you hang out with addicts."

Annie had since found out that she could have gotten the lifesaving medication without a prescription. In hindsight, she deeply regretted that she had not thought to get a naloxone kit as a precaution as soon as she placed her Craigslist ad. But she'd underestimated the foe—addiction—that she and Caroline were up against.

"I know it's a lot to digest," Josh said. "But all the terms are written out here if you want to take some time to review them." He pushed the papers toward Annie.

Annie's thoughts returned from the land of "what ifs" and "should haves" to the present.

"Did the DA say anything about getting back my camera?" she asked.

"The State's going to hold onto it until the case is resolved," Josh said. "As far as they're concerned, what's on that film is evidence, not art."

Annie sighed. "Can't they amend the charge to just plain old drug possession? That's also a misdemeanor, and I would be willing to plead to that."

Josh shook his head. "They can't charge you with simple possession because of the Good Samaritan law," he reminded her. "You're immune to prosecution for drug possession, since you're the person who called 911. But you're not immune to the felony drug dealing charge."

"I wasn't selling drugs, though," Annie said.

"I know. The prosecution could argue, though, that you were getting something of value in exchange for the pot. You were getting the rights to take people's pictures and use them in your art. And that could be seen as a sale. But it doesn't matter anyway, because they don't even need to prove there was a sale, or any intent of a sale. 'Deliver' doesn't have to mean 'sell.' Under the law, it's enough even if you just *give* drugs to someone."

"What happens if I don't plead?"

"Then we go to trial on both felony charges," Josh said. "And maybe we can convince a jury that the State's evidence isn't enough to convict you. But there's a good chance it could go the other way, too. That's the gamble that anyone takes if they go to trial."

Annie glanced toward the shelves on either side of the fireplace. Two oversized silver jacks were holding up a row of leather-bound books, acting as bookends. Annie remembered playing the game as a child, bouncing the ball and scooping up a handful of little metal game pieces. She remembered the sharp, cold feel of the jacks in her hand. What a strange game for children, she thought. They'd learn soon enough about the world's hard edges.

"Can't I just plead to the drug dealing charge?" Annie asked.

"You could . . . I can see if the DA is amenable to making a deal on that charge. But it's not going to be as good of a deal as what's on the table right now. You'd almost certainly get some jail time."

"I can survive some jail time," Annie said. "Honestly, the thing that bothers me the most about having a felony conviction is the idea of not being able to vote. Every eligible citizen with a vagina needs to vote these days."

"Your voting rights would be restored once you've served your sentence."

"Okay, then," Annie said. "I'll do it. I'll enter a plea for the drug dealing charge, assuming you negotiate the jail time down as low as you're able. I just want to get this over with."

Josh sighed. "If that's what you really want to do, I'm sure we can make it happen. But first give me a couple of days to go over the record again. If it's okay with you, I'm going to have my law students take a look, too, and do some research. Just to have some other eyes and brains on the case."

"Sure. The more brains the better. Thank you."

After Josh left, Annie went outside to clear her head and walk around the stone path that wove through the sculpture garden. The beds and mounds were black and loamy, finally free of their snowy shrouds. The air smelled sweet and verdant, but did little to lift the sadness that weighed heavily on Annie's chest. Because no matter what she pled to, no matter what sentence she served, she could not bring Caroline back.

To occupy her hands and, hopefully, her thoughts, Annie knelt on the ground and pulled a few weeds that had begun to crop up in the flower beds. When she'd cleared one bed, she moved on to the next. It felt cathartic, rooting out the dandelion sprouts and creeping Charlie vines, to make way for the perennials Betsy had planted over the years.

When she'd finished weeding, Annie's hands were covered in mud. She went inside to wash them, and nearly ran into Odin carrying a chair.

"Rearranging some furniture?" Annie asked.

"Kind of," he said. "Talk to Nell."

Annie washed her hands in the kitchen, then went into the dining room, where Nell was lining up dishes and glassware on the table.

Annie sat down on one of the few chairs that remained in the room. "Either we're moving, you've gotten a spring cleaning bug, or we're having a party no one told me about," she said.

Nell looked up. "I guess you could call it a party. I'm getting things ready for the Gallery Night we've planned for Friday, to raise money for your defense."

Annie put a hand to her chest. She couldn't believe they were going to so much trouble for her. If anything, Nell and the others should have been angry with her, for disrupting the Colony and potentially risking its reputation. Instead, they were trying to help her.

"I'm flattered," Annie said. "But if all goes as planned, pretty soon I won't have a case anymore, so there won't be any need to raise money for it." She nodded toward the office. "That's what Josh and I were talking about in there. I think I'm going to agree to a plea deal."

"What will you plead to?"

"Possession with intent to deliver."

Nell frowned. "But you're not a drug dealer."

Annie gave Nell a small, grateful smile. "I'm glad you know that."

Nell set a silver serving dish down on the table. "Of course. None of us think that. We think the charges against you have been trumped up because the DA's office is making a public effort to crack down on opioids. They need to hold someone accountable for Caroline's overdose, and since they can't pinpoint where she got the heroin from, you're getting scapegoated. Not for the heroin, of course. But the other drug charges at least make it seem like law enforcement is doing something."

"Well, hopefully all of this will be in the past soon," Annie said. "So, while I'm flattered that you want to do a fund-raiser for me, you really don't need to go to the trouble."

"Well, it's not *just* for you," Nell said. "One of Betsy's directives was that every group of residents hold a collective show at least once. I mentioned it early on when you guys first got here, but the goal sort of got swallowed up with everything else going on. So, with the Gallery Night, we can accomplish that goal and also help you at the same time."

Annie crossed her arms on her chest. "I won't accept the money. But what if we found a different cause to give the proceeds to? I've been thinking a lot about how there's so much I didn't know about what Caroline was going through. We could raise money for a nonprofit that does research on addiction or provides support services to people in recovery."

"I like that idea," Nell said. "Odin and Paige have already provided me with some pieces to show, but it won't truly be a collaborative show unless we have work from all three of you. Do you have anything you could contribute?"

Annie shook her head. "The cops confiscated my film when they took the camera. I had been planning to develop the photos all together. I'd gotten permission from one of the instructors at the technical college to use the darkroom there to do it. But now . . ."

"What about paintings or other types of work that you've done in the past?"

"Everything's in storage in New York. I suppose I could contact a friend to get a few things out of storage, but it would probably cost a lot to ship them here properly." Annie paused when she saw Nell pick up a towel and start polishing spots off wineglasses. "I can help you with that," she said. "Let me go get a rag."

Annie went to the kitchen and opened up the drawer where they usually kept the kitchen rags. It was empty. She went down to the basement, where she had thrown a load of laundry into the dryer earlier and forgotten about it. But as soon as she went downstairs, she forgot all about the towels and the wash because she remembered something else.

There *were* some photos she'd developed but never shown. She just needed to find them.

Chapter Twenty-eight

Betsy

PIECE: *Silk throw-pillow cover made from Chinese brocade.*

Cindy opened the drapes in the bedroom, and Betsy blinked in the summer sunlight streaming in. She'd already been awake for nearly an hour, but didn't have the strength to get out of bed on her own. Lately she'd been waiting for the arrival of Cindy, the hospice nurse who cared for her in the mornings, before attempting to go to the bathroom or get dressed, if she even got dressed. Many days she didn't.

"How are you feeling today, Mrs. Barrett?" Cindy asked.

Betsy cleared her throat and sat up. "You know the phrase 'I feel like a million bucks'?"

"Sure." Cindy gave her a funny look.

"Well, I feel like about five bucks. Maybe four fifty."

Cindy laughed. "You know, we can reschedule today's interview if you're not feeling up to it."

"Absolutely not. The night nurse brought up the idea of moving to the hospice inpatient facility again." Betsy sighed. "And I think she's right about that. She said they can administer around-the-clock care there, plus better pain management. Which sounds good to me." She rubbed her side, which radiated pain from where she knew, from her most recent doctor's appointment, the tumors had spread. It was hard to pinpoint, though, where the pain was coming from. She hurt all over.

"Perhaps we can do the interview up here, then?" Cindy suggested.

"No way. There will be pictures."

"I could tidy up the room a bit."

Betsy looked at the crumpled tissues on the nightstand, the clutter of jars and tubes and pill canisters. No matter how many creams and balms she applied to her lips and skin, they still felt dry as desert sand. And no matter how many medications she took, she knew she was not getting better.

"I've put so much thought, time, and money into my sculpture garden over the years," Betsy said. "I want to sit outside. And if that means you have to throw me down the stairs to get me there, so be it."

Cindy gave her a conciliatory look. "Well, then I guess we'd better get you dressed." She went to the closet and brought back the outfit Betsy had chosen—a slub silk suit in the palest shade of ice blue.

Betsy didn't like needing help to go to the bathroom and get dressed, but there was no way around it. She could barely even get up from the bed without having to grab the night table for balance. By some miracle, though, Cindy managed to help Betsy into the suit, with its zippers and hooks and buttons. She applied makeup to her face, bringing color to her pale cheeks and lips, and brushed the gray-blond wig that Betsy had special-ordered as soon as her hair began to fall out from radiation.

"Think of how much more time I'm going to have on my hands, now that I don't have to get my hair colored every eight weeks," Betsy had said when the wig arrived in the mail. Little did she know that the time she gained was quickly filled up with chemotherapy and doctors' appointments.

Then, after Betsy chose to stop radiation treatment, she finally recouped her free time. But "free" was a misnomer, because she spent almost all of it in bed. Betsy had never been good at being idle, though, so even when she was bedridden she made the most of her time, writing down ideas for the artist-in-residency program she'd be leaving as her legacy. When pain and fatigue prevented her from writing her own notes, she dictated them to Cindy or one of the nursing assistants on duty. Betsy also had them read reviews aloud to her, of art exhibits she'd never see and performances she'd never attend. Somehow it gave her comfort to know that creative expression would continue in this world long after she'd left it.

"There," Cindy said, holding up a hand mirror.

Betsy tried to look at her reflection, but the image was blurry. "I need my glasses," she said.

Cindy pushed aside papers and bottles on the nightstand until she found a pair of tortoiseshell glasses, round and over-sized. She handed them to Betsy.

"That's better," Betsy said when she'd put them on.

"You look like Iris Apfel in those," Cindy said.

Betsy laughed. "Or maybe Mr. Magoo."

"I just watched a documentary about Apfel. If I live to my nineties, I hope I have even a smidge of her energy. Here she is, this woman famous enough to have her clothing displayed at the Met, and she's running around a flea market with her cane, pawing through tables of bargain accessories."

"Normally I'd say it's dangerous to tell a woman she looks like someone older than her," Betsy said. "But in this case I'm flattered by the comparison. I've always thought it was a shame that I never got to meet Apfel when she lived in Madison. But she graduated from art school at UW in the forties, and I was just a kid then. I didn't move here until the late fifties, after I got married."

"Well, it's her loss as much as yours." Cindy straightened Betsy's wig. "Are you ready?"

Slowly, deliberately, they made their way to the hallway and down the stairs, where every step seemed like a mile. Betsy clutched the smooth handrail on one side and, on the other, she leaned her weight against Cindy's sturdy shoulders. They inched downward like that, pausing to rest on the landing where the staircase curved.

"I feel like we're in a three-legged race," Betsy said. "Good thing no one's racing against us, or else we'd surely lose."

Cindy laughed, then supported Betsy the rest of the way downstairs and out the front door.

Betsy leaned on the white wooden rails of the front porch,

taking in the view of the sculpture garden at its midsummer peak. Bush roses in white and peach hues bloomed in the beds that bordered the front porch. Clustered around the mother-and-child statue Betsy loved so much were bunches of hydrangea in shades of purple and blue, their puffy, carefree blossoms swaying in the mild breeze off the lake.

Cindy led her to the wrought-iron bench in the yard, positioned for perfect views of the sculptures. Throw pillows in various colors and textures had been placed on the seat—Betsy had had Cindy bring them all upstairs so she could select patterns that complimented one another.

Betsy played with the fringe on a rust-colored pillow with a silk brocade cover. "I bought this fabric in China," she said. "At a gift market near the Mutianyu section of the Great Wall." She closed her eyes. "Oh the steps! I know you'd never believe it now, after having to practically carry me down a single flight of stairs, but Walt and I climbed hundreds of steps that day. It was autumn, and from on top of the wall you could see miles and miles of orange and red treetops. That's why I picked out this particular fabric, actually, at one of the market stalls on our way out of town. It reminded me of the color of the autumn leaves."

A warm wind blew up from the lake, rustling the grasses in the garden. Without even opening her eyes, Betsy could picture the fronds of green and yellow ornamental grass that flanked the stone footpath leading around the side of the house. She inhaled the sweet, heady scent of the roses near the porch.

When Betsy opened her eyes, Cindy was no longer standing in the yard with her. Instead, she saw a gray-haired woman in overalls making her way up the front walk with a camera slung around her neck.

"Annie Beck?" she said. "What are you doing here?"

"I'm here to photograph you," she said. "If it's okay with you."

"Of course. I didn't put all this on just to sit out here in my own garden." Betsy swept her hand to indicate her made-up face and tailored attire. "Did the magazine send you?"

"There's no magazine," Annie said. She knelt down in the grass and started snapping pictures.

Betsy sat silent for a moment, trying to put everything together. Had she mixed something up? She wouldn't be surprised. Her head felt so foggy these days, floating from the effects of one medication to the next. But Cindy was usually pretty good at keeping track of details.

"I don't understand," Betsy said.

Annie had climbed on top of the berm that separated Betsy's yard from the neighbor's, to shoot from a different angle. From her perch Annie said, "I'm the one who called about doing a magazine article. But I made the whole thing up."

"Why?" Betsy asked. "If you'd just asked to photograph me, I would have said yes."

"We wanted it to be a surprise."

"Who's 'we'?"

"Robbie and me. That night, after my show at his gallery, I mentioned something to him about how much I'd enjoyed talking with you, and whether you'd be invited to the retrospective we're planning for a future date. He said he didn't think so. That you were sick. And once I heard that, I suddenly understood why my pictures of people who were dying—like the professor with her Proust books—resonated with you so much. I asked Robbie what he thought about me photographing you, and he liked the idea. So here I am."

Betsy scratched at her scalp, which was starting to itch from the combination of the wig and the humid summer air. She wasn't sure how to feel about all of this. On one hand, she was flattered by the gesture, but on the other, it felt like an invasion of privacy. Betsy had often kept details of her personal life private, even while publicly taking on causes she believed in. And nothing was more private than dying.

"I never told Robbie about my relapse," Betsy said. "I've hardly told anyone."

"You didn't have to. He knew you had cancer once before and said he could tell you were sick again as soon as he saw you that night, from how much weight you'd lost." Annie sat down on the bench beside Betsy and removed the camera from around her neck. "Look, we don't have to do this if you don't want to. Robbie said there was a chance you might not be up for it or that you might even be offended. But the risk of offending people usually doesn't stop me from doing something I think is worthwhile, so I figured it was at least worth a shot. Not for my series, but just because I sensed you had a lot of spirit and personality, and that you might enjoy all of that being captured while you're still here, by someone who could see it. Who could see *you*. Not for my series."

"I'm not offended," Betsy said. "I don't even care if you want to use the photos. Use them however you want. You just caught me by surprise. I was expecting an interviewer and photographer from a local magazine."

"Are you disappointed there's no magazine article?"

"Lord, no. I've done so many interviews. I don't need another article saying all the things I've already said dozens of times before: when I started collecting, what my favorite pieces are, et cetera."

"If you let me, I think I can capture something about you that hasn't been said yet," Annie said. "Or at least I hope I can. That's why I came."

Betsy thought about the photographs she'd seen at the show in New York—the beauty and grace that shared space in the images with pain and death. It was a complicated combination that many people shied away from even talking about. Annie, instead, chose to focus a lens on it. It was exactly the kind of creative courage that Betsy hoped could be nurtured by the residency program she'd dreamed up.

"Okay," Betsy said. "Let's take some pictures."

Chapter Twenty-nine

Nell

PIECE: *Letter from Annie Beck, New York, New York, to Elizabeth Barrett, Madison, Wisconsin.*

That Friday afternoon, Nell was working on hanging some of the artwork for the show when she looked out one of the back windows and saw a boat towing a big barge out on the lake. It seemed to be headed straight in her direction. It came closer and closer until, from her vantage point, it looked as if it were going to hit the boathouse at the edge of the property. Nell got up and ran outside, waving her arms at the two men in the boat.

"Stop!" she yelled. The last thing she needed was for a barge to crash ashore just hours before the Colony was supposed to open its doors for its first public show.

The driver cut the engine and turned within ten feet of the boathouse. The other man jumped from the boat to the barge, which swung around so that it was parallel to the shore. He was laughing. From where she stood now, Nell could see that there was no danger of the boat hitting anything onshore. But she'd never seen any boat get this close before, let alone one towing a barge carrying what looked like big wood pallets.

"What are you doing?" she asked, this time at a normal volume.

The man looked down at Nell, who now stood on the rocks at the lake's edge. "We're putting in your pier," he said. "We store it off-site and put it back in the first week of May every year, weather permitting. Been doing it for twenty years. Then in the fall we come and haul it away to storage."

The driver anchored the boat and, wearing waders, got into the water. The man on the barge lifted one of the wood pallets—which Nell could now see was a pier section—and lowered it into the water. Then he looked at Nell. "Did the lady who used to live here move?"

"She passed away," Nell said. "The property is owned by a trust now."

The man in the water paused. "So do you still want the pier in, or should we take it back to storage?"

Nell had never even thought about it. It occurred to her now that it should have been obvious, from the fact that there was a boathouse, that there also had been a pier at some point. But the boathouse didn't have anything inside it other than a few old canoe paddles and gas cans.

"Yes," Nell said. "Go ahead and put it in. Have you already been paid or do I need to pay you?"

"We'll send a bill to the house," said the man standing on the barge. "That's what we've always done."

By the time the two men chugged away in the boat an hour later, they'd unloaded, assembled, and adjusted an L-shaped pier with a bench built into the end of it. Nell thanked them and watched as they stopped at another house a few lots down and started the whole process again with someone else's pier. She made a mental note to ask Don the next time they spoke whether she should expect anything else to be delivered, by land or by sea. She'd sent him a flyer for Gallery Night, after mulling for a couple of days whether it was a good idea to invite him. He'd called her after he saw the short article that ran in the paper about Caroline's overdose.

"Isn't this the same block as the Barrett mansion?" he'd asked. "Is everything okay over there?"

At first, Nell had been tempted to tell him as little as possible. But then, remembering the mess she'd made in her marriage by not disclosing the whole truth, she filled Don in on what facts she knew, including that Josh was helping out with the case.

"If she gets convicted of a felony, you're going to have to ask her to resign from the residency," he'd said.

"I kind of figured that," Nell said. "I'm really hoping we don't get to that point."

The residency was nearing its end, with less than two months left. Nell had begun to review applications for the next group of artists. Even so, she hoped she wouldn't have to let Annie go before the end of the program. Not only would Annie be missed, but Nell would also feel like she'd failed in her role as director. Already she chided herself for not having paid closer attention to what Annie had been up to in the basement, and not asking the right questions.

Now, Nell went back inside the house and looked over each of the new works she'd set out and hung on the walls. She hoped she'd placed them well enough to get the attention they deserved. She didn't have enough time to rearrange them now, with just a couple of hours to go before she opened the doors for Gallery Night.

The centerpieces of the exhibition were the photos Annie had found in a dresser drawer in one of the unoccupied bedrooms. The dresser had been emptied out except for a few pieces of costume jewelry and some old photo albums. Tucked into the back of one of the albums had been pictures Annie had taken of Betsy, along with a note.

> *I hope these photos reach you at home before your move. I hope, too, that they captured some of the style, grace, humor, and generosity that I saw in their subject.*
>
> *Annie Beck*

Nell had framed the photos and hung them in the foyer, both to display for Gallery Night and to remain there, so that everyone who walked in could see the woman whose vision had made the Colony possible.

There were ten photos, five in color and five in black and white, displayed in two rows. The color photos showed Betsy from different angles and ranges, sitting on a striped woven blanket, and leaning against the trunk of the bronze tree sculpture in the garden. In her lap she held a mosaic made from blue-and-white pottery pieces. Behind her, propped against a wrought-iron bench, stood the Lee Krasner painting that now hung above the fireplace. On top of the bench was an arrangement of colorful pillows in varied textures, patterns, and colors—red, pink, orange, and purple. A stack of books also shared space on the bench seat. Nell recognized the spine of one of the books as the children's poetry collection she'd seen on the office bookshelves, inscribed by Betsy's mother. The photograph looked like something out of the pages of *Vanity Fair*.

"It's so colorful, isn't it?" Annie came up beside Nell now and said, "She handpicked all the items she wanted in the picture with her."

"She certainly had a knack for knowing what went with what." Nell turned to look at Annie. "Why didn't you tell any of us that you met Betsy?"

Annie shrugged. "I didn't want people to think I was chosen just because I knew her, and not for my work."

Nell nodded and looked back at the pictures. "I can't get over the fact that the Krasner painting is just sitting there in the grass. It makes me feel a little better about when Grady took it down from the wall and put it on the floor."

"The painting is resting on top of a little box you can't see unless you look closely," Annie said. "I promise you, it never even touched the grass. I was worried about the same thing. I didn't even want to bring it outside. What if the sky suddenly opened up into a downpour, or the wind kicked up and blew it into the lake?"

"What did Betsy say?" Nell asked.

Annie lifted her chin and lowered her voice. "'Art is like life. It's fragile, but that doesn't mean you should never take a risk.'"

Nell stood silent for a moment, thinking about just how true those words were. She knew all too well how fragile life could be. You could feel a baby kicking inside you, swift and strong, only to watch her take her last breath less than an hour later. Or, in Annie's case, you could listen to a friend talk about her strides in sobriety and photograph her young, hopeful face one day, only to lose that friend to the strangle of addiction the very next time you saw her.

Nell brushed a tear from the corner of her eye before she even realized she was on the verge of crying. Annie noticed, though, and asked, "What is it?"

Nell took a deep breath. "Josh and I lost our baby, shortly after she was born. But before that, a photographer came and took pictures of her. And I'm so glad she did. It takes a special kind of person to be able to show up under the kind of circumstances that most people would rather not think about." She gave Annie a small smile. "You're that kind of person."

"I try to be," Annie said. "I'm afraid I screwed things up with Caroline, though. I know that what happened isn't my fault, but I wonder if I could have done more to help."

"Trust me, I know exactly what you mean," Nell said.

"When I started my photography series on death and pain

management, I was really passionate about it. Like you said, I felt like I could do something—capture something—that not just anybody could. But then I stopped doing that, and shifted into doing the series on addiction, because of the promise of getting my own big retrospective show." Annie shook her head. "Once all of this blows over, I want to get back to the sort of thing I was doing initially with my *Elysium* project. Because, even if death isn't the hot topic of the day, it's something we all have to deal with. It's essential to being human. And isn't that what art is all about? Trying to create just a snippet of something real and true and permanent?"

Nell nodded. It was why she'd always loved art so much. When she thought too hard about all the things that were *impermanent*, she wanted to shut down. She wanted to shut the door to pain and discomfort, like she'd done with the nursery at home. Like she'd tried to do by keeping her debt a secret. Paycheck by paycheck, though, she'd started to chip away at the balances she'd racked up. And with every payment to the credit card company, she hoped she was that much closer to bridging the gap between her and Josh. Even more than the money, though, Annie's case had brought them closer.

Josh liked to be needed, Nell knew that. He liked having a problem he could fix. When they lost their daughter, the difference in the ways she and Josh processed their grief had wrought a chasm between them, into which all feeling fell, tumbling down to some unreachable place. The Colony, though, made Nell feel something again, besides pain. It wasn't a substitute for all she'd lost—the years of raising her daughter, the countless moments never realized—but it gave her something to nurture.

Annie's phone rang and she pulled it out of her pocket. "Your husband is calling me," she said. "I'd better take this." She went into the office. A few minutes later, Nell heard a whooping sound from behind the closed door.

Annie came running back out, her cheeks flushed.

"What happened?" Nell asked.

"The DA is dropping the charges. Caroline's parents submitted a letter to him, asking that the prosecution focus on finding 'the real threat'—people dealing black market prescription drugs and heroin—instead of going after someone who had tried to help her. Apparently Caroline had told them about my project. Between that and the Good Samaritan law, which is supposed to *encourage* people to call for help, not discourage them, Josh says the DA would have been hard-pressed to go forward with the case."

Nell jumped up and down and hugged Annie. "That is fantastic news," she said. "I knew you were in good hands with Josh, but I still wasn't sure if it would all work out."

"He went above and beyond," Annie said.

Odin came downstairs. "What's all the noise?"

Paige was on his heels. "Did I miss something?

"Annie's case got dismissed," Nell said. "Now our show tonight can feel like a real celebration."

"Speaking of which, do I look presentable?" Paige pulled at the edges of her black shirtdress in an exaggerated curtsy.

"Yes," Nell said. "But not so presentable that people won't

believe you're one of the artists. The skull tights are a nice touch."

Paige walked over to where Nell had hung a grouping of three of her *Maps and Monsters* prints. "Funny how a frame can make something look completely different."

Nell felt a twinge of anxiety in the pit of her stomach. "Oh no," she said. "Did I get it all wrong?"

"No, they're perfect," Paige said. "When I'm toting stuff around in my portfolio, it seems so one-dimensional, you know? Just a print. This makes everything look more legitimate, some-how."

"Did you get the idea from all your gaming and your geek metal friends?" Odin asked.

"God, no," Paige said. "The idea was inspired by Trent, actu-ally."

"Is he coming to the show tonight?" Annie asked.

Paige shook her head. "I didn't invite him. I haven't talked to him in a few weeks, actually." She looked at her feet, clearly uncomfortable at the personal turn the conversation had taken.

Nell looked at her watch. "I guess I'd better get changed. People will start coming soon. At least I hope so." She bit her lip, suddenly racked by doubt. "What if no one comes?"

"I *did* invite some of my classmates," Paige said. "They won't buy any art, but they'll help contribute to the legitimacy fac-tor. And probably make sure we don't have too much leftover wine."

But people did come, and not just Paige's classmates. Josh was among the first to arrive, coming straight from court. He had never looked sexier to Nell, not just because he was still in his suit, but because of what he'd accomplished that day. She greeted him with a kiss that was longer than what she'd usually be comfortable giving in front of other people, let alone in a work setting. But she couldn't hold in how proud and grateful she felt.

"*Hello*," Josh said. "Maybe I should wear a suit more often." When Nell pulled away, he gave her an approving look. "And you should definitely wear that dress more often, too."

She was wearing the red dress she'd bought for the party at the dean's residence back in January. This party was already feeling decidedly more celebratory than that one.

A group of Josh's law school colleagues showed up soon afterward. Some of them bought artwork—a few of Paige's sea monster prints and a couple of smaller pieces that Odin had done before the residency. His large heron sculpture was purchased by a couple who lived down the street from the Colony. They had long admired Betsy's sculpture garden and wanted to start their own.

Don showed up, too, and wrote a donation check to the nonprofit for addiction recovery research to which the artists had agreed to donate the night's proceeds.

"Good news about Annie's case," he said to Nell. "I was following it on the court docket and saw that the charges got dropped. Where's your husband? I want to thank him for helping out."

Nell pointed him in the direction of the dining room, where Josh had jumped in as bartender and was pouring people drinks. The house was filling up, with neighbors and other local artists, and even with people who'd just been driving by and saw the luminarias lining the front walk. They wandered up to the house to look at the memorial the residents had set up on a table on the porch. Odin had made a candelabra from bent metal shaped to look like tree branches. It held five multicolored candles that Annie had made by melting down bits of other half-used candles she'd found around the mansion. Paige had used a letterpress machine up at school to print out Caroline's name on thick, handmade paper, which she then framed, along with a description of the charity that would be receiving the night's proceeds. In the end, the Colony raised just over a thousand dollars in Caroline's name. It wasn't a huge sum of money—probably nowhere near the sums that Betsy was known for giving to charity—but they raised it together. And, after spending months wondering what Betsy wanted or what she would have thought, Nell felt certain tonight that Betsy would have been proud.

Chapter Thirty

$\mathcal{P}aige$

PIECE: *Set of eight Baccarat cut-crystal flutes.*

$\mathcal{P}$aige didn't go to the big, university-wide graduation ceremony held in the football stadium. She didn't see the point of sitting amid a crowd of people, the vast majority of whom she'd never met, only to walk across the stage for ten seconds and worry about tripping on her robe the whole time. Instead, she went with her parents to the breakfast and smaller commencement celebration held just for her program. Her parents beamed with pride when her name was called and she stood up with her classmates to be recognized. But her parents, like Paige, also weren't comfortable in crowds. The number of people packed into the banquet hall, even just for her department's commencement, was probably double the number of people who lived in the town she grew up in. She wasn't surprised, then, when her parents departed Madison early that afternoon, after some obligatory pictures on campus and a quick tour of the Colony. They seemed relieved to be going back home.

Paige, too, felt relieved to be at home, in her room at the Colony. After her parents left, she fell asleep on her bed, still wearing the dress she'd put on for the graduation festivities. She woke, disoriented, a couple of hours later to a knock at her door.

"Come in," she said, sitting up and straightening out the folds of her dress.

The door opened a crack and Nell stuck her head into the room. "We have a surprise for you downstairs."

Paige followed her down to the dining room, where twinkle lights and tissue paper flowers hung from the ceiling. A bottle of Champagne in a silver ice bucket sat in the middle of the table. Annie walked in from the kitchen carrying a white layer cake with "Congratulations" written on the top in chocolate icing. Odin came in after her, carrying stemmed crystal glasses.

Paige could feel her face turning red. "You guys didn't have to do this."

"Yes, we did," Annie said, placing the cake on the table. "After everything that's happened here, we're glad to have an excuse to celebrate something good."

Odin twisted off the Champagne cork with a pop. He filled the glasses and, when everyone had one in hand, raised his own glass in the air and said, "To Paige, who makes art look easy."

Paige almost snorted out her champagne. To make art, to create something entirely original, was hard. Like really fucking hard. But she didn't know how to live without it, and she knew the others gathered around the table felt the same way. So instead of making a self-deprecating remark, she said, "Thank you. Is that cake fair game?"

"Definitely," Nell said, picking up a knife.

When the doorbell rang half an hour later, Paige went to answer it, giddy on sugar and the half glass of Champagne she'd drunk. When she opened the door, she saw Trent standing, tall and smiling, on the front porch. In that moment, she realized just how much she'd missed him. Until then, she'd carried on by pushing him to the back of her thoughts, trying to ignore the inconvenient feeling that she'd made a mistake in letting him go.

They hadn't been in touch at all since they broke up. Paige had contemplated reaching out to him on a few occasions, but always stopped herself. Part of it was pride—she'd been the one to pull away, and she didn't want to admit that she was having second thoughts. The other part was fear. What if he had moved on? Paige certainly thought *she* would have by now.

"Hey," he said.

"Hi." Paige gave him a questioning look.

"It's good to see you," he said. "I'm glad you texted me."

"I didn't." Now Paige was really confused.

Trent pulled his phone out of his back pocket and held it up for her to see. "Then who sent me this?"

Paige looked down. On the screen was a picture of one of her framed *Maps and Monsters* prints from Gallery Night, along with a message that said, My housemates are having a graduation party for me on Sunday around 4 if u want to stop by.

"I'm not sure what happened," she said. "But I didn't send that."

"Well, this is awkward." Trent put his phone back in his pocket. "If you want me to go . . ."

"No, no, come in," she said. "The party thing is true. Do you want some cake? Champagne?"

She brought him to the dining room, where the others were still standing around the table. Paige introduced Trent.

"I think I've seen some of you around," he said. "But it's nice to formally meet you."

Nell cut Trent a piece of cake, and he sat down at the table to eat. Paige stayed on her feet, turned her back to the table, and took her phone out of her pocket. She looked through her outgoing messages, but didn't see anything that matched what had been on Trent's screen.

Annie came up next to her. "What, you don't think an old lady knows how to work an iPhone?" she said quietly, nudging Paige with her elbow.

Paige's eyes widened. "It was you?"

Annie grinned. "That dress you wore to Gallery Night didn't have any pockets. I snatched your phone when you set it down to get a drink, then deleted the message after I sent it."

"Unbelievable," Paige said, shaking her head, but she smiled back at Annie. "Why?"

Annie looked at Trent, who had finished his piece of cake and was talking with Odin. "Because I've spent a lot of my life not letting anybody get too close, and I regret it," she said. "I don't know anything about this boy, but I know that you care about him enough to be moved to make beautiful artwork. So I meddled."

Trent got up from the table and caught Paige's eye.

"Do you want anything to drink?" she asked.

"No, thanks. I was hoping we could go somewhere to talk. Outside, maybe? It's really nice out."

Paige agreed. She thanked her housemates for the surprise party and went with Trent out to the pier, where they sat on the bench at the edge. Paige lit a cigarette. She exhaled, looking out at the lake through the cloud of smoke. The water was finally blue and open after so many months of ice. A line of sailboats bobbed around a bright orange buoy. The sun sank slowly in the sky amid a swath of sherbet-colored hues. Paige would miss living on the lake when the residency was over.

"I figured out who sent the message," Paige said. "It was Annie."

Trent cocked his head to the side a bit. "Are you pissed?"

Paige shook her head. "I kind of wish I *had* sent it. I'm glad to see you."

"How have you been?" he asked. "It's been a while."

Paige filled him in on the events of the last few weeks, including Caroline's death and Annie's court case.

"You can't be serious," he said.

Paige nodded. "It's not exactly the sort of thing I could make up."

"Well, you are creative . . ." He nudged the side of Paige's foot with his sneaker. "I'm sorry you and your friends had to go through all that."

"What have *you* been up to?" she asked.

"Working and saving money. I start back up with classes next week." Trent turned his gaze from the lake to Paige. "I was glad when I got your text—I mean Annie's text," he said. "What we had was good, don't you think? I know you weren't looking for a relationship. I wasn't, either. But when I have something good, I kind of want more of it, you know?"

Paige nodded. "Yeah, it was good," she said. But then she had to look away. The bare tenderness in his eyes made her uncomfortable. Desire she could handle. Flirting, banter, sex—she was used to all of those. But tenderness? No.

"So what happened? What's underneath all this?" Trent made a sweeping gesture with his hand.

"You know very well what's underneath all this." Paige took his hand and placed it on her leg, just beneath the hem of her dress. He gave her thigh a squeeze, but then removed his hand.

"That's not what I meant. I want to know what's in here." He tapped a gentle finger against her temple and brushed a piece of hair back from her face, securing it behind her ear. Then he moved his hand down and tapped her collarbone, just above her heart. "And here."

Paige covered her face with her hands. "No you don't. Not really."

"I do."

She dropped her hands to her sides. Just as the ice had disappeared from the lake, Paige felt something melting, something softening and thawing in her chest. "I've never been good at liking myself," she admitted.

"But you *act* like you're so confident."

"Cocky," she said. "Cocky is not the same as confident. It's often quite the opposite, actually. Anyway, I've made progress. Not that long ago, when I was a teenager, it was worse than just not liking myself. I straight up hated myself."

"I know." Trent took her wrists, one by one, and kissed her on the pink, puckered skin across her scars.

Paige felt a blush burn across her face. After he'd let go of her hands, she looked at the ground and said, "I didn't tell you about all that to make you feel sorry for me. Just to explain why I've never been good at getting close."

She got up and walked down the pier, back to the shore. She scooped up a handful of flat stones, then returned and put them down on the bench. Trent selected a stone, got up, and skipped it across the water. It bounced three times on the surface before plunking under the waves.

"So . . . summer school, huh?" she asked.

"Yeah," Trent said. "And then fall semester."

"No ski season this year?"

He shook his head. "I've got to graduate." He shrugged. "It's okay, though. It feels good to actually have a plan. How about you?"

Paige bent to scoop up another stone from the bench. "I'm kind of thinking about getting a master's. My advisor thinks I should apply to the program here." She threw the stone, which skidded across the water in a line of tiny ripples before submerging.

"I think you should, too," he said. "It means you'd stay in Madison after the residency is done. "And in the meantime, maybe we can start hanging out again." He leaned in close.

"I'd like that." She closed her eyes and, when they kissed, the rush of warmth that hummed through her body felt both familiar and new at the same time.

Chapter Thirty-one

Odin

PIECE: *Bruce L. Black,* Flame. *Steel sculpture.*

Odin planned his departure from the Colony so that he'd be the first to move out. He did not want to stay long enough to watch the others take off, one by one, leaving only Nell. While she was getting the house ready for the next group of artists set to arrive in August, he'd be moving into his new apartment in Minneapolis.

When he'd packed the last of his equipment into the truck, he stood outside the mansion in the circular drive for a few moments before going inside to say goodbye to the others. He'd had a great love, once, in Sloane. He hoped there would be at least another one in his life, at some point. But in the meantime, he had his art to keep him busy. And, thanks to the recent Gallery Night, he'd signed two contracts for custom works—his first commissions.

One of the contracts was from the couple who had purchased his blue heron piece. They wanted another sculpture to jump-start their collection. He agreed without hesitation. The income would be good, but he also was excited by the prospect of creating something without being confined by the necessity for it to fit on someone's bookshelf or end table. And he loved the idea that his pieces would be outdoors, in public view, where anyone could enjoy them and where he could see them when he came back to visit the Colony in the future. Because he knew he would be back here. Nell had already said that all of the artists had a standing invitation to join the new residents for a Sunday dinner if they were ever in town.

The money from the commissions was enough for Odin to put down the first month's rent on a second-story apartment in an old house just a couple of blocks from Lake of the Isles. It had a detached garage, and the owner agreed to let him pay an extra hundred bucks in rent every month to do his sculpting work out there. It would be fucking cold in the winter—he'd have to get a space heater—but he didn't mind. He'd come to appreciate cold, how it brought him into his physical body and out of his head. Maybe someday he'd have "made it" enough to do his work in a heated studio. Until then, he welcomed the thought of the cold.

Odin looked up at the window of the room where he'd dreamed and despaired for the last six months. Then he glanced at the garage, where he'd done more of the same, but also work. Quite a bit of it, especially in the last couple of months. He had some things to show now as soon he found the right gallery to show them.

When he first arrived, he'd felt so lost. Sloane, in his mind, was synonymous with art. Synonymous with any small amount of success he'd managed to achieve. Without her, he worried he'd never create anything worthy of the faith she'd had in him, of the faith she'd somehow manage to convey to the rich, dying woman who visited the Foster Gallery on that frigid February night the year before.

But now, he knew that what Sloane had brought out in him had been there all along. And it lived on, still, even in her absence. Other people, and other things, could inspire him. Paige had motivated him to stop worrying so much about what other people thought, and to make the art he wanted to make. Annie encouraged him to always keep moving and keep creating, with the rebel nature she donned as a guard against her ever-present fear of disappearing, of losing relevance and significance. And then there was Nell.

Nell, with her heart as jagged and raw as his own, maybe even more so. When he first met her, it seemed as if her dreams had been scrambled and tossed onto the table like dice. He knew that sense of powerlessness. But somewhere over the last six months, it seemed she'd leaned into the game again.

Odin would be lying to himself if he said he would not have taken the opportunity, in a millisecond, to be Nell's lover as well as her friend. But the friendship was what he needed more. And he realized that his attraction to her served, more than anything else, as proof that his ability to connect with someone had not died when Sloane did. He just had to be patient. Still, Odin was relieved that he wouldn't be around to watch as Nell found her way back to Josh. Already the space between them had shrunk.

With his truck loaded up, he walked around the side of the house to take one last look at his favorite work of art on the property. It was a sculpture of a flame made up of several steel beams, now reddened with rust. The beams were curved and positioned in such a way that they gave the impression of a flickering fire. The plaque at its base read: IN LOVING MEMORY OF WALTER BARRETT, WHOSE SPIRIT SHINES ETERNAL.

At the sound of voices, he walked back toward his truck. Everyone came down the steps of the front porch just then. Nell squinted in the afternoon sunlight. She had on a sundress (God, he loved summer) that hit a few inches above her knees and showed off her legs, which he told himself were fine to admire silently, even if he'd resigned himself to the fact that they should keep things professional.

As usual, Paige had her phone clutched in her hand, as if it were an extension of her body. Odin felt flattered that she glanced up for a full five seconds to meet his eye and say goodbye. He hugged her, and she acted awkward and stiff at first, then squeezed him hard before she pulled away.

"You let me know if you ever make it up to the Twin Cities, okay?" Odin said. "It's worth a trip. The art scene there is pretty great."

Paige nodded. "For sure."

Annie didn't wait for Odin to approach her. She threw her arms around him and patted his back with a firm slap.

"You're one of the good ones," she said.

When Odin hugged Nell, he held on long enough to take a deep inhale of the soapy-sweet smell of her hair, then pulled away and said, "I'll be in touch."

"You'd better. I'll be keeping tabs because I expect big things from you," Nell said. She looked over at the others. "That goes for all of you."

Odin got into his truck, rolled down the driver's side window, and waved as he pulled out of the driveway. He stole glances at the mansion in the rearview mirror until, finally, he turned the corner and kept his eyes fixed forward.

Chapter Thirty-two

Nell

PIECE: *Drawing of the Mansion Hill Artists' Colony, colored pencil on paper.*

June was crazy, with all of the artists wrapping up projects and moving out. But July was quiet and, at first, Nell missed having the residents around. She missed their conversation, their ideas, the hum of creative energy that had filled the rooms while they were here. It felt strange to come to work in an empty mansion. Nell never felt entirely alone, though, just as she suspected Betsy never did—not with all the artwork on the walls, shelves, and lawn.

Nell soon slipped into the long, languid days of summer, keeping shorter hours at work and convincing Josh to do the same. A few times, he came over for lunch and they ate together on the pier, taking their shoes off and dipping their toes into the water. Things weren't perfect between them, but they were better than they'd been in a long time.

Sometimes, during those lunch breaks, Nell would take out a notepad and doodle with colored pencils—something she hadn't done since childhood. She was under no illusion that she had any particular aptitude for drawing, but it didn't matter. Combining colors on the page gave her a joy she hadn't realized she'd missed, a creative release she hadn't known she needed. She drew what she saw or what came to mind—a box tied with a pink ribbon, the peaks and valleys of the waves lapping against the pier, or the angles of the mansion, with its wraparound porch and red door.

Often, Nell took her laptop outside to work from the porch or pier, answering emails from the new crop of artists—a young man who had just graduated from the university with an MFA in studio art, a woman from nearby Spring Green who did ceramics, and a landscape painter in her late fifties. The painter had lived near and painted Lake Superior for decades and said she wanted to try her hand at abstract painting, but worried that if she stayed put, she'd chicken out and keep doing the same old thing she'd always done. Nell was pretty sure Betsy would have thought she'd chosen well.

Nell used the downtime to write some community guidelines for the incoming residents (she preferred the word "guidelines" to "rules," especially in the context of an artists' colony). Josh helped her write them. She knew she couldn't police everything the artists did, nor did she want to, but she hoped that laying out some reasonable expectations in the beginning would prevent problems down the road.

She also busied herself cleaning and organizing the house.

She could have paid someone to do it—there was money in the trust for upkeep. And, in fact, she did hire a high school kid to do the lawn and a company to wash the windows (there was no way she was leaning out of that third-floor cupola to get at the highest ones). But the rest of it Nell did herself, and she sort of enjoyed the process. It gave her a chance to really notice things, like the way the light coming in from the windows at different times of day could completely alter the mood of a painting or print.

Nell settled so well, in fact, into the slower pace of summer that it took her a while to realize her cycle was off. She had to count back days on the calendar to realize that she'd missed a period. The realization brought a glimmer of hope, followed almost immediately by a wave of terror and sadness. She remembered the last time she'd missed her period, the twenty-two weeks she'd carried her and Josh's daughter, and all that had gone wrong.

Today, Nell left work early, stopped at the pharmacy on the way home, and picked up a box of home pregnancy tests. As soon as she got home, she went into the bathroom and, with shaking hands, ripped open the box and dumped out the two tests. She picked one up. The crinkly wrapper rattled around in her sweaty fingers. She didn't even know fingers could sweat, but apparently they could. Somehow, she managed to tear open the package and take out the plastic stick inside.

Nell didn't need to read the directions. She'd taken dozens of this same brand of test before, always with a negative result, except for that one time. She'd gotten used to seeing the single, lonely pink line in the test window, with nothing but stark white space where the second pink line was supposed to appear.

Back when she and Josh were doing fertility treatments, she used to hold the stick in her hands and watch the result window for the entire three minutes the test instructions said to wait before reading the result. Nell remembered how she'd watch the control line come up, straight and scientific. So bold, that control line. Always bright pink, just to prove to her that the test was not faulty. As if to say, "The test is working. Yep. Definitely working. Just in case you're hoping there's a manufacturing defect or some sort of user error or *something* to explain the big fat negative you're about to get, again." Sometimes, her eyes used to play tricks on her. She'd swear she saw the faintest second line only to realize it was a reflection from the light fixture.

Now, after taking the test, Nell placed it on the bathroom counter, set the timer on her phone for three minutes, and left the room, shutting off the light and closing the door behind her. She went downstairs and out the back door, so as to curb any temptation to look at the result before the timer went off.

She walked around the perimeter of the small yard behind their bungalow. She'd been so busy with getting things ready for the next session at the Colony that she'd barely noticed that the border perennial garden was in full bloom. The grass was soft underneath her feet as she walked across the lawn to inspect the flower beds bordering the back edge of the property.

She remembered that she'd planted lilies there the previous fall. With Josh engrossed in the start of the semester, she'd been desperate for something to distract her between appointments at Dr. Lynch's office. She'd never been much into gardening—when she lived in Chicago, she never had a yard. The closest she came to gardening had been to buy a couple of potted herbs from Trader Joe's and then set them on the kitchen windowsill of her and Josh's apartment, where they slowly turned brown and died. But when Nell purchased Stargazer lily bulbs at the farmers market, the vendor had promised her that no special skills were required to plant them.

"Just dig a hole, put 'em in the ground, and wait. Come next summer, if all goes well, you'll have fragrant, showy flowers like these here." He'd pointed at a laminated picture of how the plant was supposed to look when it was in bloom, with clusters of big, six-petaled pink-and-white flowers.

Nell had gone home, cleared the fallen leaves from one of the flower beds behind the house, and done what the man said. She doubted that anything would actually grow from the musty little clusters of bulbs she covered with soil, smoothing the back of her spade over the earth where she'd upset it. Not even a week after she spent an entire afternoon planting, she saw a squirrel digging in one of the beds, then running off with its cheeks puffed out, leaving a trail of chewed-up brown bulbs behind it.

After that, consumed by first their IVF treatments, then her work with the Colony, Nell forgot all about the flowers she'd planted, until now. The flower bed was crowded with plants that the previous owners had planted—bee balm, hostas, and coneflowers. But she didn't see her lilies anywhere.

The timer on her phone went off with a chime. Nell was about to go back inside when something pink near the back fence caught her eye. She walked across the few feet of mulch and foliage and bent down to get a better view.

There, protected by the fence, stood a single pink lily in full bloom. Its long stalk shook in the wind, but the blossom was open to the sun, revealing a bright yellow center. She understood, now, the appeal of perennial plants. Because to plant them was to plant hope. There was something bold, almost brazenly optimistic, about hiding something away in the soil and then hunkering down for a hard freeze and having faith that there would be life and beauty on the other end.

Nell piled up a small mound of mulch around the flower, to better protect it from the wind. Then she went inside and upstairs, where she hesitated outside the bathroom door.

She remembered something Josh had said to her, back when they had been arguing over whether or not to do any more fertility treatments.

"This doesn't just affect you," he'd said. "I'm in this, too." She also thought about how he'd stuck by her despite everything that had happened—the debt and deception, the distance between them. There were times when Nell thought she could practically hear the tension humming between them, like the high E string on a guitar tuned just a little too tightly, ready either to snap or sing.

She called him at work.

"I just took a pregnancy test," she said.

"I thought we didn't have any in the house," he said.

Nell let out a small laugh. Back when they'd been doing IVF, Josh had made Nell promise to turn over any pregnancy tests she had stashed in the bathroom, so as not to be tempted to test early. He'd helped her double-check all the drawers and cabinets, just to make sure she didn't have a secret stash hiding somewhere.

"I went and bought a box of them today," Nell said. "My period is two weeks late."

"*Oh.*"

Nell read so much into that single syllable. Not just understanding, but also fear. The memory of all the frustration and the fighting. But also, above everything else, she heard hope. Hope she hadn't known he still held on to.

"I haven't looked at the result yet," Nell said. "I was going to wait until you got home to even test, but I was so sure it would be negative . . . I didn't see the point in dragging you along for the emotional roller-coaster ride. But then I remembered what you said about wanting to share things. About how we can't be there for each other if we don't really let each other know what's going on. So that's why I'm calling. I'm going in to look at the test."

She heard Josh let out his breath on the other end of the line. "Okay," he said. She could practically picture him rubbing his thumb over his beard, getting out of his office chair to pace.

"Are you okay?" Nell asked.

"Yeah," he said. "Just . . . this is a surprise, that's all."

"Well, we don't know what it's going to say."

"Right," he said.

"It will probably be negative," Nell said.

"Right."

"But maybe it won't be."

"Maybe," Josh said. He paused. "Are *you* okay?"

Nell thought about it. So many possibilities lay behind that door. Her heart thumped hard and fast with equal parts hope and trepidation. She'd just begun to feel confident at the helm of the Colony. She worried about having to disconnect from it, even for something as temporary as family leave, just as she was hitting her stride. She was getting ahead of herself, though. Even if the test turned out to be positive, she knew there were no guarantees about what would happen next. There was no way she could think about a new pregnancy, a new baby, without thinking of the one she'd lost.

But she'd learned, from the artists at the Colony, that there was value in contrast. Annie, with her photography, created beautiful and haunting images from the interplay of light and darkness. Odin coaxed smoothness and fluidity from something sharp and static. And Paige, with her monster prints, showed how beauty and fear could coexist. So, too, could joy and sadness. Neither one would mean anything without the other for contrast.

Nell answered, truthfully, "Yes."

"Either way? Really? You'll be okay?"

"No," she said. "I'll be more than okay."

She turned the door handle and switched on the light.

Acknowledgments

As always, I owe a deep debt of gratitude to my husband, Bill Parsons, to my parents, Frank and Kerry Gloss, and to my in-laws, Bill and Peggy Parsons. Without the support of family, I never could have finished this book.

Special thanks is also owed to my agent, Christina Hogrebe, and her colleagues at the Jane Rotrosen Agency, as well as to my editor, Rachel Kahan, editorial assistant Alivia Lopez, and the rest of the team at William Morrow for believing in me as a writer and making it possible to get this story out into the world.

The members of my critique group—Rebecca Brown, Erin Celello, Aaron Olver, and Angela James—provided invaluable feedback in the drafting phase, while the amazing women of Tall Poppy Writers provided moral support. Murali Jasti lent his expertise with criminal law practicalities, and Karla Schmidt and Christa Archual-Nie encouraged me to keep going with a difficult topic.

Finally, I'd like to acknowledge and remember some very special babies, lost too soon. Among them are Kenley, Sawyer, Kristina, Zachary, Arabella, Baby Girl, Grayson, Kamryn, Anastasia, Parker, William, Addison, Adair, Jackson, Elizabeth, Asher, Tavin, Casey, Orion, and Caleb. They, and so many others not named here, are loved and remembered.

About the author

2 Meet Susan Gloss

About the book

3 Reading Group Guide

6 Interview: Author Susan Gloss
on Fashion, Blogging, Her Novel
Vintage & How Every Seam
Has a Story

Insights,
Interviews
& More . . .

Meet Susan Gloss

Nick Wilkes

SUSAN GLOSS is a graduate of Notre Dame and the University of Wisconsin Law School. She lives with her family in Madison, Wisconsin. When she's not writing fiction, Susan can be found working as an attorney, blogging at GlossingOverIt.com, or hunting for vintage treasures for her Etsy shop, Cleverly Curated. ◠

Reading Group Guide

1. The loss of a child, and longing for a child, threaten to overwhelm Nell's life. Why do you think having a child is so important to Nell? Is it as important to Josh?

2. When Josh starts using the nursery for an office Nell feels as though Josh has moved on from the loss of their daughter: "She knew for the first time, then, that Josh had moved on from their loss, leaving her behind, still in the midst of mourning." Do you think Josh had really moved on from the loss of their daughter? Why was his grief different than Nell's, and how did he process it?

3. Betsy established The Elizabeth Barrett Trust for the Fine Arts to allow artists from all over the country to focus on their art and bring attention to the Madison art scene. Does the artist colony live up to her vision? Does it fulfill other needs besides what Betsy might have envisioned? ▶

Reading Group Guide *(continued)*

4. "Inside there are plenty of pieces by artists from all over the country, even the world, but Betsy said she felt strongly that if she was going to put artwork outside the house, where everyone would see it, she wanted it to be 'native,' just like the flowers she had planted." Discuss the role Wisconsin plays in the novel. Is there a similar art/cultural scene where you live?

5. When each artist arrives they almost instinctively gravitate toward different spaces. Paige the attic, Annie the basement, and Odin the garage. Why do you think they choose those parts of the house to work in? What do their choices say about each character?

6. Nell racks up credit card debt in secret for fertility treatments she hides from Josh. Would you have done the same? What would you have advised Nell to do in that situation if you were her best friend?

7. Paige, Annie, and Odin were accepted to the colony because of they hadn't yet reached their full potential. Did the colony help them achieve that? If not, in what ways do they still need to grow as artists? How did they grow as people apart from their artistic endeavors?

8. How does Nell's time working at the colony change her as a person? How does it change her relationship with Josh?

9. What do you think Nell and Josh's lives are like ten years after the novel? What about Paige, Annie, and Odin? ∽

Interview:
Author Susan Gloss
on Fashion, Blogging,
Her Novel *Vintage*
& How Every Seam
Has a Story

This interview by Doreen Creede first appeared on her lifestyle blog, Style Maniac. Read more at stylemaniac.com

In 2010, after Susan Gloss wrote a poignant guest post for Style Maniac about why she loves vintage fashion, I commented:

> *Susan, I am thrilled that you wrote this post for Style Maniac. You captured so much of my own feeling about vintage style. We are truly kindred spirits in so many ways. When you are a famous novelist I'll be tickled to say you appeared on Style Maniac way back when. . . .*

In fact, Susan had just begun writing her book, *Vintage,* and it's with such delight that I've followed her four-year journey as she went from manuscript to published novel. Since its debut in March 2014, *Vintage's* charming tale of friendships forged among women brought together by a vintage boutique in Madison, Wisconsin, has received rave reviews from *Booklist* and *Library Journal* plus fans around the world.

In this Style Maniac interview, Susan shares her publishing journey, the role blogging played, her best vintage find ever, and how she believes every seam has a story.

Q: *When did the idea for* Vintage *come to you?*

A: I came up with the idea for *Vintage* in 2010. At the time, I was living in a house that had a thrift store in its backyard. Literally. I could toss a tennis ball to play fetch with my dog and the ball would hit the brick wall of the thrift store.

Q: *Tell us a bit about the process of getting an agent and publisher.*

A: For me, getting an agent took two years, two manuscripts, and more rejections than I care to advertise, but let's just say that Kathryn Stockett ain't got nothin' on me. Once I signed with my agent, she sold *Vintage* quickly, though, within a couple of months. ▶

Interview: Author Susan Gloss on Fashion, Blogging, Her Novel *Vintage* & How Every Seam Has a Story   *(continued)*

Q: Did having a blog help with writing a book? Getting it published?

A: I think it helped in building my platform. My agent and editor, before signing me or the book, could see that I had an online presence and had built a portfolio of work. They both told me that they googled me prior to signing me.

Q: Did blogging hinder writing a book? Will you continue to blog?

A: I have definitely slowed down my personal blog due to other commitments, including writing my next book. But I've been blogging a lot, just not on my own site! Last September, I was chosen to be a part of the 2014 class for The Debutante Ball—a group blog for debut authors that's been in existence since 2008. It's launched the careers of several bestsellers, including Eleanor Brown, Sarah Jio, and Sarah Pekkanen. It's been great, and I've really enjoyed connecting with the other authors and a new group of readers.

Q: What's the best thing about being a published novelist?

A: The absolute best thing has been hearing from readers who enjoyed the book and relate to the characters. That, and seeing my book on bookstore shelves. It never gets old.

Q: I loved your dedication—"For my grandmother, Sally Baker, who taught me that every seam has a story"—which incorporates the title of the guest post you wrote for Style Maniac in 2010! What influence did your grandmother have on your fashion sense/desire to write?

A: Yes, I wrote that post here on Style Maniac when *Vintage* was still in the drafting phase, but what I said then is still true now: I owe my interest in fashion to my maternal grandmother. She was a pattern maker and seamstress for many years, and she taught me about different fabrics and what makes a quality garment. I also had the most gorgeous, unique outfits for my dolls when I was a girl. My grandmother used to design and sew them for me, and I've hung on to all of them. She came to my launch book party in March. ▶

Interview: Author Susan Gloss on Fashion, Blogging, Her Novel *Vintage* **& How Every Seam Has a Story** *(continued)*

Q: In Vintage, *each chapter opens with an inventory item of a vintage piece. Are these based on pieces you own?*

A: Sadly, I don't own any of the items. Most of the items in *Vintage* are things I wish I owned! But some were inspired by real-life objects. For example, there's scene where Violet, one of the main characters, packs up her belongings to leave her small hometown for good. She puts everything into a yellow Samsonite suitcase. That fictional suitcase was inspired by a real, 1960s luggage set that a wanderlusting friend of mine bought on Etsy.

Q: What's your favorite vintage find of all time?

A: That would have to be a vintage navy blue and gold Dior evening bag, complete with a gold chain strap and the original tag still on it. Believe it or not, I bought it for two dollars at a garage sale. ∿